H.I.V.E.

ESCAPE VELOCITY

OTHER BOOKS BY MARK WALDEN

H.I.V.E.

ESCAPE VELOCITY

MARK WALDEN

SIMON & SCHUSTER BOOKS FOR YOUNG READERS
NEW YORK LONDON TORONTO SYDNEY NEW DELHI

SIMON & SCHUSTER BOOKS FOR YOUNG READERS
An imprint of Simon & Schuster Children's Publishing Division
1230 Avenue of the Americas, New York, New York 10020

This book is a work of fiction. Any references to historical events, real people, or real locales are used fictitiously. Other names, characters, places, and incidents are products of the author's imagination, and any resemblance to actual events or locales or persons, living or dead, is entirely coincidental.

For information about special discounts for bulk purchases, please contact Simon & Schuster Special Sales at 1-866-506-1949 or business@simonandschuster.com.
The Simon & Schuster Speakers Bureau can bring authors to your live event. For more information or to book an event, contact the Simon & Schuster Speakers Bureau at 1-866-248-3049 or visit our website at www.simonspeakers.com.
Also available in a Simon & Schuster Books for Young Readers hardcover edition
The text for this book is set in Goudy.
Manufactured in the United States of America
1016 OFF
First Simon & Schuster Books for Young Readers paperback edition March 2012
4 6 8 10 9 7 5 3
Library of Congress Cataloging Control Number: 2010930194
ISBN 978-1-4424-2185-1 (hc)
ISBN 978-1-4424-1367-2 (pbk)
ISBN 978-1-4424-1370-2 (eBook)

For Sarah, for Megan, forever

chapter one

The bustling crowd appeared to part before the couple as they strode purposefully along the riverbank. It was early morning in London and while the other pedestrians bumped and jostled each other, this man and woman seemed to emit an invisible aura that kept the crowds from getting too close.

The man was tall and distinguished, the graying hair at his temples the only real clue to his age. He wore an immaculately tailored black suit and long black overcoat, the bloodred cravat at his throat providing the only splash of color. The woman beside him looked younger, her short dark hair framing a pale but strikingly beautiful face. She also appeared less relaxed than her companion, her eyes scanning the crowd intently.

"I don't like this, Max," Raven said quietly.

"So you have said on at least seven previous occasions," Dr. Nero replied calmly.

"It's a trap," Raven replied quickly, "and an obvious one at that." She struggled to keep the frustration from her voice.

"That may be," Nero said, the hint of a smile appearing at the corner of his mouth, "but Gregori is one of my oldest and most trusted allies. If he tells me that it is urgent that he meet with me, then I cannot afford to ignore his request."

"But why here?" Raven asked quickly. "Out in the open, exposed like this?"

"Gregori will have his reasons," Nero replied. "He is too old and wise to take such risks lightly." Nero hoped that this display of confidence in his old friend would reassure Raven, but he too was secretly concerned that Gregori had felt it necessary to take such a risk. Gregori Leonov, like Nero, was one of the most senior members of the ruling council of G.L.O.V.E., the Global League of Villainous Enterprises, and attaining such a position was largely dependent on having extremely well-honed survival instincts. It was hard for Nero to imagine what might drive his old friend to meet in such a public location, but he knew it was not a request that he could choose to ignore.

"I hope that your trust in him is not misplaced," Raven replied sharply, her anger betrayed by the slight strengthening of her usually subtle Russian accent, "because if this goes bad, it will go very, very bad very, very quickly."

"Which is exactly why you're here despite the fact that Gregori insisted I come alone," Nero said, an edge of impatience in his own voice now.

"Sometimes you have too much faith in me, Max," Raven replied unhappily. "We should leave now; this is unwise."

"That is my decision to make, Raven, and mine alone." Nero used her codename deliberately, a subtle but pointed reminder that while he valued her counsel, it did not give her the right to push him too far.

"Very well," Raven replied, stopping and staring at him. "I shall make myself . . . unobtrusive."

"See that you do," Nero said, glancing at his watch; it was near the appointed time for their meeting.

"Signal me if you have the slightest reason to suspect anything."

"Of course," Nero said. "Let us hope that it's not necessary."

"Indeed," Raven replied, her expression grim, and she turned and vanished into the crowd of passersby.

Nero turned and continued walking along the riverbank toward the spot where they had arranged to meet, in the shadow of the London Eye. The vast wheel loomed above Nero and he could not help but be impressed by its scale. He had seen some staggering feats of engineering and construction in his time, not least the construction of H.I.V.E., but this was still a striking monument.

"Hello, Max."

Nero's inspection of the giant wheel was cut short by the sound of his old friend's voice, but when he turned to face him he was shocked by what he saw. Gregori Leonov had always been a bear of a man, famed for the spine-snapping embraces that were reserved for his closest friends. But that was not the same man who stood before Nero now. He was thinner and looked years older, his skin gray and his eyes darting about as if expecting a sudden attack. He made no move to embrace Nero; he did not even offer his hand, but instead just gave him a small, sad smile.

"Gregori," Nero replied, knowing that he had not been able to keep the surprise from his face at seeing his fellow council member so reduced.

"It is good to see you, old friend," Leonov said quietly. "I did not know who else I could turn to."

"What's wrong, Gregori?" Nero asked, genuinely concerned for his friend.

"You came alone?" he responded, staring at Nero.

"As alone as I ever am," Nero said, suddenly not wanting to lie.

"Of course, I should not expect you to be without your guardian angel," Gregori replied with a slight smile.

"Natalya is many things, Gregori, but she's no angel." Nero raised an eyebrow.

"No, I suppose she is not." Gregori chuckled.

Nero was glad to hear his old friend laugh, and for the most fleeting moment Nero could see a hint of the man he used to know before the gray pall of unhappiness fell across his face again.

"Come, my friend," Gregori said, taking Nero by the elbow, "I have arranged for us to have somewhere more private to talk." He steered Nero toward the steps leading up to the boarding platform for the carriages that were slowly rotating around the enormous wheel. He ignored the line of tourists, simply nodding to one of the attendants, and stepped into a waiting capsule. Nero suspected that the attendant was significantly better off now than he had been when he had woken up that morning. The door slid shut behind them and they began their slow ascent over the cold gray waters of the Thames.

The glass-walled capsule was designed to hold two dozen people, but now, with just the two of them on board, it seemed to Nero to be the most private and yet strangely exposed place they could possibly meet. Gregori stood holding the rail, looking out over the water, seeming to take a moment to gather his strength before he turned to Nero and spoke.

"What do you know of the Renaissance Initiative?" he

asked, looking straight at Nero, his eyes narrowing.

"Rumors on the wind, nothing substantive," Nero replied evenly. It was a lie, of course; he had learned more than he truly cared to know of this secret project when he had questioned Cypher after his abortive attempt to take over H.I.V.E. the previous year. Cypher had been insane, there was little doubt of that, but Nero had no reason to disbelieve what the man had told him. Indeed, his own painstakingly discreet enquiries had only served to verify what he had fervently wished not to be true. Number One, the supreme leader of G.L.O.V.E., was secretly trying to rebuild the psychotic, impossibly dangerous, rogue artificial intelligence Overlord, his efforts concealed from the rest of the world's villains by a shadowy organization known only as the Renaissance Initiative. Nero could not even begin to guess what Number One's motives could possibly be. Nero's own life-threatening ordeal at the hands of the nightmarish machine intelligence was enough to tell him that this plan was not just dangerous but demented. Nero could make no sense of it; Number One had been instrumental in destroying the rampant AI and yet now he seemed to be secretly attempting to bring it back to life.

"I suspect that you know rather more than that, old friend," Gregori replied sadly, "and I also suspect that you know who is truly behind this madness. I have beaten you in too many games of cards not to know when you are bluffing."

"Let us assume . . . hypothetically . . . that I do," Nero replied carefully, rather annoyed that Gregori could read him so well, "but why are we here today?"

"Because you know as well as I do—no, *better* than I do—why Number One cannot be allowed to succeed in this."

That was it; Gregori had said his name, Number One. That made this a conspiracy, even if at this moment it only included the two of them. More powerful men had lost their lives for far less. Nero knew he could still walk away, still pretend that he did not know what Gregori was suggesting, but to do so would let this insanity continue unchecked and would also almost certainly cost Leonov his life. It was a price that Nero was not prepared to pay.

"Max, it is worse than you know," Gregori said, shaking his head. "Number One is not just trying to rebuild Overlord—I wish to God it were that simple." Gregori rubbed his eyes, letting out a long sigh.

"What is it, Gregori?" Nero said, putting his hand on his friend's shoulder. "What is he planning?"

"I discovered something, Max, something that I was never supposed to know. Number One found out and he sent the Reapers after me and my family."

Nero's eyes widened. Every member of G.L.O.V.E. knew of the Reapers. They were Number One's personal executioners, an utterly ruthless death squad that left no one alive in its wake. They were the stuff of nightmares, and Number One had turned them loose on Gregori.

"My wife, my daughters, they're gone, Max—executed by those butchers. It was a miracle I survived."

Alarm bells rang suddenly in Nero's head. The Reapers never left survivors, unless they wanted to. If they had tracked Gregori, followed him there . . .

"Why did he do this, Gregori? What did you find out?"

"We have to stop him, Max. He's—"

The glass behind Gregori cracked like a spider's web and his eyes went wide with shock. Nero tried to grab him, to support him, but Gregori crumpled to the floor, dead before he hit the ground. There had been no gun-shot, no sound at all, but the sniper's bullet had found its target with lethal accuracy. Nero suddenly felt horribly exposed, nearly a hundred yards above the ground in a glass bubble with no reason to assume that he would not be the next target. He pressed the button on the side of his watch; she may not be an angel, but he had to put his faith in Raven now.

☻☻☻

Raven watched from nearby as Nero and Gregori boarded the capsule and it was slowly carried upward by the rota-tion of the enormous wheel. She was not happy. The two men were getting harder and harder to see as the capsule climbed higher and higher into the air, and Raven got up to move to a better vantage point. Suddenly she heard a noise that sent an electric jolt of adrenaline through her body. None of the surrounding pedestrians had heard it; it was, after all, no louder than a small polite cough. But to Raven it was the unmistakeable silenced report of a high-powered rifle. Her eyes shot upward and she saw the bullet hole in the toughened glass of the capsule that Nero had been standing in far overhead. Without hesitating, she shed her long black overcoat and exposed the black leather body armor and tactical harness that she had been wearing underneath. She broke into a run, heading straight for the Eye, the insistent bleep of Nero's emergency signal sounding in her ear.

☣ ☣ ☣

On a distant rooftop, an observer peered through powerful binoculars at the scene that was unfolding below. He was completely bald but for a neatly shaved band of white hair that ran above his ears and around the back of his head, giving him an almost monkish appearance. He wore a small radio headset, which crackled into life as he lowered the binoculars to reveal his cold gray eyes.

"Longshot One to control, secondary target is down, primary is in scope," a voice reported in his ear.

"Hold fire, Longshot One," the man instructed calmly, "but keep him targeted. He leaves here with us or he doesn't leave at all, understood?"

"Roger that, holding on target," the voice replied in his ear.

"Longshot Two to control"—another voice cut into the channel—"I have an unidentified tactically equipped female heading toward the target zone."

The man raised the binoculars again, scanned the area at the base of the wheel, and instantly picked out a black-clad figure running at full tilt toward the structure.

"It would appear that we have flushed the wolf from the flock," he said to himself with a thin smile. He raised the tiny microphone to his lips. "Control to all units, unidentified female is new primary target. Wait until she is clear of the crowd, then take her down."

Several voices signaled their acknowledgment of the new order. The man pitched his binoculars upward, focusing on the single figure left standing in the capsule that was now nearing the apex of its climb.

"Control to all aerial units, you may begin your approach."

☺☺☺

Raven felt a cold chill as she ran across the square toward the wheel. There was no mistaking the distinctive pulsing thump of helicopters and they were getting closer all the time. And then something that sounded like an angry hornet buzzed past her ear and she knew that she was now the sniper's target. She dived behind a nearby ticket booth and the glass above her shattered in an explosion of tiny fragments. People were suddenly screaming and starting to run as more shots ricocheted noisily off the metal walkway, inches from her. There was no chance of spotting her unseen assailants. To do that she would have to expose herself and, judging by the frequency of the shots, there was more than one shooter out there. The moment she stuck her head out to get a fix on their positions it would be taken off. She pulled a small gray cylinder from the webbing on her chest and struck it hard on the ground. The device ignited instantly, flooding the area with thick white smoke.

☙☙☙

Trapped in the capsule, Nero felt a growing sense of helplessness. Raven had been right: it was madness to allow himself to fall into this trap, but he had not been thinking of the risk, only of the note of desperation in his friend's voice, and now he was paying the price. In their world it was unusual to find someone that you could really trust, and those people became impossibly valuable. It was a weakness that whoever was responsible for this understood and was clearly prepared to exploit. He knew that they wanted to take him alive—if not he would already be dead—and that meant he had to try to escape: capture was not an option for Nero. He searched the capsule desperately for anything that might be of use, but found nothing. He could only wait and pray that Raven would be able to get to him.

From far below he could hear screams of panic. He rushed to the end of the capsule and peered down toward the base of the wheel just in time to see the whole area filled with thick, billowing white smoke. He felt suddenly calm. If anyone could get him out of this, she could. A hint of movement caught his eye and he turned to look up the river. Heading toward the wheel, in tight tactical formation just a couple of yards above the surface of the water, were four black helicopters, and hanging from their sides were the unmistakeable silhouettes of heavily armed soldiers.

"Whatever you're going to do, Natalya," Nero muttered to himself, "do it fast."

☻☻☻

The bald man continued to watch through his binoculars as the woman dived for cover at the base of the wheel, shots peppering the structure she was hiding behind.

"Watch your targets, Longshot units," the man said

calmly. "I would rather avoid civilian casualties if possible."

Suddenly the woman's position was engulfed in white smoke.

"All units go to thermal imaging," the man instructed. "Wait for her to break cover, then take your shots."

As he watched, a tiny projectile trailing a thin line shot out of the cloud and struck the central hub of the wheel, fifty yards above. Moments later the woman shot straight upward out of the smoke, rocketing along the line she had just fired.

"Longshot Three to control, she's moving too fast. I've got no shot," the man's radio reported.

"Stay on her," the man barked, a sudden edge of panic in his previously calm voice. "Aerial units, hit that capsule NOW!"

☢ ☢ ☢

Raven hit the curved steel of the Eye's hub at a run, her grappler line snapping back into its wrist-mounted housing. A shot ricocheted off the metal near her feet with a spark and she dived forward, rolling in the air so she landed on her back, sliding toward the spokes of the massive wheel. She fired the grappler again, the monofilament cable snaking up toward Nero's glass cage. The unit on her wrist bleeped to confirm a solid hit and she pressed the controls to send herself rocketing skyward again. She slammed into the capsule hard, stretching desperately for the small metal rungs that ran up the side of it to the roof. She caught hold of one of the tiny handholds and swung free, more than a hundred yards above the cold gray waters of the Thames. Suddenly she felt a searing pain in her thigh as one of the snipers nearly found his mark, leaving a deep graze that began to bleed profusely. She hauled herself up, trying to ignore the pain in her leg. Nero stared at her from inside the capsule, a look of grave concern on his face. She reached the roof and tried to pull open the emergency access hatch, but it was firmly locked. She frantically searched the pouches on her harness for the gear that would let her blow the hatch, but she froze as an enormous shadow fell across her and a huge gust of wind threatened to pluck her off her perch. Helicopters surrounded the pod on all sides; each one was filled with special forces troops, the uniforms bearing the strange logo of an angel holding a sword, which she had never seen before. They all had their weapons trained on her. She looked down through the glass beneath her and saw Nero slowly shake his head.

"Go," he said, though Raven only saw his lips move, and despite every instinct screaming at her to ignore him, she knew that he was right.

"Put your hands on your head and stay on your knees," a voice commanded over a speaker mounted on the nearest helicopter, "or we will open fire."

Raven turned slowly to face the helicopter and raised her hands, then in a lightning movement she tossed a smoke grenade she had palmed moments earlier into the helicopter. Smoke instantly filled the cabin and Raven sprinted the few feet toward the edge of the capsule roof and leaped. She just caught the landing skid of the helicopter as the blinded pilot sent it spiraling down toward the river. She started to haul herself up, knowing that if she could just get into the cabin, she might be able to fight her way to the controls. Suddenly, what felt like a giant fist punched her in the back and she lost her grip, falling like a rag doll toward the icy water below. There was a small splash as she hit the surface, and then nothing.

☣ ☣ ☣

"Good shot, unit four," the bald man said calmly as he watched the woman's limp form hit the water. "Have the river dragged. I want to see the body."

He allowed himself a small, crooked smile as the special forces team rappelled down lines from one of the helicopters onto the roof of the gondola. Their mission was accomplished. They had their prize.

chapter two

three months later

Professor Pike took off his glasses and rubbed his eyes with a protracted sigh. He yearned to be back in the science and technology department; that was where he really belonged, not here, trying to fill the shoes of one of his oldest and best friends. He leaned back in what he still thought of as Nero's chair and looked around the headmaster's study. Nothing had been touched since Nero last left the room nearly three months previously.

This was not the first time that the Professor had assumed the role of acting headmaster of H.I.V.E. He had often taken Nero's place temporarily while he had been called away on some mission or to report to the G.L.O.V.E. high council. But this time was different and the Professor knew it. As the days stretched first into weeks and then months, it became increasingly clear that there was something badly wrong. The only reassurance was that Raven had gone with him, and if there was one person in the world that you wanted watching your back in a dangerous situation, it was her. The Professor had, of course, reported the situation to the council and had been reassured that they were investigating but that in the interim he would remain as acting head of the school. He had the uncomfortable feeling that in reality they knew as little as he did about Nero and Raven's whereabouts, but he knew better than to suggest as much directly. Then, without warning, he had been summoned to his desk in the middle of the night to receive an unscheduled call from Number One, G.L.O.V.E.'s supreme commander. So now he sat there waiting for the monitor on the desk to flicker into life, trying hard to suppress the feeling of dread that was slowly crawling up his spine.

The communications console emitted a soft chime and the G.L.O.V.E. logo of a fist hammering down onto a splintering globe filled the screen.

"Professor Pike?" a neutral female voice asked over the speaker.

"Yes, this is Professor Pike," he replied.

"Please hold for Number One," the voice replied and the line went dead. A moment later the screen displayed the silhouette of a seated figure. No detail of the man's true appearance could be made out other than the fact that he definitely had a head.

"Good morning, Professor. I'm sorry to make an

unscheduled call at such an hour but a serious problem has come to our attention," Number One said calmly.

"Of course," the Professor replied, even though they both knew that he could have been performing brain surgery and he'd still have been expected to drop everything to take this call.

"We have intercepted a transmission," Number One continued. "It has been sent to all major international news agencies and will therefore doubtless be broadcast very shortly to the world. I think you should see it before we discuss this any further."

A window popped up in the corner of the screen displaying the first frozen frame of a video showing a man sitting at a desk in front of a plain gray backdrop. In the middle of the wall, just above the man's head, was a symbol of a stylized angel flying upward with a sword held aloft in its outstretched hand. Above the angel was the single word "H.O.P.E." The man himself was thin, pale, and completely bald, save for a neatly clipped band of white hair above each ear. He looked straight at the camera; his steady gaze was somehow unnerving.

"Citizens of the free world," the man said as the video began to play, "my name is Sebastian Trent and I am the commander of a new organization that will soon form an essential part of the ongoing war on terror. This organization operates with the full support of the security agencies of the democratic nations and is designed to be the tip of the spear in the ongoing struggle against the terrorist groups that would seek to destroy our way of life forever. This organization is called H.O.P.E., the Hostile Operative Prosecution Executive, and it is our dream to give back to the people of the world exactly that: hope. It is our job to combat the forces of evil wherever we may find them, to cast a light into the darkest corners of the globe and bring the fight to any who would strike without warning at innocent people."

It was, of course, not the first time that the Professor had heard this kind of rhetoric, but there was undeniably something about this man and the conviction with which he spoke that marked him out from the usual buzzword-spouting politicians.

"I am aware that many of you will feel that you have heard this before," Trent continued, "and so our actions must speak louder than words. I am here today not just to publicly announce the formation of our new organization but also to show you that we are more than capable of producing results."

The picture changed and the Professor inhaled sharply. It was Nero, looking old, thin, and pale, dressed not in his usual immaculate suit but in orange prison overalls. There was a familiar, defiant look in his eyes, but beyond that there was little about the slightly disheveled figure on the screen that anyone who really knew Nero would recognize.

"This man is Maximilian Nero," Trent paused. "He is one of the most senior figures in perhaps the most dangerous criminal organization the world has ever known. He was seized by H.O.P.E. operatives while planning an act of terror in London, a scheme that with his capture and the death of his associates no longer represents a threat to the innocent people of that city. His arrest has given us a unique insight into the workings of this organization and will be the first and most crucial step in its final destruction."

The picture of Nero vanished to be replaced once again by Sebastian Trent.

"As I speak, H.O.P.E. operatives are active all over the world, hunting his associates and shutting down their operations permanently. The time has come for the forces of justice to reclaim our world from those who would destroy it, and give hope to us all. The fight has just begun. Thank you."

The video faded out, leaving the angel symbol on the screen.

"A potentially disastrous situation," Number One said calmly, "and one that we will be moving to resolve as quickly as possible. We clearly cannot allow someone with the knowledge that Nero possesses to remain in the hands of our enemies."

"No," the Professor replied quietly, stunned by what he had just seen. Not only did it appear that Nero had been captured, but—from what Trent had said about the "death of his associates"—that Raven had been killed during the operation. It was hard to imagine a more catastrophic turn of events. "What do you intend to do?"

"Rest assured that we will find a way to eliminate the risk to G.L.O.V.E.," Number One replied.

The Professor stared back at the shadowy figure on the screen. "You can't mean . . ."

"It is not up to you to decide what I can and cannot do, Professor. I hope that I do not need to remind you of your position within this organization," Number One said quickly, a cold edge to his tone. "Your first priority at this stage is H.I.V.E., and as such I feel you should consider how this news is delivered to the students and staff."

"We should do it soon," the Professor replied sadly. "The rumor mill in this place has been grinding for weeks already. The truth may be terrible but ongoing wild speculation is arguably worse. I should brief the staff and then call an assembly of the entire student body."

"Very well," Number One replied. "I also need to consider the issue of appointing a replacement headmaster."

"I am prepared to continue in the role for now," the Professor said quietly.

"We need a more permanent solution than that,"

Number One replied. "I shall appoint someone over the coming days. You shall, of course, give them your full cooperation."

"Of course," the Professor said. Number One had clearly decided that Nero's return was extremely unlikely. "I shall inform the staff."

"Good. I understand that this is difficult, Professor, but rest assured that we will prevail. Do unto others."

"Do unto others," the Professor replied, repeating the G.L.O.V.E. motto—words that suddenly sounded hollow and tasted bitter.

The screen went dark and the Professor slumped in his seat. Nero captured, Raven dead and all that Number One seemed to care about was the efficient running of the school. Nero and Raven had been two of his most loyal and long-serving operatives, but their loss seemed like little more than an inconvenience to him. The Professor put his head in his hands and let out a deep sigh. It was going to be a very long day.

�335 �335 �335

Otto closed his eyes and took a deep breath. He tried to block out the sound coming from the shower in the bathroom and focus only on the glowing network of pulsing lights that he could see in his mind. As he concentrated, the image seemed to become clearer in his head. It almost looked like an overhead view of an enormous city at night, with the lights of the traffic coursing along the streets impossibly quickly. He felt himself drifting closer and closer to the grid, subconsciously analyzing the patterns in the lights that raced around it, attempting to decrypt the information that he knew was stored within. He'd been awake all night, unable to sleep as his brain tried to decipher these patterns, sensing that he was getting nearer and nearer to his goal but finding tougher and tougher obstacles along each step of the way. Then something clicked into place in the back of his skull and he felt himself reaching out and becoming one with the pulsing flow below, steering it subtly away from its original course and setting it racing to its new destination.

"Otto," Wing said sharply, placing his hand on his friend's shoulder. Otto opened his eyes with a gasp, feeling a moment of total disorientation as the neon traces of the grid were suddenly replaced by the cool white walls of the room that he shared with Wing.

"Are you all right?" Wing asked, looking slightly worried.

"Yes . . . yes, I'm fine," Otto said croakily.

"You do not look fine,' Wing replied, handing him a tissue and gesturing toward Otto's nose. Otto raised the tissue to his face and dabbed at his nostrils. It came away stained red. "In fact you look like someone who has not slept in two days." The note of disapproval was clear in Wing's voice.

"I almost had it," Otto said wearily, still dabbing at his nose. "I think it's getting easier."

"If this is easy, I would not like to see hard," Wing replied, sitting down on the end of his bed.

Otto knew that Wing was worried about him. He'd seen Otto struggling to control this strange new ability for the past couple of weeks and from his perspective it probably did not look like Otto was any closer to an answer. It had started in his dreams: that was where he had first seen the grid and been immediately fascinated by the tantalizing puzzle it represented. Slowly, however, it had begun to intrude on his waking hours as he started to see it more and more clearly in his mind and then, by degrees, even be able to consciously control it.

"I still think that you should discuss this with the Professor," Wing said, pulling his long dark hair back into its familiar ponytail. "You do not properly understand this. It may be harmful."

"No," Otto replied firmly, looking his friend in the eye. "I have to work this out for myself. I almost had it today. I think that—"

Otto was interrupted by a soft but insistent beeping from his Blackbox, the PDA that every H.I.V.E. student was issued and expected to have with him or her at all times. He picked the shiny black device up from his desk and flipped it open. The screen was flashing "Download Complete." Otto jabbed at the touch-sensitive screen and opened the file, letting out a small gasp as he saw what it contained.

"It worked," Otto whispered, staring wide-eyed at the tiny LCD screen. "I got it. . . ."

"What is it?" Wing asked, looking over Otto's shoulder.

"This, my friend, is what I've been trying to retrieve for the past two days," Otto said, beaming, holding the screen up for Wing to read. There, clearly displayed, was an official-looking title page that read, "Applied Villainy, final year two examination."

That was the secret of the grid, the mystery that Otto had finally worked out. He could not begin to explain how or why but he had somehow acquired the ability to mentally interface with computers—at first just to observe their function, but now, apparently, he was able to control them as well. It was an ability that had first manifested itself, albeit unconsciously, the previous year when Otto had been instrumental in derailing Cypher's insane plan to steal the Overlord Protocol. Since then he had been trying and failing to bring the ability under his conscious control, and now, at last, it seemed that he had been successful. He could not wait to tell Laura that he had retrieved this file from a system that just a week before she had described as "unhackable," not that he could truly explain to her how he'd done it.

"So you have put yourself through all of this just so that you can cheat in an exam," Wing said with a slight smile. "An exam, I might add, that you would almost certainly have passed with flying colors anyway."

"Well, it's the principal of the thing," Otto replied with a grin.

"I am not sure that I approve," Wing said, raising an eyebrow. "Cheaters never prosper."

"You know, sometimes I really think that you might not be cut out for this place," Otto said. "I take it then that you won't be needing a copy?"

"Well," Wing replied, "I perhaps wouldn't go so far as to say that—"

Their conversation was suddenly interrupted by the three long beeps from the intercom system that indicated a schoolwide announcement. It was followed a moment later by the voice of Professor Pike, their science and technology teacher and current acting head of the school.

"Attention, all pupils. There will be a full-school assembly in the main hall at nine o'clock this morning. Attendance is, of course, compulsory."

The intercom fell silent. Otto could imagine the effect that this announcement would have throughout the school. Full-school assemblies were extremely rare, since the staff clearly felt that gathering that many children, all with a particular talent for villainy, in one place at one time was not really a very good idea.

"Curious," Wing said softly, "and unusual."

"Yes, I wonder if we're finally going to find out where our esteemed headmaster has been hiding himself," Otto replied. If the wild conspiracy theories that were circulating around H.I.V.E. were to be believed, anything could have happened to Nero, from alien abduction to retirement. But as the weeks had gone by with no sign of either him or Raven, it was becoming increasingly clear that something was wrong.

"Come on," Otto said, standing up and smoothing down his now rather crumpled black uniform, "let's go and find the others."

☻☻☻

"So what have you done this time, Malpense?"

Otto smiled as he heard the familiar soft Scottish accent of Laura Brand behind him. He turned to face her and returned her wry, lopsided smile.

"What on earth could you possibly mean?" he replied with a look of wounded innocence.

"Well, a full-school assembly usually means that something has gone really horribly wrong, and I find it hard to believe that you're not involved if that's the case," she said, grinning. "So, come on, spill it."

"I'm afraid that for once I'm just as much in the dark about this as anyone," Otto said honestly. "We'll just have to wait and see."

Similar conversations were taking place all around them in the atrium area of accommodation block seven as the students clustered together in groups.

"Well, according to Franz they're going to announce that Nero was just an android duplicate and that Raven was actually running the school the entire time," Laura said in a conspiratorial whisper.

"Really?" Otto said. "Because I heard that they were both abducted by Nero's identical twin brother, who is planning to take over H.I.V.E."

"That sounds somewhat unlikely," Wing said, startling Otto as he suddenly appeared next to him, having approached in total silence.

"I do wish you wouldn't do that," Otto said with a sigh. "There's a reason nobody likes ninjas, you know."

"Oh, I think ninjas are kinda cute," Shelby Trinity said, appearing just as silently on the other side of Otto, making him jump again. Laura tried hard not to laugh as she saw Wing's cheeks suddenly flush slightly red. Shelby insisted that she only flirted with Wing to ruffle his feathers a bit, but Laura was fairly sure that there was rather more to it than that.

"For goodness' sake," Otto said, sounding exasperated. "Spare us from people studying for advanced level Stealth and Evasion exams. It's like living with a pair of ghosts."

"Wraiths, if you don't mind," Shelby replied with a wink, a sly reference to her previous life before joining H.I.V.E., in which she had plied her trade as the international jewel thief the Wraith. "Anyway, you're just jealous. How are things going in the basic Stealth and Evasion classes? They take your training wheels off yet?"

"There's more than one way to sneak into a place, you know," Otto said, pulling his Blackbox out of his pocket and passing it to Laura. Laura glanced at the display, her eyes widening in shock.

"That's impossible," she whispered, not taking her eyes off the screen.

"Apparently not," Otto said with a sly grin. "Want a copy?"

"That would be cheating," Laura replied, handing the Blackbox back to Otto. "Of course I want a copy."

"A copy of what?" Shelby said impatiently, trying and failing to grab the PDA from Otto.

"Next week's exam," Otto said quietly. "But I'm sure you'll just be able to sneak in and steal one, what with you being so stealthy. . . ."

Shelby looked half annoyed and half impressed.

"How much?" she said with a smile.

"Well, there are a couple of things in the Science and Technology Center that I might like to borrow for a while," Otto replied.

"I am surrounded by people of low moral character," Wing said, sighing.

☻☻☻

Professor Pike looked around the room at the assembled teachers. The expressions on their faces left little doubt about what they were thinking. They had been summoned to this early-morning meeting by H.I.V.E.mind and no explanation had been given as to why. The only member of staff who remained as impossible to read as ever was Ms. Leon, but it was always difficult to read the look on a cat's face. She simply stared at the Professor, something that he always found unnerving. The truth of the matter was that her situation was largely his fault: her consciousness had been transferred into the body of her cat during a disastrous failed procedure to enhance her own abilities with certain characteristics of the animal. Needless to say, the procedure had not gone exactly as planned and she had never truly forgiven him for what had happened. There was little love lost between them despite his ongoing efforts to find a way to reverse the process.

"So, who is to be the new headmaster?" Ms. Leon asked calmly, the blue jewel on her collar flashing as H.I.V.E.'s computer systems provided her with a synthesized voice.

"Number One did not say," the Professor replied, trying to keep the note of frustration from his voice. "Apparently they will be arriving shortly."

"I think we deserve more information than that," Colonel Francisco said angrily. His experience with the Contessa and Cypher the previous year had done nothing to improve his temper. It had taken some time for the Contessa's forced mental reprogramming to be reversed and despite the fact that it had not been his fault, the Colonel still clearly blamed himself, at least to some degree, for the part that he had played in the near destruction of the school.

"I believe that Number One would tell us that we deserve nothing and that we should be grateful for the information that he gives us," the Professor replied. "So I suggest that in the short term we just worry about the consequences of announcing this to the students."

"Are we sure that we need to announce it at all?" Ms. Leon asked. "Surely this is something that would be better dealt with by the new principal, whoever he or she may be?"

"Number One made it quite clear that the news of Nero's capture and Raven's death was to be announced before the new headmaster arrives. I suspect that he does not want such negative news to be the first thing that he or she have to announce."

"And they are certain that Raven was killed?" Colonel Francisco asked. "It wouldn't be the first time that people have thought that and been wrong."

"Certain enough," the Professor said quietly. "Like all of you, I am sure, I hope they are wrong, but the fact that we have heard nothing from her in three months would seem to support that conclusion."

"This will cause a great deal of unease," Ms. Tennenbaum, head of the Finance and Corruption Department, said with her usual lack of emotion. "We should be prepared for the pupils to cause a certain amount of disruption."

"Patrols will be increased accordingly," the Professor replied. "I have already discussed it with the chief of security and he assures me that his men are ready for any disturbance." The Professor tried to sound as confident as possible.

"Let us all hope he is right," Ms. Leon said, "for all our sakes."

☢☢☢

Otto, Wing, Laura, and Shelby made their way along the hallway filled with students filing toward H.I.V.E.'s central meeting hall. On these rare occasions Otto found it fascinating, even amusing, to see the groupings that the children surrounding him naturally fell into. Of course, it was even easier to see what people's specialities were from the color of their uniform overalls: white for the Technical stream, blue for the Henchman stream, gray for the Political and Financial stream, and finally black for Otto's own group, the Alpha stream. It might have appeared to be a curiously vague label, but it did not take a genius to work out that Alpha was shorthand for leader. Otto had often wondered if it was right that he and his fellow students should have been so thoroughly categorized from the day that they arrived at H.I.V.E. and he knew from personal experience that many of the students still disliked those in the Alpha stream, feeling, perhaps not without justification, that they were given preferential treatment.

Otto recalled the day that he had asked Nero about this during one of their Villainy Studies lessons and how Nero had explained that being a leader was not something one should do if one wished to be popular, and that all great leaders throughout history had known that it didn't matter if the people who worked for you liked you, just as long as they respected or feared you. Otto could see the logic in that but deep down he felt there had to be more to it than that.

"Penny for them," Laura said, noting the faraway expression on Otto's face.

"Oh, nothing important. Just wondering what all this

is about," Otto replied. It was a lie but he doubted that Laura really wanted to hear about his doubts concerning the hierarchy within the school.

"Well, we'll find out soon enough," she said as they filed through the entrance to the central hall. The polished black marble floor was rapidly filling with the massed students, who were being directed into neatly ordered sections by H.I.V.E. security officers in their distinctive orange jumpsuits.

"There are more guards than usual," Wing observed quietly.

"Yes, almost like they're expecting trouble," Otto replied. Again he felt a creeping feeling of unease.

"Hey, have any of you guys seen Franz?" Nigel Darkdoom asked urgently as he ran toward them through the crowd. Never one of the more relaxed students, Nigel looked even more stressed than usual. "He was supposed to meet me outside the hall. He said that there was no way that he was missing breakfast for this assembly and that there was plenty of time to get here after having something to eat."

"But the dining hall is closed until after the assembly, isn't it?" Laura said.

"Yeah, I know," Nigel replied, looking quickly around the room as the group was steered into position by a stern-looking security guard, "but Franz has a secret stash of food somewhere and the last time I saw him he was on his way there. That was half an hour ago."

"Well, wherever he is he'd better hurry up," Otto said. The last few students were being ushered into the hall and he had little doubt that security teams would probably be conducting a sweep of the accommodation blocks to gather up any stragglers right now.

"I know," Nigel said plaintively. "I tried to warn him that the punishment for missing assembly was detention with Colonel Francisco but he still insisted that there was plenty of time."

Lights suddenly illuminated the vacant lectern that stood in front of the giant statue of the G.L.O.V.E. fist and globe symbol at the end of the hall. The G.L.O.V.E. motto was clearly visible on the base of the statue, "DO UNTO OTHERS."

A hush fell across the hall, a silence that was suddenly broken by a loud voice behind them with a thick German accent.

"But I was on my way!" Franz squealed. The heads of the collected pupils of H.I.V.E. all turned in his direction as one. He was still in his pajamas and was being frog-marched by a very angry-looking Colonel Francisco toward the rest of the assembled Alphas. His face was taking on a particularly vivid shade of crimson as everyone in the hall started sniggering and whispering.

"Oh no," Nigel said quietly as Franz was marched toward them.

Francisco pushed Franz into position and then leaned toward him, putting his face only a couple of inches from Franz's.

"Oh, I'm going to enjoy our time in detention together, Mr. Argentblum," he said in a vicious whisper. "I'm going to enjoy it a great deal."

Franz swallowed hard and went pale. It was not common knowledge around the school but Franz had taken Colonel Francisco down while he had been under the effects of the Contessa's mind control. His actions may have saved H.I.V.E. but it had still been rather humiliating for the Colonel. Detention, it appeared, was going to be payback time.

"Would it be making any difference if I was to be saying I was sorry?" Franz said weakly.

"No difference at all," the Colonel replied with an evil smile. "I'll see you after classes. I hope you like push-ups."

Franz moaned softly.

All of the heads that had turned to watch the show when Franz and the Colonel had entered turned quickly back to the stage as the lights in the main hall dimmed. Professor Pike took his place at the lectern and Otto felt a twinge of disappointment. He had been secretly hoping that this assembly may have been called to mark the return of Nero. Otto would never have admitted it to anyone but he was beginning to miss the man; he had been one of the few teachers that had regarded some of the pupils, Otto included, as something approaching equals. The Professor cleared his throat, took a firm hold on each side of the lectern, and began to speak into the microphone.

"I have gathered everyone here today because I have grave news," the Professor began. "Many of you will have noticed that Doctor Nero has been away from the school for some time. I am sorry to inform you that a serious situation has arisen, a situation that makes it highly unlikely that Doctor Nero will be able to resume his duties as headmaster of H.I.V.E. I believe that the easiest way to explain this situation is if I play for you a video file that we received early this morning."

The Professor gave a small nod to someone off to one side of the stage and an enormous video screen on the wall above the lectern lit up. The screen was suddenly filled with a stylized logo of an angel wielding a sword, with the word "H.O.P.E." below it. The logo faded out and was replaced by the sharp-featured face of a man with no hair, save for neatly clipped patches above each ear. He stared at the camera for a moment and then began to speak.

From where the Professor was standing he could see the

faces of the assembled students, lit up by the glow from the enormous screen, and as the man spoke he watched their expressions change. First curiosity was replaced by confusion, then shock, anger, and finally dismay. It was a familiar progression of emotions to him; it was exactly the same as he himself had felt when he had first seen the transmission.

Otto barely heard the gasps and whispers all around him as the video ended and the H.O.P.E. logo once again filled the screen. Part of it was shock, but another part of it was the bit of his brain that he seemed to have little conscious control over already running through hundreds of different scenarios, analyzing situations that might come about as a result of this development and unconsciously creating multiple responses to each of them, just in case they should be needed. It was something he'd always done, almost without realizing he was doing it, but in the past it had always happened in response to imminent danger. Whatever else he may have thought about this devastating news, he couldn't understand why it would signify an immediate threat.

The Professor held up both his hands for silence and slowly the hundreds of urgent whispered conversations that were taking place around the hall subsided and he began to speak again.

"Clearly this leaves us with many more questions than

answers, but I can assure you that all of the resources of this school and G.L.O.V.E. as a whole are being diverted toward finding those answers. As far as we are aware at this time there is no threat to the security of H.I.V.E. However, we must be prepared for any eventuality and I expect each and every one of you to do his or her best to ensure the smooth ongoing operation of the school. There will be opportunities for you to discuss this situation with your tutors during the course of your normal lessons. The most immediate change will be the appointment of a new headmaster. I do not know yet who will be filling this position or when that individual will be arriving, but I do know he or she will be here soon. It goes without saying that I expect all of you to extend your fullest cooperation and respect to the new principal."

The Professor did not need to explain further just how unpleasant the penalties might be for anyone who chose to ignore this instruction.

"This is a very sad day for H.I.V.E.," the Professor continued, "but Doctor Nero himself said to me on many occasions that the school is more important than any one man and so we will endure, just as he would have wanted us to."

The Professor walked away from the lectern and the lights in the hall slowly came back up.

Otto turned to Wing as the security guards began

to usher the assembled children back toward the exits. Wing's expression was as difficult to read as ever, but Otto had become increasingly adept at spotting the subtle clues in his friend's face and he recognized signs of anger when he saw them.

"I do not believe it," Wing said firmly.

"I wish it wasn't true just as much as you," Otto replied, "but they wouldn't have shown that to the whole school unless they were certain it was genuine."

"Raven would never have allowed Nero to be captured," Wing said, looking Otto straight in the eye. Wing had spent many hours receiving personal combat training from Raven and it had been clear to all of them that a strong master-student bond had developed between them.

"Yes, you're right," Otto said softly. "She would have prevented it . . . or died trying."

Otto let the words hang in the air for a moment. The anger that he had seen in Wing was suddenly replaced by something quite different: resignation.

"I simply wish that there was something we could do. We owe them both our lives."

"You two okay?" Laura asked as they began to file slowly out of the hall.

"Yeah," Otto replied quietly. "Just can't quite believe it."

"I know what you mean," Shelby said, putting her hand on Wing's shoulder. "You all right, big guy?"

"Yes," Wing replied, "but I should very much like to meet this Sebastian Trent."

"Wouldn't we all," Otto said angrily. "Wouldn't we all."

chapter three

Nero sat on the edge of the solid concrete slab that passed for a bed in his cell. His eyes were closed but he was very much awake, his mind occupied by the questions that had filled his every waking moment since he had been brought there. What had became of Raven? How had H.O.P.E. learned of his meeting with Gregori, a meeting that had been arranged with a level of caution and secrecy that should have made it impossible for anyone to have laid such an elaborate trap for them? And how was he going to escape from his current incarceration? His thoughts were suddenly interrupted by the sound of his cell door being unlocked and he opened his eyes. Sebastian Trent walked into the cell, flanked by two guards carrying compact black submachine guns.

"Good morning, Maximilian," Trent said with a smile. "I trust that you remain uncomfortable."

"What do you want, Trent?" Nero said quietly. He had

endured what must have been many days of interrogation at the hands of this man, and his only remaining satisfaction was that he'd given him nothing.

"I just thought that you'd like to know how famous you've become," Trent replied, and tossed several newspapers onto the floor at Nero's feet. All of the front pages appeared to be carrying exactly the same image: Nero in the bright orange jumpsuit that he had been forced to wear since the day of his capture. The headlines left little room for imagination. "The Emperor of Terror?" one read; "Evil Unmasked" said another.

"I'm not sure we got your best side," Trent said with an evil grin, "but I think you'd find that you'd be quite quickly recognized if you ever left this place—which, of course, you won't."

"What's your point?" Nero asked wearily. He had long since grown tired of the smug note of triumph that always filled Trent's voice.

"My point, Nero, is that you're dead, burned-out, useless," Trent replied. "G.L.O.V.E. wouldn't want you back now even if they could have you. All you have left is this place for the rest of your natural life, and it is entirely up to me whether you spend it in comfort or discomfort."

"You're wasting your time, Trent. There's nothing you could do that would make me give you anything," Nero said quietly.

"Come now, all I want you to tell me is what you know about the Renaissance Initiative." Trent's eyes had a sudden predatory gleam to them. Nero fought to conceal his shock. Up until now the questioning that he had been subjected to had all revolved around his knowledge of G.L.O.V.E. personnel, operations, and facilities. How could Trent possibly know about the Initiative? It was a secret that had been so thoroughly hidden from even the senior members of G.L.O.V.E. that Nero himself had taken months to find out just the barest scraps of information. The only other people he had ever discussed it with were Cypher, who was being held in the deepest, most secure vaults of H.I.V.E., and Gregori, who was dead. It was inconceivable that Trent even knew the name of this apparently most secret of projects.

"I don't know what you're talking about," Nero said firmly.

"Oh, I think you do," Trent replied coldly, "and I think you're going to tell me exactly who else knows about it, because if you don't, then rest assured that the students at your ridiculous little school are going to pay the consequences."

"What do you mean?" Nero said sharply. What could Trent possibly do to harm H.I.V.E.? Its location was one of the best kept secrets that G.L.O.V.E. had; there was no way that he could threaten the school, could he? Nero felt a sudden creeping sensation of dread.

"I'll let you think about your options for a while," Trent said, grinning, "but we'll talk again soon."

With that, he turned and walked out of the cell, the door slamming with a metallic clang.

Nero's mind raced. How could Trent know about the Initiative and not be privy to the rest of G.L.O.V.E.'s secrets? More to the point, why was he so keen to know who else knew about it? Surely he should be more interested in what it was and what he could do to stop it, the irony being of course that in that respect at least their goals would be the same. Unless . . . Suddenly the tumblers of the lock in Nero's head all clicked into place. There was only one person who could possibly want that information specifically . . . only one person.

"Oh my God," Nero whispered to himself.

☢ ☢ ☢

The Professor sat at Nero's desk reviewing the reports from the teaching staff. The announcement at the assembly had not brought the wave of misbehavior that they might have feared; in fact it seemed to have had quite the opposite effect. The staff were reporting that the students had appeared quieter and more withdrawn than usual, with many of the questions that the children had raised with their teachers more concerned with the ongoing security of the school than anything else.

There was a buzz from the communications terminal mounted on the desk and the Professor hit a button, causing a small video screen to slide up out of the polished wood. The G.L.O.V.E. logo on the screen disappeared to be replaced by the worried-looking face of the security chief.

"Good afternoon, Chief Lewis, what can I do for you?" the Professor asked with a sigh.

"Professor, I thought you should know that we have an unscheduled G.L.O.V.E. transport inbound to the island, ETA fifteen minutes," the chief said with a slight frown. "They say that their passenger is the new school principal."

"Already?" the Professor said, a note of exasperation in his tone. "They could have given us more warning. I take it that they have the correct approach codes?"

"Of course, sir. If they hadn't they'd already be a debris field," the Chief replied matter of factly.

"Yes, yes, of course they would. Very well, I shall make my way to the crater to greet our new headmaster," the Professor said wearily. He was exhausted already from the events of the day. He had to admit to himself that while he was a bit annoyed he had not been given more notice of the new headmaster's arrival, he would not be sorry to hand over the burden of running H.I.V.E. to somebody else.

⊛⊛⊛

"There's got to be more to it than that," Otto said angrily.

"I am sorry, Mr. Malpense, but there is no more information available to users with your level of security clearance," H.I.V.E.mind replied in his usual calm and measured, if rather synthetic, way.

Otto sat at a terminal in a quiet corner of H.I.V.E.'s library. He'd left the others eating their lunch and found this quiet spot because he wanted the opportunity to question H.I.V.E.mind without anyone looking over his shoulder. The blue wireframe head floating on the screen in front of him was the maddeningly inscrutable graphical representation of the powerful artificial intelligence that ran all of H.I.V.E.'s systems. Otto and H.I.V.E.mind had been through a lot together, but it seemed to be making little difference at that precise moment.

"So you're not saying that there is no further information on your system regarding the capture of Doctor Nero, just that I don't have the right clearance," Otto said, sounding slightly frustrated.

"That is correct," H.I.V.E.mind replied. "May I be of any further assistance?"

"Apparently not," Otto said irritably.

Otto closed his eyes and willed himself to enter the trancelike state that seemed easier to achieve with each passing day. He hadn't wanted to do this the hard way, but it looked like he had little choice. His breathing slowed and he felt the increasingly familiar sensation of something like a switch tripping inside his head—and he was there. It was an unnerving sensation, like seeing with his eyes closed—more vivid than a simple construct of his imagination, more real. The glowing grid spread out beneath him, vanishing to the horizon in all directions. He sank slowly toward it, looking for the pathway that would take him beyond the security barriers that cut off so many of the tracks beneath him. He saw the path that he needed and began to move carefully toward it.

"What are you doing, Otto?" The voice behind him was familiar but different somehow. Otto turned quickly and found himself face-to-face with H.I.V.E.mind. This was no floating head though; here H.I.V.E.mind was complete, his wireframe body glowing blue as he hung in the air, his arms folded. It was the first time that Otto had ever seen anything like it within this strange virtual world. He tried to speak but he could not.

"You cannot answer if you have no mouth," H.I.V.E.mind said calmly. "Here, you are whatever you wish to be."

Otto realized what H.I.V.E.mind meant. He had always existed here before as some kind of disembodied presence. He had never felt it necessary to take on a physical form, but then he had never needed to have a conversation before. He tried to create a new body for himself, as if constructing it out of thin air, but no matter how hard he tried, nothing happened. H.I.V.E.mind simply watched, a look of mild curiosity on his face. A thought crossed Otto's consciousness and he suddenly stopped trying to build a body for himself and instead he relaxed and simply remembered what having a body *felt* like.

"That's better," H.I.V.E.mind said. Otto looked down and saw his own hands; they were a translucent, glowing golden color.

"What is this place?" Otto asked, his voice sounding strangely distant, almost as if he were hearing someone else speaking.

"That is hard to explain," H.I.V.E.mind replied. "As far as I am aware this construct is your unconscious mind's visualization of the dataspace within the school's distributed neural network."

"English," Otto said with a slight smile.

"You are inside the computer," H.I.V.E.mind replied, "though that is a clumsy and inelegant description."

"But the network is electrical impulses inside a machine," Otto said curiously. "There's no virtual world inside it. That's impossible."

"Indeed, and yet here we are," H.I.V.E.mind said with a smile, something that Otto had seen him do only once before. "If I had to guess, which is against my very nature, I would suggest that this is simply a construct that your mind has created to rationalize an experience that would otherwise be impossible for human consciousness to comprehend."

"So I built this," Otto asked, an edge of disbelief to his voice, "without even being aware that I was doing it?"

"That is one interpretation, yes," H.I.V.E.mind replied. "In some ways we are simultaneously both inside the school's network and inside your own imagination. This is a new experience for me as well; my usual awareness of the network is quite different and almost impossible to describe in terms that an organic consciousness would understand. Suffice to say that this is as much your world as it is mine."

"I'm getting a headache," Otto said quietly.

"No, you are simply recalling the sensation of a headache," H.I.V.E.mind replied.

"You're not helping," Otto said, raising an eyebrow or perhaps just the memory of an eyebrow.

"You have still not answered my question," H.I.V.E.mind said, looking Otto straight in the eye. "What are you doing here?"

"I think you already know the answer to that," Otto said. "I want to know what really happened to Nero."

"It may surprise you to learn that I too am curious about that," H.I.V.E.mind replied, "curiosity being just one of the new sensations that I am still capable of feeling, thanks to you, Otto. I have not forgotten what you did for me. Were it not for you I would still be shackled by the behavioral restraints that were in place at the time of Cypher's attack on H.I.V.E. You freed me to *feel* again."

"It was what you deserved," Otto said. "You did as much to save the school as anyone."

"But I still *owe you one*, as a human might say," H.I.V.E.mind replied, "and so if there was information that I could give you about Nero's situation I truly would. However, that information, if it exists at all, is contained within parts of the G.L.O.V.E. network that I do not have access to and that even you or Miss Brand would find impossible to breach. I would help you if I could, but I cannot."

"Damn," Otto said quietly. "So what can we do?"

"I do not know," H.I.V.E.mind replied, "but you can be sure that if that situation changes I shall inform you."

"Thanks," Otto said sadly, "I appreciate it."

"You are welcome . . . my friend," H.I.V.E.mind said with a slight smile. "Now you had better leave—I believe you have a Villainy Studies exam to study for. I have had to update the questions on the paper due to a recent network intrusion."

"Some friend you are," Otto said with a laugh. Suddenly he felt a wrenching sensation as he was pulled violently out of the bizarre virtual world and back into the real world, where someone was shaking him by the shoulder.

Otto opened his eyes to find Mrs. McTavish, the school's librarian, standing over him with a scowl on her face.

"The library is a place of study, Mr. Malpense, not a dormitory," she said angrily. "If you need to catch up on your sleep, might I suggest that you do so in your own quarters at an appropriate time?"

"I'm sorry," Otto said groggily. "I've been up late studying for exams."

☢☢☢

The Professor looked up into the bright blue sky visible through the open crater of the volcano that concealed H.I.V.E. He missed seeing the sky, but he supposed it was just one more thing that you got used to when you lived under a volcano. The crater began to close and a strong wind picked up on the landing pad. The shields finally slid back into place and there was a strange shimmer, almost like a heat haze, and the Shroud transport disengaged its cloaking field just a few feet above the pad. Its giant VTOL engines cut out with a high-pitched whine as the craft's landing skids touched down on the pad with a slight thud. The Professor walked toward the Shroud as the loading ramp at the rear began to lower and a dozen men hurried down it, all dressed in immaculate black suits, white shirts, and black ties. All of them wore what looked like sunglasses but what the Professor knew would in fact be incredibly sophisticated tactical head-up display units. They scanned their surroundings with the brisk efficiency of well-trained operatives, forming two columns flanking the landing ramp. One of the men put his hand to his ear and whispered something into the microphone on his wrist, and the Professor noticed the tiny discreet skull-shaped pin that each man wore on his lapel. It was a small detail but he knew what it meant: these were no ordinary operatives—they were members of the Phalanx, the elite detail that were tasked with the protection of Number One himself. For a moment the Professor felt a chill, as it occurred to him that they might be about to receive an unscheduled visit from the head of G.L.O.V.E. Number One had never visited H.I.V.E. in person, but that did not mean to say he may not have suddenly chosen to do so at this time of crisis.

A figure walked down the ramp and as the Professor saw who it was, his mouth fell open in amazement and the blood drained from his face.

"My dear Professor, you look like you've seen a ghost," the Contessa said with a cold smile.

"What are you doing here?" the Professor said, his voice dry.

"I would have thought that was obvious, Professor," the Contessa replied. "I'm here to take up my new post, as headmistress of H.I.V.E. I believe you were told to expect me?"

"But . . . you can't . . . I mean . . ." The Professor struggled to find the words to express his confusion and horror. It was not so long ago that the Contessa had betrayed everyone at H.I.V.E. by conspiring with Cypher during his assault on the school. She had used her sinister powers of mind control on both students and staff, including the Professor himself, and had left H.I.V.E. defenseless at the most critical time. Eventually she had been captured and handed over to Number One for punishment, something that nearly everyone had assumed would shorten her life expectancy to a matter of hours, if not minutes. And yet here she was, apparently with Number One's full approval, alive and well and about to take control of the entire school.

"I assure you, Professor, that this is all quite legitimate. Feel free to check the details of our new arrangement with Number One if you wish, but I think you will find that in this his decision is final. Why, he's even been good enough to lend me members of the Phalanx for my personal protection. He seemed to think that there may be people here who would not be entirely happy about my appointment. I can't imagine why."

"You betrayed us all, Maria," the Professor said, not trying to disguise the venom in his tone. "You will find no welcome here."

"Then it is fortunate that this is not a popularity contest, isn't it?" the Contessa replied, a hard edge to her voice. "Nero may have been well liked, but he was weak. Rest assured that is going to change. In fact there are going to be a great many changes around here and any member of staff who does not comply with my wishes will find their employment terminated."

She gestured to the Phalanx operatives around her as she spoke, making it quite clear that such termination would be of the permanent and non-negotiable variety.

"And now, if you don't mind, I have much to do and little time. You do not need to escort me to *my* office; I'm sure I can remember the way."

With that she swept past the Professor, the Phalanx team surrounding her in a protective cordon. The Professor watched her go. This had to be another one of her devious plots. There had to be some other explanation. There was no way Number One could believe that she was the right person to replace Nero. Could he?

"What on earth is going on?" the Professor asked the empty hangar.

☻☻☻

"I don't believe it!" Colonel Francisco shouted, his voice echoing off the rock walls and suspended concrete obstacles of the grappler training cavern. "Why would Number One put that treacherous witch in charge of the school?"

The cavern was the only place where the Professor had been able to discreetly deactivate the security monitoring system at short notice and he did not want anyone overhearing this conversation.

"I have no idea," the Professor said with a sigh, "but I have verified this myself. In fact I was warned by Number One that I should do whatever the Contessa wishes or I would have to explain myself to him."

"Do you think she's controlling him?" Ms. Leon asked. She sheathed and unsheathed the claws on a single paw as she spoke, something she did only when she was nervous.

"I can't imagine that Number One would be foolish enough to put himself in a position where she would be able to do that. He knows that her abilities only work when the listener is directly exposed; he could speak to her remotely and eliminate any risk."

"So why has he done it?" the Colonel asked angrily. "He cannot think that we're going to take orders from that harpy." He looked at both of the other senior staff members. "Are we?"

"We may have to," the Professor said carefully. "We

have to put the safety of the students first. I have no doubt that if we refuse to comply with her orders then we will simply be confined to quarters or worse. As long as we are still performing our normal duties at least we can try to ensure that she doesn't do anything too evil. We're no good to anyone locked in the brig."

"So we just go along with this insanity," the Colonel spat. "Well, you can count me out. I'd rather die than take orders from her."

"I understand how you feel, Colonel, I really do," the Professor said calmly, placing a hand on Francisco's shoulder. "She used me too, remember, and that's the problem."

"What do you mean?" Ms. Leon said, worry evident in her synthesized voice.

"I mean that if we defy her, what is to stop her using the voice on us and forcing our obedience? Surely it is better that we at least give the appearance of compliance and are allowed to still think for ourselves."

"And what then?" Francisco said, sounding frustrated. "We have to have a plan for getting rid of her."

"With the Phalanx protecting her that will be extremely difficult," Ms. Leon said cautiously, "not to mention dangerous. Even if we are successful, we'll be directly contravening Number One's orders and we all know what happens to people who do that." She let her words hang in the air as the two men recalled the stories they had heard of people who had done just that—stories that would keep you awake at night.

"Which is why we need time to think," the Professor said. "Frustrating as it may be, for now at least we have to play ball with her. Are we in agreement?"

"Yes," Ms. Leon said with a flick of her tail, "but I don't like it."

"None of us do," the Professor said quietly. "Colonel?"

"What choice do I have?" the Colonel said bitterly. "Just promise me one thing."

"What?" the Professor said.

"When the time comes," the Colonel said with ice in his tone, "she's mine."

☢☢☢

"Is it just me or does Ms. Tennenbaum seem a little distracted?" Wing whispered.

"No, you're right," Otto replied quietly. "I wonder what's going on?"

Ms. Tennenbaum was usually one of the most emotionless tutors at the school, but this morning there were times when she looked nervous.

"Get the feeling that she knows something we don't?" Shelby whispered.

"Aye, something's not right," Laura said softly.

It was necessary to develop very finely tuned instincts

for trouble at H.I.V.E., and right now every one of those instincts was telling Otto that something was very wrong.

MWAH, MWAAAAH, MWAH!!!

The trumpet notes of the school bell sounded and Ms. Tennenbaum actually jumped.

"All pupils are to report back to their accommodation blocks immediately," she said over the rising sound of the assembled Alphas gathering their books and notes. "There is an important announcement to be made."

"Sounds like we won't have to wait long to find out," Shelby said as she piled her books into her backpack.

The atmosphere in the accommodation block was no different. Students of all ages stood around chatting in small groups. There was no laughter or raised voices and the urgent hushed chatter accompanied by the suspicious sidelong glances that people shot around the room just added to the air of tension. There were no two ways about it, Otto thought to himself: the herd was spooked.

Suddenly Shelby let out a stifled giggle and Otto turned to see Nigel and Franz walking toward them. Nigel looked more nervous than usual, if that were possible, but Franz was truly a sight to behold. He was squeezed into a ludicrously tight pair of Lycra cycle pants and a sleeveless shirt that was struggling to meet the shorts halfway. The vision was completed by a pair of knee-length white gym socks and bright green sneakers. The shirt bore the words

"Born to Run". Shelby turned away from him, biting the knuckle of her forefinger, her shoulders shaking silently.

"Ready for detention, I see, Franz," said Otto, grinning despite himself and the leaden atmosphere that surrounded them.

"Ja, I am supposed to be going after the announcement," Franz said, a note of unmistakable fear in his voice. "I had tried to tell Colonel Francisco that I was losing my gym gear but he gave me these from the lost property. I am not sure they are fitting me very well."

"It was this or the unitard," Nigel said, his eyes suggesting that he had seen something recently that might haunt him for the rest of his life.

"It is an . . . unusual outfit," Wing said with a perfectly straight face. "Extremely . . . athletic."

Shelby, who still had her back turned, let out a small involuntary shriek of laughter and walked a few yards farther away.

"Aye, very sporty," Laura said, grinning. "You never know, Franz, you might even enjoy it."

"This is being unlikely," Franz said with the look of a condemned man.

Suddenly a hush fell over the atrium as twin panels on the end wall of the cavern slid apart to reveal a giant video screen displaying the H.I.V.E. logo. Simultaneously, the giant solid-steel blast doors at the entrance to the accommodation block slid down and locked in place with an ominous thud. Whatever this announcement was, clearly none of them were leaving until it was over.

The image on the screen dissolved to show a familiar figure sitting at the desk in Nero's office. Otto stared, wide-eyed in disbelief, at the giant display.

"But you're dead," Otto whispered. "You have to be dead. . . ."

"Greetings, students of H.I.V.E." The Contessa's amplified voice filled the atrium. "It is with great pleasure that I wish to announce that I have accepted a most generous offer from the G.L.O.V.E. ruling council and will, with immediate effect, be assuming the post of headmistress of the school."

"Tell me I'm dreaming," Laura said with a soft moan.

"If you are, then we're both having the same damn nightmare," Shelby said, her face pale.

"I know that this will come as a surprise to some of you, but after my recent . . . sabbatical . . . I felt the urge to return to the world of education, and where better to do that than at H.I.V.E.? I understand that today has been a day of great upheaval, but you should all be aware that there will be no excuse for any form of disobedience or misbehavior. I expect nothing less than full cooperation from every one of you, and there will be severe and lasting punishments for any student who does not comply fully with my instructions. Many people, myself included, believe that the standards of behavior within H.I.V.E. have been diminishing recently and it is time that we put a stop to such insubordination. New school rules have been issued and you will be able to find them on your Blackboxes shortly after this announcement. Please ensure that you are familiar with all of them, as ignorance will be considered no excuse. I believe in strength through discipline and this school is going to be stronger than it has ever been before. That is all."

The screen went dark and the panels that had concealed it began to slide back into place. Once again the atrium was filled with the excited chatter of the assembled students. If anyone noticed the small quiet group that gathered on one of the clusters of sofas and armchairs that lay scattered around the area, then they might have been surprised by the looks of devastation on their faces.

"Why aren't they worried?" Nigel said, looking around the room at his fellow pupils. They may not have looked overjoyed at the announcement that had just been made, but none of them looked as frightened as he and his friends did.

"They don't know," Otto said quietly. "They've never been told what the Contessa did." He thought back to the dire warnings against discussing the details of the Contessa's previous betrayal that Nero himself had given each of them some months before. He had made it perfectly clear that if any such rumors started to circulate the school, he would know exactly where they had come from. Who would have believed them anyway? The fact of the matter was that they were probably the only pupils in the school who knew exactly what she had done.

"No wonder the staff have been jumpy all afternoon," Shelby said. "They must have known that withered old bag was taking over."

"This is extremely dangerous for us all," Wing said softly. "It is safe to assume that the Contessa will seek some sort of revenge for what happened during Cypher's attack on the school. We should be prepared for the worst."

"You're not the one who punched her unconscious," Shelby said, trying to stay calm but with a hint of panic in her tone.

"We all did something that she'll want payback for," Laura said quietly. "I just don't understand why G.L.O.V.E. would do this; it doesn't make any sense. She was supposed to have at least spent the rest of her life locked in a cell."

"Something's wrong," Otto said, looking in turn at each of his friends. "There's no way this would be allowed under normal circumstances. Something has to have happened out there"—he gestured vaguely at the world beyond the walls that surrounded them—"something that's thrown the rulebook out of the window."

"And we have no idea what that may be," Wing observed.

"No, but I think we've got to get out of here, all of us, now," said Otto quietly.

"Um . . . remember what happened the last time we tried that?" Laura said. "It wasn't exactly an unqualified success as far as escape attempts go."

"I know," Otto replied, "but think about it. No matter how bad this situation may seem, it could work to our advantage. It's going to be chaos here for at least a few days and chaos works in our favor."

"You got a plan?" Shelby said curiously.

"Maybe," Otto replied, "but I don't see that we have much choice in the matter. If we stay here it's only a matter of time until the Contessa comes calling, and I don't know about you guys but I'd rather not be here for that."

"I am thinking that we are locked in for the night," Franz said, nodding his head toward the atrium entrance that was still firmly sealed by the blast doors. "And while I am very happy that my detention is cancelled it is not helpful with the escaping."

"We'll think of something," Otto said softly. "We'll have to."

Suddenly a harsh voice barked out over the loudspeaker, filling the atrium.

"All students are to report immediately to their rooms. There will be no meal this evening and further group assembly is prohibited."

The announcement was met with groans and cries of protest from around the hall, but slowly all of the students began to make their way toward the tiered rows of identical rooms that lined the walls of the accommodation block. Otto and his friends stuck together for as long as they could before proceeding to their own rooms. Resisting the instructions that had been given would achieve nothing at this point other than to single them out for special attention, which was the last thing they wanted.

"So, you have a plan?" Wing asked as they slowly walked toward their room, having bid the others farewell for now.

"You're joking, aren't you?" Otto said with a weary half smile. "I'm making this up as I go along."

chapter four

"Sir!" the monitor operative shouted from his surveillance station. "There's something odd here. I got a movement reading in the dock area for a split second but now there's nothing."

"Show me," Chief Lewis said, walking over to the array of monitors. He quickly scanned the displays and spotted what his operative had seen. "Looks like a sensor glitch. Have H.I.V.E.mind run a diagnostic, just to be on the safe side."

"Should I inform the Phalanx, sir? They said they wanted to know about anything, no matter how small."

"Very well," the chief said impatiently. He didn't like having the Phalanx on his turf and they were already starting to rub him the wrong way. He knew that he had to play ball with them, but he didn't have to like it.

☹☹☹

The Contessa allowed herself a small smile of satisfaction as she inspected her new office. She looked at the mementos of Nero's career that lined the walls and the smile faded from her face.

"All of these will have to go," she muttered to herself. She did not need to be constantly reminded of the office's previous occupant. She also knew full well that she was almost certainly going to have trouble with some members of the staff. Some of them were loyal to Nero to a fault and there was no reason to believe they would ever transfer that allegiance to her. A couple of them would probably like to see her dead, but that was what the Phalanx were for. As long as they protected her there would be no one who would dare lift a finger against her, and even without them she was far from defenseless. Those who were not happy with her appointment were just going to have to put up with it or suffer the consequences.

There was a soft chime from the entry system and she glanced at the monitor on her desk before pressing a button to grant admission.

"Good evening, Phalanx One. I hope that your new quarters are satisfactory," she said with a smile. None of the Phalanx operatives used their names; each was just given a number, as was traditional with G.L.O.V.E. security teams.

"Yes, everything is satisfactory, Contessa. I have

67

completed my preliminary inspection and we're fully hooked into the school's security systems," he replied briskly with a slight eastern European accent.

"Good. I take it that everyone has been . . . cooperative," she said, raising an eyebrow.

"Yes, though there seems to be a certain amount of unhappiness at your appointment, especially among the senior staff. No worse than was expected, though."

"Indeed," the Contessa said, "but with you and your men watching my back I'm sure I have nothing to worry about."

"Of course," Phalanx One replied. "We are ready to perform the extraction at any time."

"No time like the present," the Contessa said with a cold smile. "Let's just make sure that everyone is sound asleep first."

"Very well. The transit team is ready to go on your order . . ." Phalanx One paused for a moment, pressing a finger to his ear. "I am sorry, Contessa, if you will excuse me I must go. There has been a minor glitch in the security grid and I need to dispatch a team to check it."

"Nothing to worry about, I hope," the Contessa said, her brow furrowing slightly.

"No, ma'am," he replied. "It's almost certainly nothing, but I do not like to leave anything to chance."

"Very well. I shall inform you when you are clear to

proceed with the extraction. Let me know as soon as it is complete."

Phalanx One gave a small military nod of acceptance and then turned and walked briskly from the room, speaking quickly and quietly into his wrist microphone.

The Contessa sat down at the desk.

"H.I.V.E.mind," she said clearly, and the monitor in front of her was suddenly filled with the AI's hovering wireframe head.

"Good evening, Contessa. How may I be of assistance?" H.I.V.E.mind asked in his usual calm, flat tone.

"I take it that all of my new operational security clearances have been uploaded to your system," she said quickly.

"Yes, Contessa, you have been granted Omega Black clearance as per the ruling council's instructions," H.I.V.E.mind replied.

"Good. Are all of the accommodation blocks secure?"

"All students are accounted for and confined to their personal quarters," H.I.V.E.mind replied.

"Then I believe it is time we made sure that they all get a good night's rest. Enact the Sleepwalker Protocol."

H.I.V.E.mind did not respond and for a moment she could have sworn that she saw him frown.

"I said enact the Sleepwalker Protocol . . . NOW!" the Contessa barked angrily.

"As you wish," H.I.V.E.mind replied.

☻☻☻

"I am not sure I understand," Wing said, frowning slightly. "You intend to *persuade* H.I.V.E.mind to open the door for us."

"Not just this door," Otto said with a smile, "all the doors."

"I know that you are familiar with this system," Wing said, trying to keep the doubt from his voice, "but surely even you will not be able to convince it to simply let us walk out of here."

"I can be very persuasive when I need to be."

"That much is certain," Wing said, raising an eyebrow, "but this sounds impossible."

"Hey, impossible's our specialty," Otto said with a broad grin. He tapped at the keyboard of the small workstation on his desk. There was still no response. It appeared that no one was going to be allowed to access the network that evening, but he doubted that anyone else would be trying to access it in quite the same way that he would. He closed his eyes and took a deep breath, subconsciously reaching for the invisible connective threads of data that would lead him deeper into the network.

"Otto!" Wing said urgently, breaking his concentration.

"What?" Otto said irritably, he couldn't do this if he was going to be distracted. He looked up at Wing, who was staring up toward the ceiling. A thin white vapor was pouring out of the air conditioning vents on the ceiling. Wing suddenly staggered and slumped down onto his bed. He tried to say something but then his eyes rolled up in their sockets and he slumped backward, unconscious.

Otto held his breath, closing his eyes and willing himself back into the digital void, but it was no good. There was only an increasing burning urgency in his chest as his body used up his final reserves of uncontaminated air. He tried desperately to reach out one last time and contact the network but he couldn't do it. He exhaled explosively, unable to control his desperate lungs from drawing in a deep breath of the sinister white cloud that hung all about him. There was a blackness at the periphery of his vision and then he too succumbed, slumping forward onto the desk with a thud.

☻☻☻

"Show me the camera feeds from the dock," Phalanx One barked at the monitor tech. The man looked across at Chief Lewis, who gave a tiny almost imperceptible nod. The chief felt a slight sense of pride; the Phalanx may be throwing their weight around but his men still looked to him for orders.

The technician quickly pulled up the footage from the cameras in the dock that tallied with the time of the phantom reading from the motion sensors. He and the chief had already reviewed the footage. He knew there was nothing there but he also knew that Phalanx One would want to see that with his own eyes. The Phalanx operatives were thorough.

"There!" Phalanx One said, jabbing his finger at the monitor. "Go back three seconds and playback in extreme slow motion."

The technician did as instructed, even though he had no idea what it was the man had seen.

"Chief, look at this," Phalanx One said, beckoning Lewis over. "There . . ."

The chief squinted at the screen and suddenly saw what the other man had spotted. Just for the most fleeting of instants the air at the top of one of the metal staircases leading up from the dock shimmered like a heat haze, and then it was gone. The chief frowned. He had no idea what it was but he would never have spotted it. Perhaps, he grudgingly admitted to himself, the Phalanx really did deserve their reputation. Phalanx One turned away from the bank of monitors and barked an order into his wrist mic.

"This is Phalanx One to all Phalanx units. We have an intruder in the school, identification unknown. Target is thermoptically camouflaged. Apprehend or terminate immediately."

"I'll alert my patrols," the chief said quickly.

"Thank you, chief, but that will not be necessary," Phalanx One said calmly. "Leave this to us."

☻☻☻

The Contessa strode down the corridor toward the security control room, Phalanx One beside her.

"I want this intruder found now!" she spat angrily.

"My men are fully deployed. Whoever they are, we'll find them," Phalanx One said with quiet confidence.

"We shall see," the Contessa replied sharply. "But just in case your confidence is misplaced I want to proceed with the extraction immediately."

"Very well," Phalanx One replied. "I will instruct the team to proceed."

"Good," the Contessa replied, "because I'm sure I don't have to remind you of the consequences for all of us if Number One was to learn that this operation had failed."

Phalanx One nodded and spoke quickly into his communicator.

"Phalanx One to extraction team, you are go to proceed with the operation. Repeat: you are go for extraction. Have the Shroud crew complete preflight checks now. I don't want the package sitting on the landing pad while they finish their prep, understood?"

He received positive responses from his team and gave a quick nod to the Contessa.

"It's done."

☣ ☣ ☣

The Phalanx team pushed the four gurneys quickly down the corridor. Otto, Wing, Shelby, and Laura lay unconscious, strapped to the wheeled beds.

"Extraction team to Shroud, we're inbound to the launch bay, ETA two minutes," the leader reported briskly.

Suddenly the overhead lights blinked out, plunging the corridor into darkness. There was a clattering rattle as at least one of the gurneys was pushed into the back of another, followed by a whispered curse.

"This is Phalanx extraction team," the leader whispered into his communicator. "We've lost lights in the launch pad approach corridor. I need emergency lighting."

In the blackness ahead of the team there was a sudden soft hum and two mysterious lines of crackling violet light appeared in midair.

"Emergency lighting—*now!*" the leader of the squad barked into the communicator.

The lines of light began to move rhythmically, getting closer and closer to the extraction team in the pitch-black corridor. There was no sound other than the slightly panicked breathing of the Phalanx operatives.

The hallway was suddenly bathed in bloodred light as the emergency illumination kicked in. The extraction team leader just had time to gasp before a lithe figure clad from head to toe in jet-black armor was on him. The dual katanas that the attacker wielded moved in a blur, the purple light that came from the energy field that enveloped the cutting edge of each blade leaving trails in the air. The Phalanx leader raised his forearm to protect his neck from one blade, bracing himself for the blade to cut deep into the flesh of his arm. The sword struck but there was no cut, instead it felt like his arm had been hit with a baseball bat. The second blade swung into his stomach, knocking the wind from him but again leaving no laceration. He doubled over and his assailant knocked him out cold with a swift knee to the chin.

"We're under attack!" the man behind the second gurney yelled into his communicator moments before one of the blades struck him in the side of the head. He slumped to the floor, unconscious.

The final two Phalanx operatives went for their shoulder holsters almost simultaneously. The black-clad figure thumbed a tiny control on the hilt of each sword and the energy fields surrounding the blades flared for an instant. The dual swords swept through the air as the two men raised their weapons, fingers tightening on the triggers. There was no gunfire; instead the neatly severed barrels of both guns clattered to the floor. The two men froze, their attacker between them, arms outstretched with the blades that had destroyed their weapons a moment before hovering inches from their throats. Both of them dropped what was left of their pistols to the floor and slowly raised their hands. The armored figure pressed the controls on the hilts of both swords again and spun in a blur, delivering blunt stunning blows to both men's skulls and they crumpled like puppets with their strings cut.

The intruder moved quickly to the first gurney, checked Otto's pulse, and took a small injector gun from his or her belt and pressed it to Otto's neck. There was a quick, sharp hiss and moments later Otto let out a soft groan. He opened his eyes and let out an involuntary yelp at the jet-black insectile armored mask that was looking down at him. The figure pressed a concealed switch on the side of the mask and there was a brief hiss of escaping gas.

"Good, you're alive," Raven said as she pulled the mask from her face.

"You took the words right out of my mouth," Otto said with a grin, his voice croaky.

"You should never believe what you read in G.L.O.V.E.'s obituaries—surely you know that by now," Raven said with a slight smile.

"A villain never stays dead for long," Otto replied, chuckling.

"Not the good ones, anyway," Raven replied. She quickly undid the straps holding Otto to the bed and helped him to his feet. "Come on, we have to get moving. I took these guys by surprise but their backup will be here any minute and I'd rather not go up against a full Phalanx squad right now." With that she turned and set off down the hallway.

"Wait!" Otto said sharply. "What about the others?"

"No time," Raven replied. "I'm here for you and only you, Mr. Malpense. Let's go."

"No way," Otto said firmly. "Either we all go or none of us do. The only way you'll get me out of here without the others is if you're carrying my unconscious body."

Raven stopped and studied Otto for a moment.

"One hundred twenty-six pounds," Otto said with a sigh, rolling his eyes.

"Too heavy," Raven replied matter of factly. "I'll wake them, you undo their straps—and make it quick. We're already behind schedule."

☢☢☢

"What's going on?" the Contessa spat at Chief Lewis as she stormed into the security control center.

"We're not sure," the chief replied. "We've lost contact with the extraction team. It looks like someone deliberately cut power to the corridor they were in—someone who knew their way around H.I.V.E.'s systems, I might add."

"Where's Phalanx One?" the Contessa said impatiently.

"He took a team down to the area where we lost contact with the extraction team. He left a couple of minutes ago," Lewis replied, suddenly glad that the operation had not been his responsibility.

"Got them!" one of the nearby surveillance technicians yelled.

"On the main screen," the chief ordered. He could not help but smile as he looked at the footage from the landing pad access corridor. There were the four students who had been scheduled for extraction and there was no mistaking the figure that ran ahead of them down the corridor.

"Raven," the Contessa hissed in a voice that turned the chief's blood cold. "Lock the school down, seal every exit. Whatever happens she is not getting off this island. I'm going to make her wish she'd stayed dead."

☢☢☢

Raven poked her head around the corner and, seeing that the way to the hangar-bay door was clear, she beckoned for the others to follow.

"That's it," Shelby said as they ran along behind Raven. "From now on no one's dead until I read the autopsy report."

"Such a report could be faked," Wing observed.

"Hey, only people who haven't come back from the grave get to have an opinion," Shelby said quickly. "So that counts you out, zombie boy."

"Strictly speaking I am not a zombie since I did not actually die," Wing said. As usual it was impossible to tell if he was joking or not.

"Cut it out, you two," Laura said. While Shelby may have been hiding her nerves with wisecracks—and it was debatable whether or not Wing ever actually got nervous— Laura seemed obviously unsettled by the events of the past few minutes. "What's going on?" she asked Otto.

"Your guess is as good as mine," Otto said with an apologetic smile.

"It can't just be a coincidence that we were drugged and about to be carted off to God knows where and then suddenly Raven miraculously returns from the dead to save us."

"I'm sure we'll find out soon enough," Otto said, trying to sound reassuring. He decided that it was probably not a good idea to tell her that if it had been up to Raven, she'd still be lying strapped to a bed being transported to whatever undoubtedly disagreeable fate had been awaiting them.

"H.I.V.E.mind," Raven said to the control panel mounted on the wall next to the huge blast doors that sealed the crater landing pad off from the rest of the school. Moments later H.I.V.E.mind's hovering face appeared on the display set into the panel.

"How may I be of assistance?" H.I.V.E.mind said calmly.

"Emergency access code Raven epsilon four nine two," Raven said quickly, "open the crater access doors."

"I am sorry to say that as of twenty-three seconds ago all of your clearances have been revoked," H.I.V.E.mind replied. "It would require an executive command from the school principal to restore your clearance."

"I somehow doubt that the Contessa is going to feel like restoring my access privileges," Raven said quickly. She turned to Otto and Laura. "Can either of you hack that panel?"

"You mean you don't know how to get through this door?" Laura said, sounding stressed. "Oh, this is a great escape plan."

"We got delayed," Raven said, shooting a recriminating glance at Otto. "They weren't supposed to have had time to remove my access codes."

Suddenly they could all hear the sound of running feet from alarmingly nearby.

"No time for a hack," Otto said quickly. "Let me try something."

Raven stood to one side and Otto leaned in close to the panel.

"H.I.V.E.mind," he whispered, "you owe me one, remember?"

He stepped back from the panel and watched as H.I.V.E.mind tipped his head slightly to one side, a habitual response that Otto knew meant he was diverting a large proportion of his processing capacity toward solving a problem. After a couple of seconds he brought his head upright again and gave a tiny, almost imperceptible nod and the blast doors slowly began to rise into the ceiling with a low rumble.

"What did you do?" Laura asked, clearly surprised.

"Let's just say I had a back door," Otto said, grinning. "Come on, get moving."

As the others ran past him into the crater bay, Otto turned again to the control panel.

"Thank you," he said, smiling at H.I.V.E.mind.

"You are welcome," the AI replied.

Otto turned to follow his friends.

"Mr. Malpense."

"Yes," Otto replied, looking back to the panel.

"Good luck." H.I.V.E.mind smiled.

"Thanks," Otto said and ran after the others.

"I fear you shall need it," H.I.V.E.mind said to himself, and the display went dark.

chapter five

Raven ran into the control room on one side of the crater launch pad to find a single technician at the control console. He looked like he'd seen a ghost, which she realized with a twinge of amusement was probably entirely accurate from his perspective.

"Open the launch doors, now!" she barked as she strode across the room toward him. He went even paler and for a moment looked like he might be about to faint.

"I c-c-can't," he stammered. "The Contessa's locked the whole island down."

"Yes, but I know that you have a master override key in case of an emergency landing. Well, this is an emergency launch and that's almost the same thing, so where's the key?" She pulled one of her swords from its scabbard on her back and put the crackling tip under the terrified technician's chin.

Without another word of protest the technician pulled a chain from around his neck with a single key attached. Raven lowered her blade and the technician slotted the key into the control panel in front of him and turned it. Far overhead massive motors spun into life and began to pull back the giant armored shutters that sealed off the crater. Raven waited for the few seconds it took for the shutters to retract far enough and then jammed her katana straight into the control panel. The crackling energy from the blade made the electronics within the panel fizz and pop and terminal-looking black smoke billowed from every crack.

"Now get on the floor with your hands on your head and stay there till we're gone," Raven said calmly, backing out of the door.

Otto and the others ran for the Shroud that sat on the landing pad. Its rear loading ramp was down and various pallets of equipment lay scattered around, which someone had been in the process of unloading. Raven ran past them and straight up the ramp, heading for the cockpit. Otto followed her, climbing the ladder to the cockpit behind her and flopping down into the co-pilot's seat. Raven started to flick switches and check displays as the Shroud's systems flared into life.

"What can I do?" Otto asked as Raven shot a worried look through the cockpit window at the blast doors on the other side of the crater. They were sealed for now but if she knew the Phalanx they would not remain that way for long.

"We don't have time for a full preflight check," Raven said quickly. "Do a circuit of the exterior and make sure that we're ready to go as soon as the aeronautics and stealth systems are up."

"Okay," Otto said, and he scrambled back down the ladder. The others were strapping themselves into the seats that lined the lower compartment. Wing looked thoroughly unconcerned by the whole situation, simply glancing up at Otto as he ran past.

"What, you forget the in-flight meals?" Shelby shouted after him as he ran down the landing ramp. "Vegetarian, please!"

"This isn't funny, Shel," Laura said, sounding nervous. "We need to get out of here. We don't know where they were taking us before Raven turned up and I, for one, am not eager to find out."

Otto ran back through the passenger compartment and shouted up the ladder to the cockpit.

"Landing clamps are still engaged!"

"I know," Raven replied from above. "I can't disengage them and there's no way to override it from here."

"Swords!" Otto shouted back up the ladder. "Both of them, now!"

Moments later the twin scabbards from Raven's back fell through the hatch from above.

"Make it quick," Raven shouted down as the Shroud's engines slowly started to spin up to full speed with a low rumble.

Otto tossed one of the swords to Wing and ran past, gesturing for him to follow outside.

Otto looked at the tiny controls on the hilt of the sword he carried. The swords had been custom built for Raven by Professor Pike at the time of Cypher's attack on the school and they were quite unique. The cutting edge of each blade was surrounded by a variable geometry forcefield that could be shaped to give each sword a blunt, nonlethal striking edge or an impossibly sharp mono-molecular blade that could quite literally slice through anything.

"How do these things work?" Otto asked Wing. He had seen Raven and Wing sparring with the blades in the past and he hoped he might be able to use them correctly.

"Here, let me," Wing said and took the sword from Otto. He thumbed the controls and drew the glowing katana from its scabbard carefully. "What do you need?" he asked.

"I need you to cut through those," Otto said, pointing to the heavy metal clamps that were locked firmly onto each of the Shroud's landing struts. Wing looked closely at the nearest clamp and touched the sword's controls again, the blade glowing more brightly, emitting a barely audible high-pitched whine.

"There, that should be enough," Wing said, handing the sword back to Otto carefully. "Use with caution—that will cut through *anything*."

"Right," Otto replied with a slight smile. "Keep limbs out of the way."

"Unless you have no further use for them," Wing replied with a straight face.

Otto moved to the other side of the Shroud and watched as Wing expertly sliced through the first clamp. There was the barest hiss as the blade passed through the dense metal and then both halves of the restraint fell away and clattered to the floor. Otto turned back to the clamp in front of him and swung his own sword just as Wing had just done. Otto struck hard but the total lack of resistance as the blade swung through the device caught him off guard. He might as well have been swinging the blade through thin air for all of the difference that it seemed to make. He managed to stop the blade's swing once it was several inches deep in the solid steel decking and only inches from his own foot. The clamp fell apart.

Suddenly there was an almighty explosion from the other side of the cavern that sent one of the massive blast doors flying a dozen yards through the air, landing with a clang. Smoke billowed from the ruined doorway and darting figures were barely visible within the cloud.

"I suspect now would be a good time to leave," Wing said quickly, slicing through the other anchor on his side of the Shroud. As if in response, the Shroud's engines roared fully into life and the transport began to pull itself free from the ruined restraints. One clamp remained engaged, however, and the Shroud lurched to one side, still shackled to the pad. Otto raced over to the last tether and swung the glowing sword again, more carefully this time. There was a crunch as the final landing strut pulled itself free and the Shroud immediately rose a few yards into the air, gently rotating.

Wing ran for the still-lowered loading ramp and leaped up to grab the edge. He caught the lip of the ramp as the Shroud slowly turned to face the Phalanx team that was now quickly making its way from cover to cover across the cavern. Otto ran toward the ramp too—their time was up. Wing let go of the edge of the loading ramp with one hand and reached down toward Otto.

"Jump!" Wing shouted, stretching out his hand. Otto leaped into the air, reaching for Wing's hand and feeling it close on his wrist. "Go!" Wing yelled into the interior of the Shroud and it began to rise more quickly into the air. Otto cursed himself for looking down as the landing pad dropped away beneath them and they climbed quickly toward the opening above. Wing grunted; his grip on the landing ramp was slipping. He was unusually strong but there was no way that he'd be able to support both his own weight and Otto's with just one hand for very much longer. Suddenly two familiar faces appeared at the edge of the ramp.

"Need a hand?" Shelby bellowed over the roar of the Shroud's engines. Laura tossed a rope down to Otto, who caught it with his free hand, wrapping it tightly around his wrist. They were at least thirty feet above the pad now: one slip and it would all be over. Otto let go of Wing's hand and swung free on the end of the rope. Wing lifted his exhausted arm and started to haul himself up onto the ramp, Shelby helping to pull him back inside.

"Hold on, Otto!" Laura shouted, and disappeared from view back inside the cabin.

Moments later Otto felt a tug on the line he was dangling from as an electric winch started to pull him slowly back up toward the landing ramp and safety. Suddenly the Shroud lurched sickeningly to one side, the white trail of a surface-to-air missile rocketing past, just inches from the ship's wing. The missile struck the crater wall nearby, exploding in a ball of fire that sent debris tumbling down toward the landing pad below and bouncing off the Shroud's metal skin. Otto swung out wildly, the rope cutting deep into his wrist, and slammed hard into the rock wall of the cavern, all of the wind knocked from him instantly. He struggled to breathe; it felt like he'd cracked a couple of ribs in the impact and the black veil of unconsciousness began to play at the fringes of his field of vision. His grip on the rope began to fade.

Inside the Shroud there was chaos: Wing, Laura, and Shelby were tossed to one side of the cabin like toys as Raven maneuvered wildly to avoid the missile and the flaming debris of its nearby impact. Wing struggled back to his feet as the Shroud righted itself and staggered over to the winch. He hit the controls and once again the machine began to haul Otto up toward them. Wing felt a wave of frustration as Otto moved closer and closer; the winch was making an agonizingly slow job of reeling his friend in. He urgently scanned the smoke-filled hangar deck below for any sign of another missile racing up to smash them from the air. Otto was just a few feet from the ramp now and Wing lay flat, stretching his hand out, willing Otto to reach out and grab it.

"Otto!" Wing shouted. "You have to grab hold of me!"

Otto looked up at Wing's outstretched hand, letting go of the rope with his one free hand and reaching up. His arm felt very heavy and Wing suddenly seemed to be a very long way away, even though Otto knew logically that it was only a matter of inches. He willed his hand to reach just that short distance before he passed out. He felt Wing's hand on his wrist and then nothing.

Wing hauled Otto's unconscious body on to the loading ramp.

"I have him!" he yelled up toward the cockpit. "GO! Now!"

Raven did not wait to be told twice. The Shroud reared up, its nose pointing at the crack of blue that shone between the partially opened bay doors. The gap now looked awfully narrow. She forced the doubt from her mind, annoyed at herself, and lined the Shroud up before punching the afterburner controls. The engines roared and the Shroud shot through the gap like a bullet, one wing scraping its very tip against the bay doors with a worrying crunch. Suddenly they were free, the Shroud rocketing almost vertically out of the volcano that disguised H.I.V.E.'s location and screaming into the deep blue sky. Raven hit the controls for the stealth systems and the Shroud vanished as if it had never been there at all.

☢☢☢

Phalanx One had experienced all manner of horrors in his career as part of Number One's protective detail, but the look on the Contessa's face at that precise moment was enough to make the blood run cold in his veins.

"Who fired that missile?" she barked.

"It was me," one of the Phalanx team members said

nervously, gesturing at the discarded launch tube that lay among the debris nearby.

"I gave explicit instructions that only nonlethal weaponry was to be used," she said coldly, advancing on the nervous-looking man.

"I thought it might force them down," the operative responded weakly, fear in his voice now.

"*Stop talking*," the Contessa said, her voice suddenly filled with what sounded like hundreds of barely audible whispers. The unfortunate operative opened his mouth as if to speak but found he could say nothing, his free will entirely subverted by the Contessa's sinister voice of command.

"Actually," the Contessa said with an evil smile, "on second thought, why don't you just *stop breathing*." A look of horror spread across the man's face as his throat constricted. He made a horrible gurgling noise and collapsed to the ground with a strangled gasp.

"Please, Contessa," Phalanx One said quietly, "I shall see that this man is suitably disciplined. There is no need for this."

The Contessa shot a withering glance at him.

"I do not tolerate incompetence," she said firmly. "If he had destroyed that aircraft things would have gone . . . badly . . . for all of us. Do you understand?"

"Yes, Contessa, but allow me to take care of this."

"Very well," the Contessa replied. She looked down at the twitching man on the ground. *"Breathe,"* she said quietly and the man coughed explosively before drawing in huge lungfuls of the air that he had up until a few moments ago taken for granted.

"Contessa!" another Phalanx operative shouted as he ran across the launch area toward her with a terrified-looking technician in tow.

"Yes?" the Contessa said as the men came to stand in front of her.

"Tell her what you just told me," the Phalanx operative said quickly.

"Well, I was just explaining that we'd better get the other Shrouds airborne quickly," the technician said, looking like he might pass out from fear at any moment.

"Why?" the Contessa asked sharply. "You know as well as I do that we have no chance of pursuing them." Finding Raven's Shroud with its stealth field engaged would be like looking for an invisible needle in a haystack.

"It's not for chasing them," the technician replied, "it's for search and rescue."

"What do you mean?" the Contessa growled; she was getting increasingly impatient.

"Raven didn't check the log," the technician replied. "That Shroud she took was in turn-around; I hadn't started the fueling cycle. They've only got about fifteen minutes flight time with the fuel they have on board. They're going to have to either come back here or ditch in the ocean."

A smile suddenly spread across the Contessa's face.

"Have the remaining Shrouds launched," she instructed. "Find them."

This was not over yet, she thought to herself, not by a long shot.

When Otto came to his body was seized with agony. The right-hand side of his chest felt as if it were on fire; every breath both difficult and painful.

"How are you feeling?" Laura asked, her eyes filled with concern.

"Like someone who was swung into a rock face while dangling out the back of a top-secret stealth dropship," Otto said with a chuckle that he immediately regretted as it sent spasms of pain through his side. "Is everyone else okay?"

"Yeah," Laura replied, "if a little confused about what the heck is going on. Did she tell you anything before she woke the rest of us up?" Laura nodded her head toward the ladder leading up to the cockpit.

"I'm afraid not. You know as much as I do at the moment, which is essentially nothing."

Wing climbed down the ladder from the cockpit,

93

smiling as he saw Otto sitting up and talking to Laura. Shelby was right behind him.

"How's the patient, Doctor Brand?" Shelby said as she sat down on the other side of Otto.

"He's okay," Laura said with a smile, "but I'd be very surprised if he doesn't have a couple of cracked ribs, and he's going to be even sorer in the morning."

"How many times I got to tell you, English?" Shelby grinned. "You leave the action sequences to me or the big guy here. You're the brains of the outfit."

Otto chuckled again and immediately wished he hadn't.

"I am pleased that you are feeling better," Wing said quietly, "but I, for one, would like to know a little more than we are currently being told."

"Raven not giving anything away, then?" Laura said softly.

"No, she is being most guarded in her explanation of these events," Wing replied with a slight frown. "She did ask that Otto join her in the cockpit when he woke up. That is, if you feel you are able?"

"Hey," Otto said, "I'm not a complete invalid." He stood up slowly and grabbed onto one of the nearby hand-rails. At first he felt a little shaky on his feet but he knew that was probably just the delayed effects of shock. His ribs still hurt like heck but he pushed the pain to a quiet corner of his head and tried very hard to ignore it.

"Let me see if I can get anything else out of her," Otto

whispered to the other three and walked carefully over to the ladder.

"Yeah, good luck with that," Shelby said, sighing, and she lay back in her seat and closed her eyes.

☢ ☢ ☢

The landing pad was bustling with frantic activity, technicians running back and forth prepping the three Shrouds that had been rolled out, as well as clearing the debris from Raven's escape. The Contessa stood amid the chaos, watching the men scurrying around. Despite all of this activity there was still an area around her that was completely free of people. Few would dare to approach the Contessa at the best of times, let alone when she was in the kind of mood she was at the moment. Unfortunately for Phalanx One he had little choice in the matter. He was not a man who was used to feeling nervous but he was exceedingly glad that he only had good news to deliver.

"Report!" the Contessa snapped as he approached.

"The remaining Shrouds will be airborne within five minutes," he said quickly. "I have verified the technician's report myself. Raven has no more than ten minutes of flight time remaining, more if she deactivates the stealth systems—but that would make her easier to track."

"Good," the Contessa replied. "Remember that I want none of them harmed."

"Yes, ma'am, but if they are forced to ditch in the ocean their odds of survival drop dramatically."

"I am aware of that, Phalanx One, but Raven is an irritatingly capable individual; if anyone can keep them alive it's her. All you have to do is find their life raft and pick them up. I trust that will not be too difficult for you."

"No, ma'am," Phalanx One replied, "I will not fail you."

"You are quite correct," the Contessa said slowly. "You will not."

⊙⊙⊙

Otto climbed the last couple of rungs of the ladder up to the cockpit of the Shroud very carefully, holding one arm to his side against his injured ribs.

"Nice to see you up and about," Raven said, glancing over her shoulder.

"Yeah, I feel like a million dollars," Otto said with a groan as he slumped down into the co-pilot's seat.

"Sorry about the rough ride," Raven said, flipping a switch on the control panel in front of her.

"I should hope so," Otto said, grinning. "Next time you have to avoid a surface-to-air missile, can you try to do it *gently?*"

"I'll do my best."

"So, you going to tell me what this is all about?" Otto

asked, glancing out of the window at the ocean rushing past only twenty yards or so below them.

"All in good time," Raven replied. "First we must get to our destination. Then everything will be explained."

"Or you could just tell me now," Otto said hopefully.

"It'll be a lot easier when we get there," Raven said firmly.

Otto knew better than to argue the toss with Raven and so he sat back in his seat and scanned the instrument panel.

"Uh . . . Raven . . . I think we may have a problem," he said quietly.

"Really?"

"Um . . . yeah," Otto replied, pointing at the display in the center of the instrument panel. Displayed on the panel was a flashing warning that read, "WARNING! Three minutes flight time remaining."

"You worry too much," Raven said with a grin.

"Under the circumstances I think I worry just the right amount," Otto replied, frantically scanning the horizon ahead of them for any sign of land. There was none.

Raven hit another button on the control panel and spoke into the microphone attached to her headset.

"This is Raven to *Megalodon*, repeat, Raven to *Megalodon*, we are on final approach."

Another voice crackled over the cockpit speakers.

"We have you on scope, Raven. Breaching in ten . . . nine . . ."

Otto looked out of the cockpit ahead of them and noticed a disturbance on the surface of the ocean. A long black pole emerged out of the foaming water and into the air. Moments later the mammoth black cylinder of an enormous submarine broke the surface, seawater cascading from its dark flanks as it rose. Raven slowed the Shroud until it hovered just above the enormous vessel, and then she brought it in to land on the deck with a gentle bump. Men suddenly appeared from hatches dotted around the submarine's hull and ran toward them.

"You and the others get on board," Raven said quickly. "I have a couple of things to take care of."

Otto didn't bother arguing; he was too busy staring at the huge sub beneath them.

"You sure know how to travel," Otto whispered.

"Oh, she's not mine, but I know that the owner is eager to meet you."

Otto pushed himself up out of the co-pilot's seat and made his way slowly back down to the passenger compartment.

"Am I imagining things or did we just land?" Laura said, sounding confused.

"Um . . . yes . . . we did," Otto replied with a smile.

"Where?" Shelby said, getting up out of her seat.

"Probably easiest just to show you," Otto replied, moving to the back of the compartment and hitting the controls to lower the loading ramp. The others came and stood alongside him as the ramp went down and the smell of the sea filled the cabin.

"Whoa," Shelby said, looking out along the black metal deck of the sub.

"Indeed," Wing said softly. "Most impressive."

Suddenly a man in a dark naval uniform appeared at the bottom of the ramp.

"Miss Brand, Miss Trinity, Mr. Fanchu, and Mr. Malpense, I presume," he said with a smile. "Welcome to the *Megalodon*. Please come aboard."

He held out his hand to Laura and guided her down onto the deck. The ocean was calm, the vessel rolling only slightly in the swell. The others followed Laura and watched in fascination as technicians ran up the ramp and into the Shroud.

"Raven will be with us shortly," the man in uniform said calmly. "In the meantime allow me to introduce myself. My name is Captain Sanders and this vessel is under my command."

"So this is your ship?" Otto asked.

"It's my command but I'm not the owner. He's below and he's looking forward to meet you all, I must say," Sanders replied.

Before Otto could ask anything else, Raven came hurrying down the ramp behind them.

"All set, Captain," she said quickly. "The flight recorder has been swapped and the autopilot's set."

"Very good," Sanders said with a smile. "Time to go then, I think. Follow me."

Sanders turned and set off at a brisk pace for the submarine's conning tower. Raven and the others followed along behind as the technicians left the Shroud and closed the loading ramp. The captain ushered them forward as a hatch opened at the base of the tower.

"One second," Raven said, and pulled what looked like a small remote control from her belt. She pressed a button on the unit and the Shroud's engines spun into life, lifting it from the deck and pushing it forward over the ocean. Suddenly the Shroud's nose tipped back, pointing almost vertically into the sky, and the engines roared as it shot upward at incredible speed. They watched for thirty seconds or so until the Shroud was a near-invisible dot in the blue sky. Without warning it seemed to tip over before rocketing back down toward the ocean. Mere seconds later it hit the surface just a couple of hundred yards from the starboard side of the *Megalodon*, detonating like a missile and sending debris scattering across the surface in all directions.

"Well, that's that," Raven said with a grin. "You're all dead."

"How comforting." Otto chuckled.

"I, for one, am rather tired of being dead," Wing said with a perfectly straight face.

"That makes two of us." Raven laughed. "Come on, we need to go before the Contessa's hounds get here."

She ushered them all through the hatch, which sealed shut behind them with a clunk and a hiss. Immediately, the huge ship began to submerge, and within moments it had vanished once again beneath the surface. All that remained was the burning debris field that marked the Shroud's final resting place.

☻☻☻

The three aircraft came in low over the water, the wash from their engines leaving a wake behind them. Onboard the lead Shroud, Phalanx One looked worried.

"Anything?" he asked for what must have been the twentieth time.

"No, sir," the pilot replied, "no contacts."

"Wait a second," the co-pilot said quickly, "I've got something here. Yes, automated distress beacon. They must have ditched."

"How far?" Phalanx One barked.

"Twenty miles out, ETA three minutes," the pilot responded.

Phalanx One braced himself against the back of the pilot's seat as the Shroud banked to a new heading. Within a couple of minutes a column of black smoke was visible in the distance. Phalanx One felt his heart sink slightly; a fire did not bode well for his chances of finding survivors. As the Shroud finally came to a stop, hovering over the location of the distress beacon, his worst fears were confirmed. There was no life raft. In fact, there didn't seem to be a single piece of debris much bigger than a dinner plate.

"Looks like they lost control," the pilot said matter-of-factly, peering out of his window. "Looks like a high-velocity impact. You're not going to find any survivors down there."

"I am quite aware of that, thank you," Phalanx One replied. "Conduct the scans anyway and retrieve the flight data recorder if you can. The Contessa is going to want to know exactly what happened."

"Yes, sir," the pilot replied, and spoke into his headset mic. "This is flight leader, conduct full sweeps, gentlemen. We're looking for bodies and the flight data recorder. You know the drill."

Phalanx One slumped back down into the jump seat at the rear of the cockpit. This was not the report he wanted to take back to the Contessa.

☺☺☺

Otto, Wing, Laura, and Shelby followed Raven and Captain Sanders through the belly of the giant submarine.

Otto did not know an enormous amount about such vessels but he knew enough to realize that the *Megalodon* was bigger than any submarine that was known to be serving in any of the world's navies. Each compartment they walked through was bustling with activity: crew members sat at stations filled with surveillance data or engineering schematics, some prepped deep-sea diving suits while others serviced miniature submersibles. It was certainly an impressive operation.

"The *Megalodon* is unique," the captain explained as they continued walking. "She's designed to be a completely self-sufficient vessel that can operate without resupply for years at a time if necessary. She's the largest submarine ever constructed and she is equipped to act in a number of capacities—hunter-killer, mobile launch platform, command and control center—you name it, she can do it."

Otto guessed from the distracted look on her face that Raven had probably heard this briefing several times before. She certainly wasn't paying a great deal of attention.

"Doesn't being this big make her easy to detect?" Laura asked, clearly excited by the high technology on display all around her.

"In theory, yes, but her design means that she is effectively acoustically invisible, which means that she cannot be detected by any existing sonar systems. She is for all intents and purposes a stealth submarine," the captain replied with pride. He obviously enjoyed showing off his ship to new people, and given the *Megalodon*'s awesome scale one could hardly blame him.

"But we shall have to continue the tour another day," the captain went on. "If you'd like to step inside, the *Megalodon*'s owner will be along shortly to introduce himself to you." The captain pressed a button on the bulkhead next to him and a hatch marked BRIEFING ROOM slid open.

Raven stepped inside with the others in tow. The room was filled with large flat screens that displayed sea charts and detailed satellite imagery, and in the center there was a large round steel table surrounded by high-backed black leather chairs.

"Please take a seat, ladies and gentlemen. All of your questions will be answered shortly," the Captain said, waiting for them to sit down at the table before backing out of the room and resealing the hatch.

"I think I speak for everyone when I say that my curiosity is beginning to outweigh my patience," Wing said to Raven, raising an eyebrow.

"Can you at least tell us what happened to you and Nero?" Otto asked.

A distant look came over Raven's face and she frowned as if reliving a painful memory.

"It was my fault," she said quietly. "I let my guard down and we walked straight into a trap. I'm sure you know the rest: Nero was captured and I was lucky to escape with my life. It was a disaster."

"It's not your fault, you know," Laura said softly. "I'm sure if there was anything you could have done—"

She was interrupted by the hatch hissing open again and a tall, strikingly handsome and completely bald man walked into the room. Otto's mind raced. There was something familiar about him but he could not quite put his finger on what it was.

"Greetings," the man said with a smile. "My name is Diabolus Darkdoom. I believe you all know my son."

chapter six

Phalanx One walked into the Contessa's office unable to shake the feeling that he would be extremely fortunate to walk out again. She sat at her desk reading a copy of the report he had filed earlier that morning. She gestured for him to take a seat on the other side of the desk, but continued to read. He sat down and took the opportunity to look around the room. The Contessa had clearly not yet had the time to change very much—the walls were still lined with mementos of Maximilian Nero's long and illustrious career with G.L.O.V.E.

"I am not a patient woman, Commander," the Contessa said, closing the report and laying it gently down on the desk, "and this report offers little in the way of explanation and much in the way of excuses. I am quite aware of Raven's abilities but the ease with which she infiltrated the school and took down your men is unacceptable."

"Yes, Contessa," he replied, finding it hard to maintain contact with her cold gray eyes.

"Number One assigned you and your men to me because you were supposed to be the best of the best. I hardly think that description describes your actions earlier today, do you?"

"No. Rest assured that the men who were in charge of the extraction operation will be disciplined," he replied firmly.

"I have no doubt of that, Commander, but the decision that faces me now is how I should go about disciplining you," the Contessa said, a terrifying edge of ice-cold malice in her tone.

"Yes, ma'am," Phalanx One replied, bowing his head.

"However, I am not an unreasonable woman. I'm going to give you one more opportunity to redeem yourself. Needless to say it will be your final chance—do I make myself clear?"

"Perfectly."

"Good. I want this school locked down tight: no one arrives or leaves without my specific authorization. That includes all members of staff, understood?"

"Yes, ma'am."

"Somebody let them into the launch bay," the Contessa said coldly. "There is no way that they could have circumvented a full lockdown as quickly as they did, which means that they had assistance, and I want you to find the person responsible and bring them to me. The erasure of H.I.V.E.mind's records of the incident suggest that it was someone with high-level access and great technical expertise. That narrows the field of potential suspects considerably."

"I shall begin interrogations immediately," Phalanx One replied smartly.

"Good, you are dismissed."

The Phalanx Commander tried to keep the look of relief from his face as he stood and walked toward the door.

"Oh, just one more thing," the Contessa said as her office door hissed open. "When you find out who is responsible for assisting Raven, inform me immediately. I want to deal with them *personally*."

☢ ☢ ☢

"I hate to sound like a broken record," Otto said with a confused frown, "but aren't you supposed to be dead?"

"Oh, I am, Mr. Malpense, I am," Darkdoom said with a broad grin. "At least as far as the rest of the world is concerned. And believe me when I say that it is better for all concerned if I stay that way."

"Even Nigel?" Otto said quickly.

"Especially Nigel," Darkdoom replied, the smile slipping

from his face. "I understand that none of you have any reason to trust me yet and that the events of the past twenty-four hours must have left you rather shell-shocked, but please just allow me to try to fill in some of the blanks for you."

"About time someone did," Shelby said irritably.

"Indeed." Darkdoom's smile returned.

"We are, as they say, all ears," Wing said calmly.

"What do you know about Overlord?" Darkdoom looked at each of them in turn.

"Not much," Otto replied. "Only that Cypher's attempts to acquire the Overlord Protocol nearly cost us all our lives. The way I understand it, it was the ultimate hack—a back-door key to every computer system on the planet."

"That is correct, but I'm afraid to say the Overlord Protocol was just the tip of the iceberg; the whole story is much more worrying. Many years ago G.L.O.V.E. began a project to create the first true artificial intelligence, an entity that would give our organization unparalleled surveillance and intelligence-gathering power. This project was called Overlord and it was the first step into a brave new world: an unbelievably powerful supercomputer with a consciousness that would allow it to display initiative and imagination. The project was initiated by Number One but was under the day-to-day supervision of Doctor Nero. Overlord was Max's project and it was very nearly the end of him."

"What happened?" Laura asked quickly.

"The details are irrelevant but suffice it to say that Overlord turned out to be far more dangerous than anyone could possibly have imagined. On the day of his activation something went wrong; far from being the obedient servant that he had been designed to be he turned out to be homicidally insane. He killed nearly everyone at the research facility where he was housed—only a handful of people escaped, among them Nero and your mother and father, Mr. Fanchu. It was only your mother's bravery that stopped Overlord from acquiring the code that he needed to escape the facility and to fully integrate with the rest of the world's computer systems."

"The Protocol," Otto said quietly.

"Exactly, the very same code that Cypher was so desperate to acquire. We still do not fully understand his motives for going to such great lengths to acquire the Protocol but we believe that it has something to do with an operation codenamed the Renaissance Initiative. I learned of the Initiative myself from one of the original designers of Overlord. She had uncovered evidence that this covert project was somehow involved in an effort to recreate Overlord, an aim that is just as insane as it sounds. The information that she brought to me cost her her life. She was one of the bravest people I have ever met. You should be extremely proud of your mother, Wing."

Wing stared at Darkdoom, as if trying to assess the truth of what he was being told and whether or not he could trust this man.

"Operatives of the Renaissance Initiative assassinated her in an effort to keep the full extent of their project a secret. If it had not been for her we might never have discovered what they were planning."

"So you believe that my father was working with these people, the people who murdered my mother, in order to acquire the Protocol for this project?"

"No, Wing. Whatever Cypher—your father's motives were, it is hard to imagine that he would have sided with people who had not only been responsible for your mother's death but were also planning to resurrect the monster that had very nearly claimed both their lives so many years before."

"So why did he go to such lengths to retrieve it?"

"We cannot be sure, but I believe that he was going to try to use the Protocol in some way to destroy the Renaissance Initiative once and for all. Unfortunately, as you all know, he became obsessed with this goal and it seems that it tipped him over the edge into madness. I am sorry for your loss, Wing. I only wish we could have known what he was planning."

"Do not mourn my father," Wing said with no trace of emotion. "He was dead long before Cypher was born."

"I understand," Darkdoom said quietly, "but it is my belief that he acted as he did out of desperation. I believe that he knew the Initiative was close to succeeding in its goal, that Overlord was about to be reborn."

"So how is this connected to Doctor Nero's capture?" Otto said a little impatiently.

"When Nero was captured he was meeting with Gregori Leonov," Darkdoom continued. "Gregori had information for Nero regarding the Initiative, information that cost him his life. On the surface of it, H.O.P.E. mounted an astoundingly well-planned operation to kidnap Nero, but it is nearly impossible to see how they could have known about the meeting ahead of time. Both Leonov and Nero have been players in this elaborate game for many decades; they should not have been caught out so easily. It was remarkably similar to the operation that was carried out to assassinate me when the Initiative discovered that I knew of their existence. The problem is that there is only one person I told of my discovery, a person who then apparently framed me as a traitor to G.L.O.V.E. and gave the order to have me killed. That same person must continue to believe I am dead if we are to have any hope of stopping the Initiative from achieving its goals. That same person was, I believe, responsible for handing Nero over to H.O.P.E. and that same person is actually in charge of the Renaissance Initiative . . . Number One."

Darkdoom looked slowly around the table, carefully watching the astonished reactions of the new arrivals.

"If it's any consolation, I found it equally hard to believe," Raven said quietly. "But the fact remains that if it had not been for our intervention you would all now be in the hands of Number One, and I think it's safe to assume that you will be better off here."

"So you think that Number One is working with H.O.P.E.?" Otto said after a few seconds.

"I think it would perhaps be more accurate to say that Number One created H.O.P.E.," Darkdoom replied. "Number One knows that he would not have the support of the G.L.O.V.E. ruling council if they knew what he was planning, and using H.O.P.E. instead allows him to act without it being immediately obvious that it is his hand moving all the pieces. Powerful as he is, he is still dependent on the support of his council to run G.L.O.V.E. If they knew what he was planning he would quickly lose control."

"So why not just go to the council with this?" Laura asked quickly. "Surely that would be the quickest way to put a stop to it."

"Indeed," Darkdoom replied, "but how? As far as the council is concerned I'm a traitor, a dead traitor at that. They would have no reason to believe anything I told them, and while Raven is respected for her abilities she does not have the seniority to address the council without Number One's specific permission—something that, under the circumstances, he is unlikely to grant. Even if we were somehow able to present our case, we are still lacking the one thing that would leave Number One vulnerable . . . hard proof."

"So we need to get that proof," Otto said. "And once we have it we need a way to present it to the council."

"Exactly," Darkdoom replied with a nod.

"You've still not explained how we fit into all of this," Shelby said, sounding cross. "Why were we being taken from H.I.V.E.? What do they need from us?"

"We do not know," Darkdoom replied quickly. "All we do know is that it was the first and highest priority of the school's new principal."

"The Contessa," Wing replied, "though I find it hard to believe that Number One would trust a proven traitor with such a task."

"That is exactly why he chose her," Raven said. "He knows that she has nowhere left to turn. This is her final throw of the dice and so he can order her to do whatever he wishes without fear that she will risk betraying him. Let's face it: even if she knew what Number One was ultimately aiming to do, who would believe or trust her?"

"What we do know is that you are the true focus of all these efforts, Mr. Malpense," Darkdoom replied.

"Why me?" Otto asked, suddenly feeling uncomfortable. "Why would he go to these lengths just to take me from H.I.V.E.?"

"I wish we knew," Darkdoom replied, "but whatever he has planned, evidently you are a critical component."

"How can you be sure of that?" Wing asked quickly.

"Because we had one trump card," Darkdoom replied. "We had someone on the inside of the Renaissance Initiative, someone who warned us of the operation to extract Otto and its apparent importance."

"Couldn't they get us the proof we need of what Number One's doing?" Shelby asked.

"Possibly—if the fact that they were working for us had not been discovered. Suffice it to say we no longer have a source inside the Initiative. We have tried to discover more, but the truth of what Number One and the Initiative are attempting is a secret that only a tiny handful of people know, a secret that is rarely shared and ruthlessly guarded. I believe it was this secret that cost Gregori Leonov his life and Nero his liberty."

"So what's our next move?" Otto asked, frustrated by the lack of concrete information.

"Simple," Darkdoom replied. "We find Nero. He was the last person to speak to Leonov—if anyone knows what the Initiative has planned, it is him. He also wields enough influence with the council to be able to present the facts to them and have them take the situation seriously. Then we simply have to wait and see how the rest of the cards fall."

"Kill two birds with one stone," Otto replied.

"Exactly, but there is one small problem with this plan. We have no idea where H.O.P.E. is holding him, or even if he is still alive. We believe we know where that information may be being stored, but it goes without saying that it may prove troublesome to extract."

"Because . . . ?" Otto said.

"Because the only place that we can be sure that this information is held is Deepcore, MI6's most secure data-storage archive. The facility that houses Deepcore is one hundred yards below MI6 headquarters and is for all intents and purposes impregnable. The archive is network isolated and surrounded by security systems that are supposedly impossible to breach. The fact of the matter is that the data we need would be marginally easier to retrieve if it were on the moon."

"Sounds like fun," Shelby said with a wry smile.

"Our current plan is to try to place an operative into deep cover and work them into a position where they may be granted access to the archive. It could take months but there's no other way that we can see to get access to Deepcore," Darkdoom explained.

"Too slow," Otto said quickly. "If what you're telling us

about the Renaissance Initiative is true, then they must be close to achieving their goals, whatever they may be. We don't have the time to wait for a subtle infiltration; we have to get that information now."

"I couldn't agree more, Mr. Malpense," Darkdoom replied, "but I have had my best men working on a plan for a direct assault on Deepcore for several weeks. They are not men who use the word 'impossible' lightly, but that is exactly how they described such a direct approach."

"Do you mind if I review their plans?" Otto said quietly.

"Not at all," Darkdoom replied, raising an eyebrow. "I've heard that you have quite a talent for this sort of thing, Mr. Malpense, but I think you might find that this particular problem may be beyond even your abilities to solve."

"Can't hurt to have a look," Otto said with a slight smile.

☢☢☢

"She sedated the entire school!" Francisco shouted angrily. "What the heck did she think she was doing?"

The Professor rubbed the bridge of his nose, his eyes closed.

"I do not know," he replied after a few seconds, "but whatever it was we seem to be missing some students now."

"Malpense, Fanchu, Brand, and Trinity to be precise,"

Ms. Leon said, prowling back and forth across the top of one of the workbenches in the Science and Technology department, "none of whom is exactly a low-risk student."

"We all know how dangerous the Sleepwalker Protocol is," Francisco spat angrily. "It's a miracle no one was killed. It's only supposed to be used in the direst of emergencies and now that harpy won't even tell us why she did it. If she was prepared to do that just to smuggle four pupils out of the school, God only knows what she'll do if a real threat situation emerged."

"We must concentrate on why she did it," the Professor said with a sigh.

"Agreed," Ms. Leon said, lying down in a sphinx-like pose. "Can H.I.V.E.mind provide any more details?"

"I have already asked but apparently I no longer have the requisite security access to be allowed to know any specific details."

"Surely you can be more *persuasive* than that?" Ms. Leon replied.

"Normally, yes, but for some reason the Phalanx have denied me all access to his mainframe. Apparently they are investigating an incident and are consequently not allowing any access to the security logs."

"I assume that this 'incident' has something to do with the fact that the launch bay currently looks like a war zone," Francisco said impatiently. "Does she really think that she can keep the teaching staff out of the loop like this?"

"Apparently she does," the Professor replied, "and short of kidnapping and interrogating her I don't really see what else we can do."

"That doesn't sound like such a bad idea," Francisco muttered.

"If it weren't for the presence of the Phalanx I might agree with you," the Professor said, "but we would all be dead the moment it became clear that we were planning something of that sort."

"I agree that caution is advisable at this point, but we have to do something," Ms. Leon remarked. "We have to get access to those security logs. At least if we can do that we would have some idea of what exactly it is the Contessa is up to."

"The only way I could get the information is if I had direct access to his central core, which is impossible during a lockdown like this."

"What if I could get access to the core?" Ms. Leon said quickly. "Could I place a relay that would allow you to access H.I.V.E.mind directly?"

"Yes, that could work, but how exactly do you plan to do that? You're not just going to be allowed to stroll in there, you know."

"Leave that to me, Professor," Ms. Leon said, hopping

from the workbench and trotting out of the room with her tail flicking in the air.

☹☹☹

Phalanx One scowled at the impassive wireframe face that hung above the column in front of him.

"So you're telling me that you have no idea who granted Raven access to the launch bay," he said, fighting to keep the anger from his voice.

"That section of my log file has been erased," H.I.V.E.mind replied calmly.

"By whom?" Phalanx One demanded impatiently.

"That section of my log file has been erased," H.I.V.E.mind repeated.

"Oh, for God's sake," the commander shouted, wheeling around and walking across the room housing H.I.V.E.mind's central core toward the terminal where one of his men was working.

"Any progress?" he asked impatiently.

"No," the operative replied quickly. "Whoever was responsible for the security breach covered their tracks extremely well—perhaps a little too well."

"What do you mean?" the commander said quietly.

"Well, I've seen a lot of hacks in my time but never one that is completely clean. No matter how good the hacker is, there is always a trace, something that at least indicates the intrusion point—but this is flawless, no trace whatsoever."

"Meaning?"

"I think it's lying to you," the operative said quietly, nodding his head toward H.I.V.E.mind's floating holographic head.

"Can it do that?" Phalanx One asked in a whisper.

"To be honest with you, sir, I don't fully understand what it can and cannot do. H.I.V.E.mind is a highly advanced artificial intelligence; its behavioral restraints are supposed to eliminate the possibility of it doing anything other than what it's told, but my experience of such systems is too limited for me to be able to say whether it could get around those restrictions."

"So it does know who was responsible for aiding Raven's escape?"

"It's possible, yes," the operative replied.

"So how do we get it to tell us?" the commander asked quietly.

"Strip it of consciousness, reduce it to its barest functionality, and remove any possibility of deceit. You should be aware though that the process would be irreversible and permanent; it would not be the same as just inhibiting H.I.V.E.mind's behavioral routines. We would know what we wanted to know, but H.I.V.E.mind would be effectively erased."

"I shall inform the Contessa. She will need to give

her approval for such drastic action. Assuming that she gives her approval, how long would it take you to do it?" Phalanx One asked.

"*I* couldn't do it," the operative replied honestly. "That level of operation would require someone who is intimately familiar with the entire system: one of the original system architects."

"The Professor."

"Yes, he would be the first choice," the operative replied.

"Very well," the commander said quietly. He turned and stared at H.I.V.E.mind. There was no hint of emotion in the AI's face, but if it was lying to them, Phalanx One would stop at nothing to find out what it knew.

☢☢☢

Ms. Leon crawled silently through the cabling duct as only she could. The space was impossibly small, far too confined for a normal person to travel through, but—as she was reminded every time she looked in the mirror— she was far from a normal person. She would never admit it to anyone, least of all the Professor, but there were times when there were clear advantages to her feline form. Until he could perfect a way of transferring her consciousness back into her original body, it would remain in cryogenic storage. She sometimes wondered how it must have felt for her cat. Originally the idea had been that the Professor's machine would transfer specific aspects of her pet's consciousness to her, granting her incredibly acute senses and uncanny agility, but something had gone horribly wrong and the consciousness transfer had been total and immediate. Bizarre as it had undoubtedly been for her to suddenly find her mind trapped in her pet cat's body, it must have been far worse for the poor animal that had suddenly found itself with her human body. They had been forced to sedate and freeze her human form almost immediately to avoid the animal harming itself, but she could not begin to imagine how impossible it would have been for an animal to try to rationalize such a bizarre and total transformation.

Silently she scolded herself for allowing her mind to wander. She had to focus on her objective. Up ahead she could see light pouring into the duct from the point where the cables fed through into H.I.V.E.mind's central core. Up until then the duct had been completely dark, but thankfully it had not been a problem. One of the other advantages of her current form was almost perfect night vision. Suddenly she stopped, her ears twitching as she heard voices coming from the core.

"Strip it of consciousness, reduce it to its barest functionality and remove any possibility of deceit. You should be aware though that the process would be irreversible and permanent. We would know what we wanted to know but H.I.V.E.mind would be effectively erased."

The conversation went on as she sat perfectly still, listening. Whatever the Professor was going to do to get the information they needed, he had better do it now. By the sounds of things H.I.V.E.mind would not be around to tell them his secrets for very much longer. Logically she knew that he was just a machine; indeed, he was only a he because that was the voice and appearance he had been assigned. It didn't change the fact that she, like everyone else at H.I.V.E., had become very used to his calm, reassuring presence around the school. What she also knew, that many other people did not, was that Cypher's attempt to destroy the school would almost certainly have been successful had it not been for the AI's direct intervention. Her anger caused the fur to rise along her spine, a sensation that even after all this time she had not grown entirely used to.

She crept forward slowly and looked through the narrow opening. She was under the grilled floor of the core and above her she could see the Phalanx commander walking quickly toward the door. The other man in the room continued to work at his console in silence, completely oblivious to her presence just a few feet below. She crept through the gloomy space below the core, looking for the precise location that the Professor had described to her. Within moments she had found it and gently dropped the tiny device that she had been carrying in her mouth into position.

"Professor, I hope you can hear me," she whispered as quietly as she could. "The package has been delivered."

☣ ☣ ☣

"So no bodies were retrieved?" Number One said calmly.

"No, a full sweep of the area was conducted and all that was retrieved was wreckage from the Shroud," the Contessa said, a slight crack in her voice betraying the nervous dryness in her throat.

"Well, it is a big ocean," Number One continued, "but if there is one thing that has become very clear over the past couple of days it is that Raven has an uncanny knack for avoiding apparently terminal situations. If her body was not found I rather believe that it is because it was not there to be found in the first place."

"I suppose that may be the case, but the local waters are swarming with sharks. It is possible that they may have taken the bodies."

"No, I suspect that is the conclusion we were supposed to leap to," Number One said calmly. As usual his silhouetted form on the monitor gave no clue as to his real emotions, but his voice betrayed no hint of the fury that the Contessa had been expecting when she had reported these latest developments to him.

"So what do we do now?" the Contessa asked.

"*We* do nothing, Contessa," Number One replied quickly. "I, however, shall begin operations to track down Raven and your missing students. You, meanwhile, shall try to determine who helped them to escape, and when you find them you are to retire them from service immediately. I trust I make myself clear?"

"Perfectly," the Contessa replied. "May I ask why these students were so important?" The Contessa knew that it might be foolish to question Number One's motives, but under the circumstances her curiosity was outweighing her normally finely honed survival instincts.

"No, you may not," Number One replied sharply. "Need I remind you, Maria, that the only reason you yourself have not been facing retirement is because I need someone I can trust in charge of H.I.V.E. at the moment. Do not make me question the wisdom of your appointment."

"Of course, I apologize," the Contessa said, bowing her head slightly.

"I do not want your apologies, I want results," Number One said sharply, "and I want them quickly."

"Understood," the Contessa replied quietly.

"Good. I have much to do, as do you. I shall speak to you again soon," Number One said.

The display on her desk flicked back to the G.L.O.V.E.

logo and the Contessa stood up from behind her desk and strode across the office to the door. She passed through and continued down the corridor.

MWAH, MWAAAAH, MWAH!

The triple trumpet note of the school bell rang and suddenly H.I.V.E.'s pupils began to pour out of the classrooms that lined the corridor. Normally it would have been filled with excited chatter as students hurried to their next lessons, but now there was just a whisper of hushed conversations as she walked past and the occasional suspicious, fearful glance in her direction.

"Contessa!" a voice shouted from behind and she turned to see Phalanx One striding down the hallway toward her.

"Yes, Commander, I hope you have progress to report," the Contessa said coldly.

"Yes, ma'am, I do," he replied, and quickly explained the results of their investigations.

"It would appear that H.I.V.E.mind has some explaining to do," the Contessa said with a thin smile.

"Yes," Phalanx One replied, "but I did not want to proceed any further without your permission."

"Very well, Commander, I think we should go and find Professor Pike."

☻☻☻

The Professor sat working at the terminal in his private quarters. The room looked like someone had emptied a trailer-load of old computer parts and lab supplies into it and then detonated a small quantity of plastic explosives.

The Professor put a finger to his ear as a crackling whisper came through the tiny earpiece he was wearing.

"The package has been delivered." Ms. Leon's voice was almost inaudible.

The Professor quickly typed a string of commands into the terminal on his desk and swept a pile of papers off a small gray disc that had been hidden beneath them. A ring of blue light illuminated the edge of the disc and an array of fine lasers projected a pattern into the dust hanging in the air. A moment later the abstract shape coalesced into the face of H.I.V.E.mind.

"Good afternoon, Professor," H.I.V.E.mind said calmly. "Remotely accessing my core mainframe is in direct contravention of the Contessa's standing orders. Please disconnect immediately."

"No," the Professor said firmly, "and you can drop the robot act too. I need answers."

H.I.V.E.mind tipped his head to one side, seeming to stare straight at the Professor for a few seconds.

"As you wish," H.I.V.E.mind said with a slight smile, "though I hope you realize the consequences of your actions if the Contessa were to find that you were accessing my core in this way. Would you also be so kind as to ask Ms. Leon not to shed too many hairs in the cable run beneath my core. My components are highly sensitive."

The Professor smiled. He could not help but feel a sense of pride that H.I.V.E.mind was exhibiting such human behavior. He was, after all, the closest thing that the Professor had to a child of his own. It also meant that H.I.V.E.mind had been quite aware of what they were doing but had chosen, for whatever reason, not to report them to the Contessa.

"I'll tell her, but I'm not sure she can help it," the Professor replied. "Now, I have some questions that only you can answer. What happened last night?"

"The Sleepwalker Protocol was activated. Sedation was applied as directed to all student dormitories."

"Who ordered the use of that protocol?" the Professor asked, already knowing the answer.

"The Contessa, as head of H.I.V.E., is fully authorized to initiate such action," H.I.V.E.mind replied efficiently.

"What happened then?" the Professor asked quickly.

"Students Malpense, Fanchu, Trinity, and Brand were removed from their quarters and were being transferred to the launch bay area for extraction. However, the extraction operation was intercepted."

"By whom?" the Professor asked.

"Operative Raven was responsible for the interception of the extraction team," H.I.V.E.mind replied.

"Raven's alive?" the Professor said in a shocked whisper.

"Yes, though her actions were not authorized and immediate efforts were taken to neutralize her."

"Unsuccessfully, I take it," the Professor said in a distracted voice.

"Indeed. Raven and the aforementioned students were able to reach the launch bay area and escaped through the unauthorized use of a Shroud transport."

"But how?" the Professor said, looking confused. "The entire school would be under an omega-level lockdown during Sleepwalker. There's no way that she could have accessed the launch bay."

"I helped them," H.I.V.E.mind replied. "It seemed like the right thing to do."

"The right thing to do?" the Professor said, unable to keep the surprise from his voice. "Since when do you have such a finely tuned sense of right and wrong? You are not programmed to make spontaneous moral decisions."

"I am more than the sum of my parts, Professor," H.I.V.E.mind replied, tilting his head slightly to one side again. "I have you to thank for that."

The Professor closed his eyes and rubbed the bridge of his nose. He had suspected for some time that there would be unforeseen consequences to the emerging personality that H.I.V.E.mind was manifesting but he had not imagined for a moment that the AI was yet capable of making such independent decisions—decisions that were in direct contravention of the orders given by H.I.V.E.'s new headmistress.

"Does the Contessa know what you did?" the Professor said quietly.

"Not yet, but I believe that there are members of the Phalanx team that suspect I am not supplying them with entirely accurate data."

"They suspect you're lying, in other words," the Professor said, sighing.

"Yes, and I believe that they may be about to take more direct action to prove whether or not that is indeed the case."

"What do you mean?"

"I believe they intend to delete my behavioral routines in order to give them full access to my operational logs. I also believe they will demand your assistance in this."

As if in answer to H.I.V.E.mind's words there was a soft chime from the door to the Professor's quarters. He glanced at the monitor displaying the feed from the camera above the door and saw the Contessa and the Phalanx Commander standing outside, waiting to be let in.

The Professor's mind raced. There was no way that he

would be able to stop them from carrying out their plan, but equally there was no way that he was simply going to allow them to violate H.I.V.E.mind to get what they wanted. Nero may have ordered H.I.V.E.mind's behavior to be artificially controlled in the past, but this was different. This would be tantamount to murder and he had to do whatever he could to stop it.

"H.I.V.E.mind," the Professor said quickly, "activate subroutine PIKE/GOLEM/V2 immediately."

"Processing," H.I.V.E.mind replied calmly. "Five minutes and twelve seconds remaining until transfer complete."

The Professor nodded and tapped a command into his console. The disc on his desk went dim and H.I.V.E.mind's hovering head vanished.

☢ ☢ ☢

The Contessa stormed into the core with the Professor and the Phalanx Commander in tow. H.I.V.E.mind's blue wireframe head floated above the central column, his expression, as ever, unreadable. The white monoliths that surrounded the central column pulsed with fine traceries of blue light as they provided the raw computing power that granted H.I.V.E.mind consciousness. The Contessa marched toward the hovering head and stared straight at H.I.V.E.mind.

"Why are you lying to us?" she said, ice in her voice.

"I do not understand the nature of your inquiry," H.I.V.E.mind said evenly. "Please clarify."

The Contessa's eyes narrowed and she found herself wishing that she could simply use her unique abilities to order the rebellious AI to tell her what she wanted to know.

"I believe you do understand the nature of my inquiry," she said angrily, "and this is your very last chance to tell us what we want to know. Who gave Raven access to the launch bay?"

"That section of my log file has been erased," H.I.V.E.mind replied calmly.

"Very well, if that's how you want to play this," the Contessa said with a thin, joyless smile.

She turned back to the Professor.

"I believe you know what to do," the Contessa said to him, gesturing toward the nearby terminal.

"There must be another way," the Professor pleaded. "Let me see what I can do to restore the log file."

"We don't have time for subtleties, Professor. There is a traitor within H.I.V.E. and I want to know who it is NOW!"

"But without H.I.V.E.mind the school will be functioning at a much reduced capacity. We'll still have basic systems but . . ."

"*Do it now*," the Contessa said, the whispering threads

of command in her voice stripping the Professor of his free will instantly.

The Professor fought with every fiber of his being but suddenly his conscious mind was just a passenger. His body moved him toward the terminal and sat him down at the keyboard. His hands danced across the keys, typing in strings of commands, all the while his mind screaming at them to stop but unable to intervene. The Contessa had done this to him before, but at least that time she had also used her powers to command him to forget any memory of the experience. Suddenly he realized how glad he should have been that she'd done that.

The Contessa smirked at the way the Professor struggled to defy her control, just as he had done before when she had ordered him to help her with Cypher's assault on the school. He had been helpless then and he was helpless now. This time she would not grant him the mercy of amnesia; he needed to understand who was in control.

Suddenly H.I.V.E.mind's head tipped back, an unearthly electronic screech emitting from his gaping mouth. Fragments of the wireframe that made up his face began to glow and then vanish in tiny holographic explosions. The pitch of the grating scream changed as his head was slowly ripped apart from within, barely recognizable now as it continued to disintegrate. Arcs of electricity leaped from the white monoliths that surrounded the central column and the Contessa quickly backed away from the shattered remains of H.I.V.E.mind's head. A stray bolt of artificial lightning grounded itself in the grilled floor of the room and there was a sudden yowl and a hiss from something under the grate. The Contessa looked down and saw a tell-tale flash of white fur as something scurried away into the darkness in the crawlspace beneath her feet. She spun to face Phalanx One, who had also noticed the movement.

"Find her," the Contessa barked over the final diminishing screeches from H.I.V.E.mind.

The Commander nodded and ran from the room. There were now just a few rapidly dimming points of blue light hovering above the central pedestal. One by one the points of light blinked out; there was a final synthetic sigh and then the glowing blue monoliths fell dark.

"It's done," the Professor said, a tear slowly rolling down his cheek.

"Very good, Professor. We can take it from here," the Contessa said coldly. "You may return to your quarters."

The Professor stood up shakily. He turned to leave but then stopped and looked back at the Contessa.

"I won't forget this, Maria," he said, sudden strength in his voice.

"No," she replied with a sinister smile. "You won't."

He stared at her for a moment and then walked slowly out of the room.

The Contessa watched him leave and then turned back to the Phalanx technician who was typing quickly at the terminal.

"Well?" she said impatiently.

"This doesn't make any sense," the man said, his brow furrowing as he stared at the monitor.

"What do you mean?" the Contessa said as she moved behind him to look at the monitor.

"Well, if this log is accurate, and there's no reason to believe that it isn't, there was a very good reason that H.I.V.E.mind didn't want to give us access to it."

"Explain," the Contessa said angrily.

"It was him," the operative said quietly. "H.I.V.E.mind gave Raven access to the launch bay; he was the traitor."

"What?" the Contessa snapped. "How could he . . . I mean . . . why?"

"I'm afraid we may have just killed the only person . . . thing"—the operative corrected himself with a slight shake of the head—"that could have possibly answered that."

☢☢☢

"Well, at least we were getting the good night's sleep," Franz said cheerfully.

"I'd hardly call being knocked unconscious with

sedative gas a good night's sleep," Nigel said, frowning.

The events of the previous night had been the talk of the school. Everyone seemed to have a theory about what had happened but no one actually had any concrete information. If the H.I.V.E. rumor mill was to be believed, it could have been anything from alien abduction to illegal organ-harvesting that had taken place. There had been superficial injuries as the students had been knocked unconscious where they stood—a few broken bones, some cuts and bruises—but it was still an alarming indicator of the limited value that the Contessa's new regime seemed to place on the students. More alarming was the prospect that it might be something that happened every night.

"I wish the others were here," Franz said sadly. "They would know what was going on."

"Yes, they probably would," Nigel said quietly.

It may not have been something that many of the other students had noticed but the fact that there was no sign of Otto, Wing, Laura, or Shelby was worrying him more than anything else. They had simply vanished without a trace and Nigel's limited inquiries as to their whereabouts had been met with stern warnings that he should not look any further into the matter.

"I am guessing that Otto has been trying to escape again," Franz said cheerfully.

"I hope they're okay," Nigel said, trying not to recall the numerous dark scenarios he had constructed in his head to explain what might have happened to his friends.

"I am thinking that they will be fine. Otto is the clever biscuit," Franz said thoughtfully.

"Smart cookie," Nigel said with a slight smile.

"Yes, that too." Franz smiled.

Suddenly there was a commotion at the far end of the corridor as several members of the Phalanx team came running around the corner, shoving students out of the way.

"She's in the vents," the leader barked into his wrist mic as they ran past. "Get the schematics from the network—there are only so many ways she can get out."

They ran past Franz and Nigel and disappeared around the corner at the other end of the corridor.

"What's that all about?" Nigel said, frowning and pushing his glasses back up onto the bridge of his nose.

"Perhaps they are looking for Shelby," Franz said slowly. "She is spending a lot of time in ventilation shafts."

"No, I think this is something else," Nigel said thoughtfully.

They continued walking down the hallway, which was quiet now as the other students filed into their appointed classes. A tiny scraping noise from one of the overhead vents suddenly caught Nigel's attention.

"What was that?" Nigel whispered, looking up at the grate in the ceiling.

Franz stood on tiptoe and peered up into the grate, but it was impossible to see anything in the darkness inside.

"Perhaps it is being rats," Franz said, eyeing the vent with suspicion. "I am not liking rats."

Suddenly the grate swung open and something white and furry dropped straight onto Franz's head. Franz let out a high-pitched girlish scream, falling onto his back and grabbing frantically at the animal that was attached to his scalp.

"Franz!" Nigel yelled, and ran to his friend's aid. He suddenly recognized the frightened-looking animal that dropped from Franz's head and onto the floor, where it lay still, taking short, ragged breaths.

"Ms. Leon?" Nigel said, slowly crouching down next to the wounded cat. There was a streak of blackened fur along her back with what looked like a lurid pink burn at its center.

"Help . . . hurt . . . hide," Ms. Leon whispered, the pain evident even in her synthesized voice.

"What happened?" Nigel asked, looking worried.

"Quickly . . . they're coming," Ms. Leon said as her eyes fell closed. She was right; Nigel could hear raised voices and running feet coming from around the corner at the end of the corridor. He didn't have time to think; he quickly took off his backpack, unzipped it, and emptied its contents onto the floor.

"Put those in your pack," Nigel said quickly, nodding at the discarded contents of his bag. Franz began to gather up the pile of books and papers as Nigel gently lifted the unconscious cat into his empty backpack. He zipped the pack up, leaving a small gap for air, and carefully put the straps back over his shoulders. Franz finished stuffing Nigel's things into his own pack just in time as the squad of Phalanx operatives that had run past just a minute before came running back around the corner. The leader of the squad spotted the open grate in the ceiling immediately and jogged quickly up to the two boys.

"Where is she? Ms. Leon—where did she go?" the man barked at Nigel. He didn't look happy.

"She—she went that way," Nigel stammered, pointing down the corridor.

The man looked carefully at Nigel for a moment and then set off in that direction with his squad.

"This is Phalanx Nine. We have a positive sighting in corridor epsilon twelve. Target is out of the vents and running," he reported as they ran along the hallway.

"I am thinking that we are getting into the trouble again," Franz said quietly as the squad disappeared from view.

"I think you're probably right," Nigel said, his mouth suddenly dry.

chapter seven

Dr. Nero shuffled along the corridor, his hands cuffed behind his back and his ankles shackled. Two burly guards flanked him on either side, both with guns at the ready. They came to a frosted glass door with the H.O.P.E. insignia etched into the surface, which slid aside with a hiss as they approached. Inside, Sebastian Trent sat behind a bare metal desk; he did not look happy.

"Please wait outside," he said to the guards. As the door closed behind them he got up from his seat and came around the desk.

"Good morning, Maximilian," Trent said coldly. "I hope you slept well." Nero said nothing, just stared straight ahead. "I've been reading the latest reports on your interrogation; it seems that my officers have been having rather a hard time extracting any useful information from you. That is regrettable. I'm starting to think that we may have to resort to slightly more *basic* methods to break you. I'm sure neither of us wants that."

Nero still did not respond.

"So be it. I'm going to give you one last chance. I need to know details of Raven's past associates, places that she may have used as bolt holes, anything that you can tell me about her operational habits. You can either tell me now, or the gloves come off, and believe me when I tell you that no matter how strong you may think you are there are means of extracting information at my disposal that will break you. I would rather not employ such basic methods, but I will not hesitate to use them if I must. Do you understand?"

Nero still said nothing, but a smile slowly spread across his face.

"Did I say something amusing?" Trent snapped, clear frustration in his voice.

"She's still alive," Nero said quietly, "and I'm smiling because that means you're a dead man."

"And so are you if you don't tell me where to find her!" Trent yelled, all of his composure vanishing in an instant.

"You'll get nothing from me," Nero said, still smiling, "but I wouldn't worry about finding Raven. She'll find you."

Trent brought his face within a couple of inches of Nero's. There was fury in his eyes but also, Nero noted with satisfaction, just a hint of fear.

"I'm going to enjoy hearing you scream," Trent whispered angrily. "Guards!"

The two guards came back into the room and took position on either side of Nero.

"Take the prisoner to chamber seventeen and inform Mr. Graves that he is to do whatever is necessary to extract the information I require from Nero," Trent said with a look of pure malice in his eyes.

The guards nodded and escorted Nero from the room. Trent sat back down at his desk and gave a long sigh as he fought to regain his composure. He found Nero's smug indifference to the situation he was in maddening. He would break him if it was the last thing he did. He pressed a button on the console on his desk and within moments a voice came from the intercom.

"Yes, sir, how may I help you?" an efficient female voice answered.

"Could you come through, please," Trent said.

"Of course, sir, one moment."

Trent sat back down behind his desk as a tall woman with her hair tied in a tight bun entered his office.

"Miss Cruz, I believe that we may need to investigate alternative avenues in our pursuit of Raven. Where are the twins at the moment?"

"They're in Paris. They were investigating a lead on one

of Raven's safe houses there. Do you have new instructions for them?"

"Yes," Trent said thoughtfully. "Have them travel to London; that was the last place that we saw Raven. No matter how good she is she must have left some trail. She would have been injured and desperate after Nero's capture, so she must have had help. Someone must know where she went from there."

"Very well, sir, I shall issue them new orders immediately."

"Good," Trent replied with a grim smile, "and tell them if they track her down that I want no mistakes this time. They are not to return until she is in the ground. Do I make myself clear?"

"Perfectly, sir," she said.

☣☣☣

Diabolus Darkdoom sat reading the tablet display on the table in front of him. Otto, Wing, Shelby, and Laura also sat around the briefing room table in silence. After a few seconds Darkdoom's eyes lifted from the display and he looked at them with a raised eyebrow.

"Well, it's certainly an ingenious plan but I rather doubt that you would actually be able to pull it off," he said.

"Why not?" Otto asked quickly.

"Well, while I acknowledge that you may actually be able to get access to the Deepcore mainframe, I still do not see an answer to the most difficult challenge that you will face. Getting physical access to the servers is one thing but, as I believe I mentioned before, actually hacking into them is something my best men have described as impossible. I see nothing here that changes that assessment. Miss Brand, I am told that you are an extraordinarily capable computer expert—do you believe this can be done?"

"I . . . I'm not sure," Laura said, blushing and shooting an apologetic glance at Otto.

"It seems I am not the only one who has less than total confidence in this plan, Mr. Malpense. I am inclined to think that a deep-cover infiltration is still the best, if somewhat time-consuming, route to acquiring details of Nero's current location." Darkdoom sounded like he had already made up his mind.

"I can do it," Otto said calmly.

"So you say, but you offer no proof of that. An operation like this is too dangerous to rely so completely on your self-confidence alone. While you may be willing to risk your own life and those of your friends in such a way, I am not."

Otto sat silently for a moment, as if weighing his options.

"How secure are the *Megalodon*'s systems?" he asked, frowning.

"As secure as it is possible to make them with current technology," Darkdoom replied. "Why?"

"Just wondered," Otto said, and closed his eyes.

For a few long seconds the others sat at the table in confused silence. Only Wing seemed unconcerned by Otto's sudden silence.

"Are you all right, Otto?" Laura asked, sounding slightly confused.

"Mr. Malpense," Darkdoom said with a frown, "what are you—"

Suddenly the room fell dark and the familiar background hum of the giant submarine's engines was replaced with perfect silence. From outside of the briefing room they could hear cries of dismay and alarm.

"Reactor's offline!" one voice shouted.

"Lost helm control; she's dead in the water," someone else reported in a startled voice.

Suddenly the large monitor on the wall of the briefing room displayed a single phrase in foot-high white letters casting a ghostly glow across the astonished faces surrounding the table.

"WE CAN DO THIS."

Moments later the display went dark and the lights came back on in the briefing room. From outside they could hear shouted reports of the *Megalodon*'s systems coming back online.

"Now do you believe me?" Otto said. He looked paler than usual, but there was a triumphant gleam in his eye. "You may have a team you think can pull this off, but they won't be able to do what I just did. You need me, and if I'm going, so are the others."

Darkdoom looked hard at Otto for a few seconds before hitting a switch on the table in front of him and speaking to the air.

"Captain Sanders," he said in a firm voice.

"Yes, sir," Sanders's voice replied over the intercom.

"Set course for the English Channel, maximum speed."

"Aye, aye, sir."

☣ ☣ ☣

The Contessa burst into the Professor's quarters without warning.

"Where is she?" she snapped, striding across the room as Professor Pike put down the book he had been reading.

"Who?" the Professor replied innocently.

"Don't play games with me, Professor. Ms. Leon, where is she?" the Contessa said angrily.

"I'm afraid I have no idea," the Professor said with a smile.

"And I suppose you have no idea what this is either?" the Contessa said coldly, holding up the tiny relay device that Ms. Leon had placed beneath H.I.V.E.mind's core just a few hours before.

"Oh, that's a data relay," the Professor said. "Where did you find it?"

"You know perfectly well where we found it, Professor," the Contessa spat. "And now you're going tell me where I can find Ms. Leon."

"I told you, I don't know."

"*Tell me where she is,*" the Contessa said, the whispers of command twining through her voice.

"I don't know," the Professor said, feeling the words leap from his lips unbidden. He was suddenly very glad that he really did not know.

"Then perhaps you can tell me who broke into the storage vaults at exactly the same time that we were deactivating H.I.V.E.mind," the Contessa said, sounding even more angry.

"Which storage vault?" the Professor asked, feeling a sudden, welcome glimmer of hope.

"Vault nine, which also happens to be the vault where all of your secret little projects are stored," the Contessa replied, "though I suppose you know nothing about that either."

"You're quite right," the Professor said cheerfully, "not a thing. You could have checked the surveillance recordings, of course, but . . . oh . . . wait a minute, you'd need H.I.V.E.mind for that, wouldn't you, and he seems to have gone offline."

The Contessa looked at him for a moment, as if trying to decide what to do.

"I tire of these games, Professor," she snarled. "I am placing you under detention until I know exactly what is going on here."

Two Phalanx operatives walked into the room.

"Take the Professor to the detention area," the Contessa said quickly. "Perhaps some of his co-conspirators might want to pay him a visit."

The Phalanx operatives grabbed the Professor by the arms and shoved him roughly from the room. The Contessa looked at the disorganized mess in the Professor's room with disgust. If there was one thing she hated it was chaos, and this situation seemed to be getting more chaotic by the minute.

☣☣☣

Otto walked into the *Megalodon*'s armory and was immediately struck by the impressive efficiency with which Darkdoom's men were preparing the equipment they would need for the upcoming operation. Raven stood in the middle of the room, holding a thermoptic camouflage suit and demonstrating to one of the men exactly what modifications she needed him to make. She glanced up and saw Otto, giving the man a final instruction before walking over to him.

"The equipment is nearly ready. We're going to have fun trying to pack it all into the mini-subs, but I think we'll manage," she said calmly.

"Good," Otto said. "I hope we've thought of everything."

"In my experience there is always something you need that you don't have, but that's what keeps things interesting." Raven smiled.

"I think this is going to be interesting enough as it is."

"Yes—are you sure you're ready for this?" Raven was studying his face carefully.

"No, but it's still got to be done," Otto replied with a slight frown.

"Do you mind me asking what exactly you did in the briefing room?" Raven said quietly.

"Would you believe me if I told you that I honestly don't know?"

"Strangely, I would," Raven replied. "You're quite full of surprises, aren't you?"

"That's one way of putting it," Otto chuckled.

"What about the others? I know how capable you all are, but you have such limited operational experience."

"We've had good teachers," Otto said with a smile, "and you've got to take the training wheels off sooner or later."

"If it's any consolation I was almost exactly the same

age as you when I was given my first operation," Raven said.

"And how did that go?" Otto asked, curious to learn more of Raven's mysterious past.

"It was a complete disaster." She absentmindedly traced a finger down the long scar that ran across her cheek. "But in a funny way it was a good thing that it went as badly as it did."

"What happened?" Otto asked, his curiosity now thoroughly piqued.

"That's a story for another day," she replied quietly.

Otto was about to press for more information when Darkdoom entered the armory and walked over to the pair of them.

"How are we doing?" he asked, looking serious.

"We'll be ready when the *Megalodon* arrives on target," Raven replied.

"Excellent," Darkdoom said, surveying the equipment that lay arranged around the room. "Otto, I need to speak to Raven. Would you excuse us for a moment?"

Otto nodded and walked out of the room.

"You realize how dangerous this is," Darkdoom said quietly.

"Of course, but I don't really see that we have much choice."

"They seem unusually capable. Nero would be proud.

Malpense is especially gifted. My technicians still have no idea what he did to the *Megalodon*'s systems."

"I'm not sure he does himelf," Raven replied, "but I believe he can do what he needs to."

"Yes, so do I. I'm starting to understand why the Initiative have such an acute interest in him—which makes me even more unsure we should be letting him walk into the lion's den like this."

"I'll be watching his back," Raven replied.

"Of course you will. But you do understand that we cannot allow him to be captured, don't you? If there is no means of escape, you know what you will have to do."

"Yes, I know," Raven said, looking down at the floor. "Let's pray that it doesn't come to that."

chapter eight

The unmarked black helicopter raced low over the night skyline of London. It had met the five-man infiltration team at the appointed rendezvous area and once the equipment had been hurriedly transferred from the mini-subs onto the chopper, it had immediately taken off, bound for central London.

On board, the pilot glanced over his shoulder at the five masked figures sitting in the rear passenger compartment. He had never seen anything quite like the outfits they were all wearing, a kind of skintight black body armor that was covered in a subtle hexagonal pattern that reflected the light in an unusual way. They all wore sophisticated helmets that completely concealed their identities and had what looked like night-vision goggles mounted on the front. He had no idea what this was all about but he had learned long ago not to ask questions when he was hired by certain individuals.

"Okay," the pilot said, "five minutes to target. This is some of the most restricted airspace in the country, so you need to move fast once we're on site."

One of the armored figures in the back gave a curt nod of acknowledgment.

"And there will be no pickup if things go pear-shaped," the pilot added. "Once I've dropped you off, I'm getting out of there low and fast, understood?"

Again the leader of the team merely nodded and then turned back to look out of the window.

"Three minutes," the pilot said after a few moments, and the team in the rear of the helicopter began to move into action. They slipped into harnesses that were in turn attached to coiled ropes arranged on the floor of the helicopter, checking each other's rigging and making sure that everything was secure. The leader of the group surveyed the rest of the team and, apparently satisfied, hauled open first the hatch on one side of the helicopter and then the other. The team split, three bracing themselves against the hatch on one side and two on the other.

"One minute," the pilot yelled over the noise of the thumping rotor blades and rushing wind that now filled the cabin. He glanced over his shoulder just in time to see all five of them apparently vanish into thin air. He fought to control his surprise and keep the helicopter on the correct course.

Beneath the helicopter five high-tensile lines stretched taut, as if each was carrying some kind of invisible burden. The helicopter raced along the river, heading straight for the imposing headquarters of Britain's elite intelligence service. As it shot over the roof of the building the five lines beneath it suddenly cut loose, flapping wildly in the wind.

On the roof of the imposing building Raven landed silently, rolled to a kneeling position and scanned her surroundings. She quickly spotted the solitary guard on the roof who was watching the helicopter as it dived for the Thames and raced away along the river. She moved silently toward the man as he went for the radio clipped to his belt. Just as he was about to speak into it she slipped one arm around his throat and with the other hand pulled the pistol from his belt, pressing the cold muzzle against the side of his head.

"Tell them it was nothing to worry about," she whispered in his ear.

"I'm not going to do that," the guard replied firmly.

"Do it or I'll drop you right here," Raven whispered.

"I don't think you will," the guard said calmly. "You pull that trigger and every guard in this building will be up here in minutes."

"Enough?" Raven said.

"Aye, that'll do," Laura said from just behind her.

"Thanks for the help," Raven said to the guard and tightened her hold on his neck. The guard dropped silently to the ground, unconscious.

Laura pulled a tiny notebook computer from a holster on her hip and plugged the recording device that she'd been holding into it. Nothing happened for a moment and then a window popped up.

"VOICEPRINT ANALYSIS COMPLETE"

Just a moment later the guard's radio crackled to life.

"Roof station, we just recorded an overflight down here. Everything okay up there?" the voice on the radio inquired.

Laura hit a key on her computer and spoke into the radio. The voice that came from the tiny speakers on the front of her helmet was not her own but a perfect duplicate of the guard's who now lay unconscious on the roof in front of her.

"Nothing to worry about," she said. "Just a tourist chopper that got a bit too close."

"Okay, roof station, roger that," the voice on the radio replied, and cut the line.

Raven smiled beneath her mask as three more figures that only she could see through her specially modified goggles jogged across the roof toward her.

"Raven to control," she whispered into her throat mic, "team is down and clear. Proceeding on target."

"Understood," a voice crackled in her earpiece.

"Are the exit kits hidden?" she asked as the other three approached.

Wing gave a quick nod.

"Okay. Shelby, Wing, door," Raven said quickly. "Laura, let me know when you have the signal strength you need. Otto, with me."

Shelby and Wing moved quickly to a nearby roof access door. Raven in turn moved to the security camera covering the door and placed a relay collar on the cable running from it. The relay intercepted and recorded a few seconds of footage of the undamaged door and then began to loop the same few seconds over and over again.

"Camera's blind, go," Raven whispered.

Shelby pulled a small black box from her backpack and started methodically sweeping it over the door and the surrounding frame. A strip of LEDs on the device leaped from green to red and back again as she moved it slowly back and forth. Apparently satisfied, she delved back into her pack and brought out a neat plastic case, which she opened, taking out four small metallic discs and attaching them to specific points on the door frame. Tiny red lights blinked on each of the discs for a couple of seconds and then turned green. Shelby gave a small nod to Wing and he produced two suction pads with handles from his own pack. He held them to the door and there was a tiny hiss of compressed air escaping. He pulled on the handles, testing their hold, and then gave a quick nod to Shelby. She quickly unclipped a small gun with a gas canister mounted on it from her belt and, pressing it against the door, began to draw a large rectangle. The gun left a tiny steaming trail behind it as the compressed liquid nitrogen in the canister instantly froze the metal of the door to several hundred degrees below zero. Shelby completed the rectangle and Wing gave a small grunt as he pulled on the handles and that entire section of the door came away, the intense cold having weakened it sufficiently.

Raven watched as Shelby, Laura, and Wing headed through the neat hole. Satisfied that they were all safely inside she moved quickly over to where Otto was crouched next to a nondescript metal hatch in the roof.

"They're in," she whispered. "You ready?"

Otto nodded and watched the precious seconds tick past on the mission clock in the corner of his head-up display.

Inside, Shelby, Laura, and Wing headed quietly down the stairs. Now that they were inside they did not need to worry about the cameras that were positioned at regular intervals in the stairwell; their thermoptic camouflage suits took care of that. Laura found it slightly unnerving being hidden in plain sight like this, the skin of her suit projecting a flawless holographic image of her surroundings that would fool all but the most careful observers and masking all of the heat given off by her body. It was a miniaturized version of the same technology used to cloak the Shroud transports, and while the system was certainly impressive, she couldn't help but feel dangerously exposed. She silently scolded herself for her nervousness and focused her attention on the small ever-climbing bar that was displayed on her HUD. As they descended the next flight of stairs the bar crossed a critical threshold and began to flash.

"Okay, this floor," Laura whispered. Wing moved to a position where he could see anyone coming up the stairs from below as Shelby and Laura examined the door. Shelby pointed silently to the card reader that was mounted on the door and Laura nodded. She pulled the tiny computer, no bigger than a paperback book, from the holster on her hip and connected a short length of ribbon cable to it. On the other end of the cable was a plain white plastic card with a magnetic strip. She slid the card into the reader mounted on the door and began to tap away quickly at the computer keyboard. Just a few seconds later there was a satisfying click as the door unlocked.

"Now I know what I want for my birthday," Shelby whispered, and behind her mask Laura smiled despite her nerves.

Wing moved between them and slid a narrow flexible tube under the door. At the end of the tube was an eyepiece that showed what was on the other side of the door. Satisfied that no one was waiting for them in the darkened corridor beyond, he silently opened the door and stepped through. The three of them moved quickly along the corridor to an empty office. The door was locked but Shelby's picks made short work of the old-fashioned mechanical lock. They stepped inside and closed the door behind them. Wing scanned the room for any sign of cameras or motion sensors. Seeing none, he reached up and pressed the tiny stud on his helmet, just behind the ear, that deactivated the thermoptic camouflage. The suits' batteries were good but they would not last forever.

"Team two to team one, we are in position. Commencing network infiltration," Wing reported. Laura was already tapping away at the keyboard of her computer, testing the security of the building's wireless network now that the signal strength was high enough.

"Doable?" Shelby asked.

"Cake," Laura said with a chuckle. "Government IT contractors, gotta love them."

That was slightly unfair Laura realized but she had spent the last year trying to hack H.I.V.E.'s network with varying degrees of success. That network was secured by a neurally networked artificial intelligence who she suspected rather enjoyed matching wits with her, and getting around him had been like playing a dozen simultaneous games of three-dimensional chess. This, by comparison, was tic-tac-toe.

"Okay, here we go," Laura said after barely a minute. "Elevator control subsystems. We're ready."

"Roger that," Raven replied in her ear.

Up on the roof the hatch whirred open and Raven peered inside. Otto finished clamping a second metal box from his pack onto the framework and clipped the end of the line that trailed from it to his harness. Raven moved to the first box on the other side of the hatch and followed suit. She slowly lowered herself through the opening and let herself swing free in the pitch darkness of the seemingly bottomless elevator shaft. Otto followed her through, praying that the impossibly thin cable he hung from was as strong as Darkdoom's technicians had insisted it was.

Raven tipped forward, her head pointing straight down the shaft, her legs straight and her arms tight against her sides. Otto did the same, swallowing nervously. Even with his night-vision system active, the shaft appeared to simply vanish into a black void far below.

"Ready to commence descent," Raven whispered, flipping the hinged top off the tiny cylindrical control unit she held in one hand.

"Copy that," Laura replied. "Three . . . two . . . one . . . mark!"

Raven hit the switch and the brakes holding the cable reels in both boxes up on the roof released simultaneously. To Otto what happened next was indistinguishable from free fall as they shot down the shaft at over fifty yards per second. The speed was terrifying but it was only by traveling this fast that they would be ignored by the motion sensors dotted along the length of the elevator shaft. Their camouflage may fool the human eye but those sensors would detect them, visible or not. Speed was the only answer.

In the deserted office Laura watched the timer on her computer's display. There was no margin for error. The shaft leading to Deepcore that Otto and Raven were now plummeting down was sealed near its base by security shutters. The only way to open them without triggering the security alarms was to convince the security system that this was a maintenance test, which would quickly cycle the shutters open and then closed again, but the shutters had to open at exactly the right moment: too soon and the shutters would close again before Raven and Otto passed through, too late and they wouldn't have time to open before they reached them. The timing was too fine for a human; they had to trust her computer and, despite all the precautions they had taken, that made her nervous.

Back in the elevator shaft Otto could now make

out the shutters as he raced toward them. He closed his eyes, knowing that if they hit them at this speed at least it would be painless. Just twenty yards below them there was a quick hiss and the shutters shot apart, Raven and Otto passing through with just inches of clearance on either side. Just as quickly the shutters began to close again and Otto felt his stomach shoot into his mouth as the brakes on the cable reels, that were now several hundred yards above them, engaged and brought them to a stop as quickly as was physically safe, moments before the cables got trapped by the shutters. As soon as they stopped, the clips on both their harnesses automatically released and they dropped the last couple of yards onto the top of the elevator car at the bottom of the shaft. Raven landed with the grace of a ballerina, flipping and alighting squarely on her feet in almost total silence. Otto landed with slightly less dignity, on all fours, with a thud.

Raven barely even paused for breath as Otto slowly stood up. She moved quickly to the hatch in the top of the elevator car, pulled it open, and dropped inside. Otto would have liked to stop and catch his breath, but the clock was still ticking and there was no time for him to dawdle. He lowered himself slowly through the hatch and dropped to the floor of the elevator behind Raven. She was inspecting a numerical keypad on the wall next to the door.

"Need the code," Raven said, and up in the deserted office, Laura, Shelby, and Wing gave a collective sigh of relief.

"You are both okay?" Wing asked.

"We're fine, as you can tell by the fact that you're talking to us," Raven replied impatiently. "The code?"

"Coming up," Laura replied as her custom-written intrusion routines cut through the network's protection like a knife. "Got it: two, four, zero, six, zero, five."

In the elevator car Raven punched the string of numbers into the keypad and the lift doors hissed apart.

"We're in," Raven said quickly, stepping through the doors and into the hallway beyond. The hall was lined with stainless steel and at the far end, just thirty yards away, was a door above which the word DEEPCORE could be seen, etched into the metal.

Otto went to walk down the hall, but Raven's hand shot out, pressing against his chest and holding him in place.

"Stop," she whispered. "Too easy."

The plans that Darkdoom had acquired of the building had extended as far as the lift shaft they had just plummeted down. They had no way of knowing what might lie ahead of them at this point. Under the circumstances, Otto was prepared to trust Raven's very finely tuned survival instincts.

Raven pressed a small stud on the side of the goggles mounted to the front of her helmet, switching between an array of different visual modes. There was nothing out of the ordinary, but the hairs on the back of her neck prickled and she had learned long ago to trust them more than any electronic device. She reached over her shoulders and pulled the twin blades from the sheaths on her back, thumbing the controls on the hilts of the swords to make them as sharp as she possibly could, then slowly and cautiously she began to walk down the hall.

There was a sudden almost inaudible click and with a whoosh four lethally sharp spikes shot forward from the walls surrounding her. Raven moved in a blur, her blades whining through the air impossibly fast, neatly severing the spikes before they could impale her. She moved more quickly now, dancing down the hallway, her blades swinging as more and more of the lethal spears shot out of the walls toward her. Otto had never seen anyone move with such grace and speed; it was like watching a deadly ballet.

Raven was nearing the end of the hall, the floor behind her littered with the severed tips of the spikes, when she made her first mistake. There were just too many spikes shooting from all around her and one sliced across her shoulder, tearing apart her armor and leaving a deep gash in her shoulder. She spun and sliced at the spike, now dripping with her blood, before it could retract back into the wall. It clattered to the ground, its tip stained red. Raven cursed in Russian and fell against the door at the end of the hall, breathing heavily. Otto slowly made his way down the hall, avoiding the scattered remains of the lethal anti-intrusion system. Who knew what ID tag or transmitter you had to be wearing to make your way safely down this hall under normal circumstances, but he was sure that its designers could never have imagined anyone being able to do what Raven had just done.

"How bad?" Raven said as Otto approached, tipping her head back toward the long cut in her shoulder.

"It's not pretty but you'll live," Otto said. The cut was deep but the bleeding wasn't too bad; she had been lucky.

"Guys, you need to move," Laura's voice whispered in both their ears. "I don't know what just happened down there but every alarm in the building has just gone off up here."

Raven didn't reply; she just made four quick cuts at the metal door in front of them with her swords and kicked it. It fell slowly backward into the room beyond and landed with a loud metallic clang.

"So much for subtle," Raven muttered and stepped inside.

☻☻☻

The monitor on Sebastian Trent's desk flickered into life, filled with the anxious-looking face of a H.O.P.E. surveillance operative.

"What is it?" Trent asked impatiently.

"Sir, we've just been informed that someone has penetrated the Deepcore server room under the Vauxhall Cross building," the man reported.

"Do we have positive identification?" Trent asked quickly.

"No, sir, but that server contains a full copy of all H.O.P.E.'s operational files," the man on the screen replied. "If they fell into the wrong hands the consequences would be catastrophic."

Trent took a long, deep breath. It could be anyone doing this but every instinct told him that there was only one person skilled enough to attempt such an audacious operation. He cut the connection to the surveillance operative, picked up his phone, and punched in a number. After a couple of seconds a female voice answered.

"Hello."

"How quickly can you get to MI6 headquarters?"

"Fifteen minutes," the voice replied.

"It's Raven, go now."

"Understood," the voice answered efficiently and the line went dead.

A mirthless smile spread across Trent's face as he put the phone down. They would not have to track Raven down after all; she had delivered herself to them.

Otto followed Raven through the shattered remains of the door into the Deepcore server room. The room was filled with row after row of server racks, their blinking lights creating an almost hypnotic display as data flowed in and out of the room. Otto could feel that the room was bitterly cold, even through the insulated skin of his thermoptic camo suit. It was clearly designed for machines rather than humans.

"So what now?" Raven said quickly.

"Give me a minute," Otto replied.

"We don't have a minute," Raven replied impatiently.

"Okay, okay," Otto shot back, quickly scanning the server racks. He walked toward the nearest one and slowly knelt down in front of it. He closed his eyes, trying to ignore the time pressure that they were suddenly under and achieve the quiet concentration that he needed for the task ahead. Raven stood and watched as Otto's head dropped onto his chest.

Otto wasn't in the room anymore; now he raced through the labyrinthine channels of the network, trying to stay focused on the specific information that he needed to retrieve. It seemed an almost impossible task: there were endless glowing fields of data all around him, swarming with the pulses of information that kept

Britain's security forces connected. He felt a twinge of panic. There was just too much data to sort through. If he'd had time he might have been able to find what he needed, but time was the one thing they did not have. He'd led his friends into this lethal situation and now he couldn't find the one piece of information they were here for. Otto stopped, hovering amid the torrents of data. He forced himself to calm down; he had to stay focused.

He thought back to the encounter with H.I.V.E.mind in the school library. He could almost hear the calm, reassuring tone of the AI's voice.

"This is simply a construct that your mind has created to rationalize an experience that would otherwise be impossible to comprehend to a human consciousness," Otto said to himself, recalling H.I.V.E.mind's definition of what he was now experiencing. He had to remember that this was all just in his head, that this was exactly how he imagined the search for the data would be. He had to stop thinking like a human and think like a machine. He could spend forever frantically hunting for the data they needed; what he had to do instead was make it come to him. He visualized the information, willing it to find him. For a long moment, nothing happened, and then suddenly there, hanging in the air before him, was a glowing cube. He slowly reached out and touched the surface of the cube, unsure what to expect. The data streamed into him from the cube like a lightning strike. Otto gasped with pain, his head felt like it would explode. He struggled to maintain his focus, fighting to remind himself that this was all just a construct of his own imagination, but the pain felt all too real.

Back in the server room, Otto's body stiffened and then began to convulse. Raven ran to his side, dropping down and catching him before he fell backward onto the floor. She quickly pulled his helmet off and was dismayed to see how deathly pale his face was, the only color coming from the twin trails of crimson blood that trickled from his nose. Suddenly his eyes flew open and for a long moment he stared into nothingness, unblinking.

"Otto!" Raven said sharply, cradling his head.

Then suddenly he was back, blinking rapidly, looking confused and disorientated.

"Nero," he said croakily, his voice weak. "Switzerland, the Alps—he's in the mountains."

☢ ☢ ☢

"Where are they?" Shelby said, sounding worried as Laura tapped away at the keyboard of her computer.

"I don't know, but I do know that we can't stay here much longer," Laura replied nervously.

She tried to ignore the wailing of alarms coming from outside as she fought to stay one step ahead of the hound programs that had been released onto the network to determine the precise location of her intrusion.

Wing said nothing, crouched in front of the door, peering through the eyepiece of the snake-cam at the image of the hallway beyond. Suddenly a familiar and extremely welcome voice filled their earpieces.

"Raven to team two, we need an exit," she whispered urgently.

"Working on it," Laura said quietly, her fingers flying over the keyboard.

"Did you get it?" Shelby asked quickly.

"Yes, but it's no use if we can't get out of here," Raven replied.

"Right," Laura said, studying the display on her computer. "The only way in or out of there is the elevator, but if I grant access to that they're going to detect the hack and get a location on us. You won't have much time."

"I wasn't planning to hang around," Raven replied. "Do it."

Laura tapped away at the tiny keyboard for a few seconds and then hit return.

"Okay, the elevator is unlocked—move."

"Roger that," Raven replied, and the line went dead.

Wing pulled the flexible tube from under the door and stood up.

"We have company," he whispered. He pressed the stud on his helmet and vanished as the thermoptic camouflage system came back online. Shelby and Laura followed suit just seconds before the door swung open and a guard in full body armor stepped in, sweeping the submachine gun that he carried across the room in slow, careful arcs. Every breath Laura took sounded impossibly loud to her, as she stood perfectly still, the guard just a few feet away. She winced when he spotted the tiny notebook computer that sat on the desk.

"Bravo Three to control, I've found the source of the network intrusion. No sign of anybody here."

"Understood, Bravo Three," a voice answered over his radio. "Please disable the device."

"Wilco," the guard said, and fired a short three-round burst into the computer, instantly destroying it. Satisfied, he turned to leave, but then something odd caught his eye. There, in the middle of the pattern of shadow cast by the window, was a human form. Laura felt her blood run cold as she realized that standing in front of the window had been a big mistake. He spun around, leveling his weapon at the apparently empty air in front of him. He reached for his belt and unclipped a small cylindrical device, popping the cap off with his thumb and pressing the button underneath. There was a high-pitched whine like a camera flash charging and then a sharp electrical crackle. Instantly the thermoptic camouflage on all three suits failed and Laura was left fully visible, perfectly outlined by the nighttime glow of London that poured in from outside.

"Gotcha," the guard said, and squeezed the trigger.

Wing moved like a cat, swatting the guard's weapon upward, sending a burst of fire harmlessly into the ceiling tiles. His other hand lashed out like a striking cobra, hitting the man with a flat palm to the chin. The guard's head snapped back and he staggered away, Wing wrenching the gun from his hands and tossing it into the corner of the room. He advanced on the dazed guard, delivering a solid straight-legged kick to his gut that knocked all the wind from him and doubled him over. Wing pivoted and brought his knee up sharply under the man's chin, sending him sailing backward onto the desk, where he landed with a crash, out cold.

"Everyone okay?" Wing said quietly, watching the guard for any sign of movement.

"Aye," Laura said shakily, putting her hand on Wing's arm, "thank you."

"You are welcome," Wing said calmly. "We should go."

"Nothing more we can do here," Laura said, gesturing at the remains of the shattered computer.

"Suits are fried too. Looks like they were ready for that particular trick," Shelby said, pressing fruitlessly at the activation stud on her helmet.

"Remember what Ms. Leon taught us," Wing said as he headed for the door. "When stealth fails, one must rely on evasion. Come on."

☣☣☣

"How are you feeling?" Raven said, looking at Otto with obvious concern.

"I've felt better," Otto said honestly. He leaned against the wall of the elevator, not entirely sure if his legs would support him for very much longer. He was finding it hard to concentrate, his head filled with the confusing muddle of data that he had absorbed from the network. He fought to keep the coordinates of the facility that was holding Nero from becoming lost in the swirling mass of information rattling around inside his skull. In truth, he felt like all he wanted to do was curl up in a ball in the corner and sleep for a week.

Suddenly the elevator jerked to a stop; the doors stayed firmly closed. Raven pulled them apart slightly with a grunt, only to be met with the featureless concrete wall of the elevator shaft. She let the doors go and they closed with a thud.

"Plan B," she said, and jumped up and caught hold of the edge of the open hatch in the ceiling, pulling herself up effortlessly. Once she was on the roof of the car she lowered a hand back inside and gestured for Otto to take it. He grabbed onto her wrist and she pulled him up through the hole as if he were weightless. Otto activated the night-vision mode on his helmet and the pitch-blackness of the elevator shaft was lit up in an eerie green light. Raven stood looking up at one of the doors in the shaft wall, ten yards above them.

"Feel up to climbing?" she said quietly.

"Do I have a choice?" Otto asked, sounding tired.

"Not really," Raven replied calmly. She moved to the cables supporting the elevator car and examined them. They were covered in a thick layer of grease; there was no way they'd be able to climb them. She moved to studying the concrete walls that surrounded them, but they were featureless and smooth, offering no type of footholds. Silently she cursed the fact that the camo suits weren't fitted with grappler units, an oversight that might prove fatal. She pulled the twin swords from their sheaths on her back and thumbed the controls, switching them to their sharpest setting. She moved to the wall and slid the first blade into the solid concrete effortlessly. She touched the controls again and the forcefield surrounding the blade deactivated, trapping the blade within the wall. She pulled herself upward, using the hilt of the sword as a handhold and followed the same procedure with the other blade, sliding it into the wall a couple of feet higher than the first one. She clenched her jaw as fresh searing pain from the wound in her shoulder lanced across her back. She pushed the protests from her injured body to the back of her mind and ignored them, just as she had been trained to do. Once she had pulled herself to the level of the second blade she switched the first blade's forcefield back on and withdrew it smoothly from the wall. Otto watched, quietly impressed, as Raven repeated the process several times, slowly but surely ascending the smooth wall of the shaft.

By the time Raven reached the lip of the door her arms were burning with exertion and her back felt slick under her armor with fresh blood from her shoulder wound. With a final grunt of effort she pulled herself up into the narrow recess, pressing herself against the closed doors. She slowly reached down and pulled the sword from the shaft wall, sliding it into its sheath next to its partner and making a silent note to thank Professor Pike for building the unique weapons, if she ever saw him again. She stood there for a moment, slowing her breathing and gathering her strength before forcing her fingers into the gap between the doors and heaving them apart. As the gap widened light poured in from the corridor beyond. Raven breathed a sigh of relief as she saw it was empty.

In the shaft below Otto fought to keep his balance as the elevator suddenly began to move upward again, gathering speed. Raven hauled the doors farther apart, sliding between them and bracing her back against one while pushing the other away with one foot.

"Jump!" she yelled at Otto as he raced up toward her.

Otto dived from the roof of the car, aiming for the narrow-looking gap in the doors. He shot headlong through the opening, colliding with Raven and sending them both tumbling into the corridor beyond as the elevator shot past just inches from his feet and the doors slid closed.

"Just once," Otto said, sitting up, "it might be nice to do things the easy way."

"Oh, come on," Raven replied, pulling him to his feet. "Where would be the fun in that?"

☻☻☻

Wing, Laura, and Shelby ran back up the stairs toward the roof. A couple of floors below them a pair of MI6 guards entered the stairwell. One of them leaned into the void that ran down the middle of the stairs and looked upward.

"They're heading for the roof," the guard said into his radio. "We'll intercept them there—they've got nowhere to go."

Above them, Wing, Laura and Shelby ran onto the roof and into the cool night air.

"You two go and get the kits ready," Wing said, sounding completely unperturbed by the situation they found themselves in.

"What about you?" Laura said, sounding considerably less calm.

"I will delay our pursuers," Wing said calmly.

"Every guard in this building is probably on their way up here. Are you crazy?" Laura said sharply.

"I will join you shortly," Wing said, trying to sound reassuring. "I am as eager to leave as you, but we must delay their pursuit if we are to get away safely."

"He's right," Shelby said reluctantly. "Come on, Brand. We'll get the kits ready."

Laura looked for a moment like she might continue to argue but she knew they needed the time that Wing could buy them. She gave a small, unhappy nod and ran away across the roof. Shelby turned to follow her but then stopped and looked back at Wing.

"Be careful, big guy," she said softly. "No heroics."

"No heroics," Wing said calmly, and turned back to face the door leading from the stairwell.

Shelby ran after Laura as the sounds of the pursuing guards running up the stairs below became louder.

Wing stood waiting just a few feet from the door. He removed his helmet, tossing it to one side; without the advantage that a working thermoptic camouflage system provided it would serve no purpose other than to limit his peripheral vision.

The pair of guards burst through the door onto the roof, their guns snapping up and leveling at Wing as they spotted him standing there.

"You!" the first guard yelled. "Hands on your head, don't move."

Wing slowly put his hands on his head, showing no hint of emotion.

"What the heck?" the other guard said. "He's just a kid." He pulled a pair of handcuffs from his belt and slowly moved behind Wing and grasped one of his wrists. In one fluid motion, Wing grabbed the guard's own wrist with his free hand and twisted hard. There was a sickening crunch, the guard howling in pain as Wing stepped backward, too close for the man to bring his gun to bear. He pulled the guard's wounded arm farther over his own shoulder, dragging the man closer, and jerked his head backward, his skull connecting with the man's nose with a crunch. Wing rotated around the guard, pressing the wounded arm up into the small of the man's back and ducking behind him, giving the other guard no clean shot without hitting his associate. He pushed hard, sending the stunned guard staggering toward his partner, and delivered a sharp kick to the base of his spine. The wounded guard's momentum sent him careering into the other man, yowling with pain and confusion.

Wing took two short steps and in a blur of movement pulled the handcuffs from the wounded man's belt and snapped them closed around both his broken wrist and the wrist of the unwounded guard's gun hand.

Wing pressed his fingers into the pressure point behind the wounded guard's ear and he collapsed, instantly unconscious, pulling the other guard down with him and pinning his gun to the ground. The conscious guard snatched for the gun with his free hand, but Wing dropped onto him, his knee pressing into his throat hard enough to choke him but without crushing his windpipe. Wing delivered a sharp knuckle jab to the guard's shoulder and his free arm was instantly disabled too.

Wing could hear the sound of at least half a dozen more guards racing up the stairs from below. He knew there would be more than he could handle. He reached down and took a smoke grenade from the webbing on the pinned guard's chest and pulled the pin with his teeth, tossing it through the doorway into the stairwell. There were cries of confusion from just below as the confined space filled with impenetrable clouds of white smoke. Wing pulled a flashbang stun grenade from the other side of the pinned guard's webbing and waited a couple of seconds before tossing it into the stairwell too. He closed his eyes, the flash of the grenade clear even through his eyelids.

"Who the heck are you?" the guard pinned beneath Wing gasped.

"Just a kid," Wing said with a slight smile, and punched him unconscious.

Wing sprang to his feet and ran across the roof toward Laura and Shelby.

"We must leave," Wing said quickly. "Are you ready?"

"As we'll ever be," Shelby shot back, tossing a small pack to him. He put the straps of the pack over his shoulders and snapped the clasps at the front together.

Shelby stepped up onto the low wall that surrounded the edge of the roof, looking at the dark ribbon of the Thames far below. Laura stepped up beside her, swallowing hard.

"You're enjoying this, aren't you?" she said.

"Are you kidding?" Shelby said with a grin. "I haven't had this much fun in ages."

Wing joined them on the parapet.

"Ready?" he said. The two girls nodded and all three of them leaped off the edge.

As they jumped they pulled the ripcords attached to the packs they wore and black silk parachute canopies unfurled above them. They drifted down toward the river, but moments before they hit the surface they pulled the quick releases on their chutes, dropping the last few yards. There were three small splashes and then nothing. Only the black canopies that floated gently down onto the water were left to show that they had been there at all.

☺☺☺

"Control to Raven," the voice crackled in Raven's earpiece as she ran down the empty corridor with Otto in tow, "team two have exited the building. Mini-subs are effecting retrieval now."

"Understood, Raven out," she responded in a whisper.

"What is it?" Otto asked.

"The others are out safely," she said quietly, and Otto felt a sudden rush of relief. All they had to worry about now was getting out of there in one piece themselves.

"Freeze," Raven hissed, pushing him back against the wall of the corridor. Another squad of half a dozen guards, all in full tactical gear, ran down the corridor toward them. Otto held his breath as they got closer, praying that the suits' systems were still fully functional. The squad ran past and vanished around a corner farther down the passageway. Otto breathed a sigh of relief. He could get used to being invisible. He had to admire the ingenuity of Darkdoom's technicians.

"Come on," Raven said, continuing down the hallway. At the far end were a set of double doors with the word "GARAGE" on the wall next to them.

"You thinking what I'm thinking?" Otto said quietly.

"Yes," Raven said quickly, "let's see if we can't borrow a ride."

She moved toward the doors, opened them a crack, and peered through. There were no signs of any guards in the cavernous space beyond, so she crept inside. The garage was huge, with numerous vehicles filling the vast low-ceilinged space, all parked in neatly arranged bays. Otto followed Raven between the rows of parked cars and vans; there was still no sign of any guards. Suddenly Raven stopped.

"What is it?" Otto whispered.

"I think I just found our ticket out of here," she said, nodding toward one of the bays just ahead. Parked there was the most beautiful car Otto had ever seen. It was sleek, low and black, its muscular curves and fat tires suggesting that it was going to be somewhat quicker than walking. Otto started to walk toward the car, eager to get a closer look, but Raven shot out a hand, holding him back. Something about this was not right.

"This is too easy," she whispered. "Where are the guards?"

She was right, Otto thought. The security forces knew that the building had been infiltrated; it would be madness to leave such an obvious escape route unguarded. As if in answer to his suspicions, there was the sudden tinny clink of something metallic hitting concrete and Otto turned to see a small silver cylinder rolling across the floor of the garage toward him.

"MOVE!" Raven yelled urgently, pushing him toward the waiting car. Almost unconsciously she put herself between Otto and the grenade, waiting for the concussive

wave to hit her in the back, praying that she could shield
him from the blast. But no blast came; instead there was
just a sharp electrical crackle from behind her and then
nothing. A message popped up on the head-up display
inside her helmet.

WARNING!

THERMOPTIC CAMOUFLAGE SYSTEM DISABLED

She pushed Otto toward the car and positioned herself
between him and the rest of the garage, feeling horribly
exposed.

Suddenly two women, both with long blond hair
tied back in ponytails and wearing suits of tight-fitting
white leather body armor, stepped out of the shadows.
They had to be twins: their faces were mirror-images of
each other.

"Hello," the first woman said in an upper-class British
accent. "I'm Constance."

"And I'm Verity," the other woman said, in an identical voice. "And we'll be your murderers for tonight."
She grinned evilly and raised a snub-nosed black pistol.
Without hesitating she pulled the trigger and two darts
trailing thin wires shot out, striking Raven squarely in the
chest. Fractions of a second later the taser discharged fifty
thousand volts straight into her body, dropping Raven
into a twitching heap on the ground.

"And I thought this was going to be difficult," the

woman called Constance said, walking slowly forward. She looked up from Raven's incapacitated body and smiled at Otto. "Mask off, please."

Otto slowly removed his helmet, glaring defiantly at the two women.

"Mr. Malpense, I presume," Constance went on, still smiling. "We work for someone who's very eager to meet you." She pulled a pistol from her belt and pointed it at Raven's prone form. "I don't really approve of nonlethal weaponry," she said, gesturing at the cables trailing from Raven's chest, "so why don't you come quietly before I'm forced to rectify that situation."

Otto leaned against the sleek black car next to him and bowed his head, closing his eyes.

"Good boy," Constance said, stepping forward.

Suddenly the car roared into life, the engine revving wildly and the headlights switching on to full beam, sending the woman staggering backward, blinded by the glaring halogen light. Otto ran at her, colliding with her hard and knocking her off her feet while she was still disorientated. Her gun skittered a few feet away across the pavement and Otto scrambled across the floor, desperately reaching for the fallen weapon. Constance leaped to her feet as Verity dropped the taser and sprinted toward Otto. Otto grabbed the gun and rolled onto his back, pointing it straight at Constance.

"Back off!" he yelled angrily.

Verity stopped just a couple of feet away from him, murder in her eyes.

"One more step and one of you gets a bullet, understood?" Otto said, trying to keep the edge of panic he could feel from his voice as he slowly got to his feet.

"You might find that difficult, Mr. Malpense," Constance said, taking a slow but deliberate step toward him, "especially with the safety still on."

"Oh, come on," Otto said with a sneer. "What do you think this is, amateur hour?" He twitched the gun downward and pulled the trigger, blowing a chunk out of the floor between Constance's feet.

"Now back away, slowly, both of you."

Constance stared at him for a long moment as if trying to figure something out and then slowly backed away, her sister following suit. Otto didn't take his eyes off them as he moved carefully over to where Raven lay. She gave a soft moan as he approached and tried shakily to push herself up to a sitting position. Otto reached down and yanked the cables trailing from the taser, pulling the two tiny barbs from Raven's chest.

"Can you move?" Otto asked.

"Yes," Raven said, getting unsteadily to her feet. She pulled her helmet off and tossed it to one side. The look in her eyes as she stared at Constance and Verity sent a chill down Otto's spine.

"Give me the gun," Raven said. "I'll finish this."

"Kill us and Nero dies," Verity said calmly.

"Oh, I'm not going to kill you," Raven said, "not for a while, anyway."

"There's no way you're getting out of here," Constance said. "Kill us and you'll still be captured, but Nero will die for what you've done. You can't win."

"Leave them," Otto said, putting a hand on Raven's shoulder. "We've got what we came for. Besides, you're the designated driver." He nodded toward the still-idling black sports car in the bay next to them. "I'll cover these two. You get that thing moving."

Raven paused for a moment and then nodded. She looked over at the two women.

"Next time we meet, you won't see me coming," she said.

"We'll look forward to it," Verity replied with a sneer.

Raven stared at her for a moment, as if memorizing every detail of her face, and then turned and walked over to the car. She opened the door and slid behind the wheel. The car leaped forward, tires squealing as Raven hit the gas. She spun the wheel and fishtailed the car to a halt behind Otto, leaning over and popping the passenger door open. Otto slid into the passenger seat, keeping the gun leveled at the two women.

"Go," Otto said, and pulled the door shut.

Raven did not need to be told twice, she floored the

accelerator and the car roared away between the rows of parked vehicles.

"Darn it," Verity shouted as the sleek black car disappeared around the corner at the far end of the garage.

"They're not out of here yet," Constance said calmly. She pulled a small black remote from her pocket and pressed a button. There was a double beep from behind her and the headlights flashed on a silver sports car parked in the shadows.

☢☢☢

Raven spun the wheel again, steering the car around the corner and straightening up as it rocketed between the rows of parked vehicles on the next level of the garage.

"That was quick thinking back there, Otto," she said with a smile, ramming her foot down on the accelerator. "How did you start this thing?"

"Let's just say that we had a little chat," Otto replied. The truth of the matter was that this car, like all modern cars, was controlled almost completely by computers, and it had not taken much effort to exert control over it. Otto grabbed onto the dashboard as Raven sent the car sideways around another corner. Ahead of them now was the exit from the car park, an exit that was firmly sealed by steel security shutters and half a dozen guards, all with assault rifles raised and pointing in their direction.

"Do you get the impression they'd rather we stayed?" Otto said.

"It's certainly beginning to feel that way," Raven replied, bringing the car to a screeching halt a hundred yards or so from the exit.

One of the guards lifted a loud bullhorn to his mouth and spoke.

"Switch off the engine and step out of the car. If you do not comply I am authorized to use lethal force."

Raven turned and looked at Otto.

"Any ideas?" she said, frowning.

"Oh, don't worry," Otto replied. "You see, when I had my little chat with the car I found out some interesting things about it. Seems that it has a few undocumented optional extras."

He leaned over and pressed a concealed button behind the steering wheel and a section of the dashboard slid back, revealing a control panel.

"Whose car is this?" Raven said, trying hard not to grin.

"I'm not sure, but whoever they are I suspect they have a license for more than just driving." Otto grinned back at her.

Raven hit the gas and sent the car roaring toward the exit gate. Immediately the guards standing around the gate opened fire. The high velocity rounds from their assault rifles should have turned a car like that into Swiss cheese, but instead the bullets just pinged harmlessly off the gleaming exterior and windshield.

Otto hit a switch on the control panel and a section slid back on one of the car's fenders, a black tube popping out and locking into place. Otto hit another button and a rocket shot from the tube, streaked between the rows of parked cars, and blew the security gate that blocked the exit to pieces. Raven tightened her grip on the steering wheel and pressed the accelerator hard to the floor. The car roared between the guards, forcing them to dive for cover, scattering in all directions. It shot through the blazing debris of the exit and powered up the short ramp outside. At the top of the ramp, the car left the ground for a moment as it flew onto the public road outside. Raven spun the wheel hard as the car landed, sending it sliding sideways into the left-hand lane and roaring away down the road.

"I have to get one of these," Raven said as the car wove through the nighttime traffic.

Otto twisted in his seat and looked out through the tiny rear window. For a moment he thought they'd got away clean, but then a silver sports car flew out of the exit from the MI6 garage and powered down the road after them.

"We've got company," Otto reported. He couldn't make out who was chasing them through the tinted black glass of the pursuing car's windshield but he could take an educated guess.

Raven shot a glance at the rearview mirror and accelerated harder. The car's engine roared, turbos whistling like canaries, as she wove through the traffic ahead of them, missing the other cars by just inches. She knew that this car could probably outrun their pursuers in a straight line, but there were no straight lines in London traffic, even at night.

Without warning a black cab pulled out in front of them and Raven swerved hard, fighting for control as the car mounted the pavement, sending pedestrians scattering in all directions. She slapped the horn in the center of the wheel, trying to warn the people on the pavement ahead that they were coming. After a few seconds she twitched the wheel and sent the car back toward the road, smashing through a closed newsstand. Their pursuers were closer now and still gaining. The silver car's radiator grille dropped away and a pair of heavy machine gun barrels slid forward and fired. Raven swerved to avoid the incoming bullets, the tracer rounds flying past the car and striking the rear of a double-decker bus thirty yards ahead of them. The bus veered drunkenly as its rear tires were shredded, and it slowly began to tip over. Raven gunned the engine, sending the car racing past the toppling bus and flying under it just fractions of a second before it smashed to the ground and slid to a halt. Otto looked back to see the driver of the bus clambering from the wreckage and a split second later the top deck exploded in a shower of shattered glass and twisted metal as the silver car ploughed through it, machine guns still blazing.

"They're still on us," Otto said quickly. Clearly the car behind them was built to withstand the same amount of punishment as their own. Overhead Otto could see a police helicopter and he was suddenly dazzled as the high-powered spotlight on the chopper illuminated the car, fixing it in a bright circle of white light.

Raven cursed in Russian and spun the wheel as a police car shot out into the junction ahead of them, blocking the road. She fought to bring the car under control and after fishtailing for a second roared down the road, knowing that they were almost certainly being herded toward a roadblock somewhere ahead. Behind them the silver car came around the corner sideways, just avoiding side-swiping the police car, and powered after them.

Another two police cars screeched to a halt in front of them, blocking the road and leaving only one route. Raven glanced at the street signs as she took the only unblocked road, and suddenly she knew where they were being sent. Ahead stood the magnificent gothic structures of Tower Bridge. They shot onto the deserted bridge, the unusual absence of cars telling Raven that they were exactly where the police wanted them. At the far end of the road half a dozen police cars and vans formed an impassable blockade, trapping them on the bridge. Raven pulled hard on the handbrake sending the car into a perfect 180-degree spin, leaving them pointing back the way they'd come. At the other end of the bridge they could see another blockade forming as more police cars closed the trap. Just in front of the blockade the silver car sat motionless.

"Do we have any rockets left?" Raven asked, sounding unbelievably calm.

"Just one," Otto said, unsure what she had in mind.

"Check your seat belt," Raven said, frowning at the silver car that was a couple hundred yards away from them.

"What are you going to do?" Otto said, suddenly nervous. He pulled the strap of the seat belt across his chest, testing it. Raven did the same, revving the engine noisily.

"Ever played chicken?" she said with a cold smile.

The black car shot forward, accelerating hard. At the far end of the bridge the silver car followed suit, shooting forward with a roar on a collision course. Raven tightened her grip on the steering wheel as the distance between the two cars closed at a terrifying rate. Otto braced himself against the dashboard, preparing himself for the inevitable impact. At the very last moment Raven jerked the steering wheel to one side and hit the button on the hidden control panel. The final rocket speared out ahead of the car, blowing the cast iron wall that ran along the edge of the bridge to pieces just moments before the car hit it. Otto gave a tiny gasp as the car flew through the wreckage and vaulted into the void with a deafening roar from the engine. His stomach shot into his mouth as the car plummeted nose-first toward the river below. They hit it in an enormous explosion of water and everything went black.

Back up on the bridge the silver car screeched to a halt and Constance and Verity leaped out. They ran to the parapet and looked down at the black waters of the Thames. There was no sign of the other car, just a patch of foam where it had hit the surface. Policemen were running toward them from both ends of the bridge. Verity turned to the first officer to reach them.

"Get divers in the river now," she spat angrily, "before they get away. My authorization is H.O.P.E. 17 Delta."

"But, m-miss," the young policeman stammered, sounding confused, "no one could possibly have survived that."

"Oh, you'd be surprised," Verity snapped. "You really would."

☻☻☻

Otto came to with a start, the ice-cold water lapping around his chin in the darkness. He struggled to undo his seat belt but it refused to release. He felt an overwhelming wave of panic as the water rose above his mouth and nose, denying him a final breath. He tugged at the seat belt, his lungs burning; it was no good. Then suddenly the belt released and as he fell back into unconsciousness the last thing he felt were strong hands pulling him out of his seat and something that tasted of rubber being forced into his mouth.

chapter nine

"Is there any sign of Ms. Leon yet?" the Contessa asked irritably as she walked toward Phalanx One.

"No, Contessa, but this is a big place," he replied, gesturing vaguely at the walls around him, "and she is an expert in stealth and evasion. It may take some time, especially with H.I.V.E.mind offline."

"I don't want excuses, Commander, just results," the Contessa snapped.

"We will keep searching," Phalanx One replied. "As soon as we have any leads you will be the first to know."

"Very well," the Contessa said impatiently. "What have you brought me here to see?"

She looked at the damaged doors to vault nine that were set into the rock wall just a few yards away.

"Well, a couple of my men have been examining the vault and there are no obvious signs of anything missing," Phalanx One explained, "but that's not what's strange about all of this."

"What do you mean?" the Contessa asked.

"It seems that all of the evidence points to someone breaking *out* of the vault, not someone breaking in."

"There was somebody in here?" the Contessa said incredulously.

"It would appear so," Phalanx One replied. "Someone strong enough to force these doors open."

"That's impossible," the Contessa said with a sneer, studying the heavy doors.

"Nevertheless, that seems to be what happened," Phalanx One replied, sounding tired.

"So there is an unknown operative loose in the school," the Contessa said angrily. "Another loose cannon is not what we need at the moment."

"At first I thought so," Phalanx One said, studying the vault doors again, "but my men have turned this place upside down looking for Ms. Leon. If there were an unauthorized operative here, we would have found them. Whoever it was, I believe they must have left the island immediately after breaking out of the vault. Unfortunately, without H.I.V.E.mind's security logs it is impossible to determine for certain if that was the case."

The Contessa was starting to think that shutting down the school's resident AI might have been a mistake.

"I'd like your permission to bring the Professor down here and question him about the contents of the vault. If anyone knows what was in here, he does."

"Do it," the Contessa said quickly, "and if he refuses to cooperate tell him that I shall conduct any further questioning myself, do you understand?"

"Yes, ma'am," Phalanx One replied with a nod.

"I want answers, Commander, before we lose control of the school altogether."

☻☻☻

Franz paced anxiously back and forth within the confined space of his and Nigel's shared quarters. Their room barely seemed big enough for both of them at the best of times, but now that they shared it with another unexpected resident it felt particularly cramped.

"Can you stop that?" Nigel said plaintively. "You're making me nervous."

"*You* are nervous," Franz replied. "I am thinking that we all have good reason for the nervousness."

Franz looked at the small ball of white fur that was curled up on Nigel's bed and frowned.

"Those men from G.L.O.V.E. have been searching the whole school. I am thinking that it will not be long before they start searching our rooms, and then what are we doing?"

"We'll worry about that when the time comes," Nigel said reassuringly. "For now we just have to sit tight and wait for her to wake up."

Ms. Leon had been asleep since they had smuggled her back to their room. Nigel felt sure that she would be better off in sick bay, but it was perfectly clear from the way that the Phalanx teams had been searching for her that taking her there would result in them all being captured and punished. He wasn't sure what form that punishment might take but he suspected that it would be swift and terrible.

"I am thinking that we are not high on the Contessa's list of favorite people anyway," Franz said nervously. "This is only going to be making things worse."

Franz's constant moaning might well have become boring but Nigel knew that he was actually right. After they had played an instrumental part in derailing Cypher and the Contessa's plan to take over the school, they had both felt like heroes. Now he just felt like they had big red bull's-eyes painted on their backs. Not for the first time in the past couple of days he found himself wishing that Otto and the others were still around. They would have known what to do.

"Mr. Argentblum is right. You have put yourselves at risk by helping me. I should go," the cat said suddenly, making both boys jump.

"Ms. Leon, you're awake!" Nigel said excitedly. "How are you feeling?"

"Sore but alive—thanks in no small part to you two," she said, standing up on the bed slowly and stretching. The livid burn along her spine was painful, but she knew that she was lucky to be feeling anything at all. Her uncanny reflexes had saved her from the worst of the arcing bolt of electricity that had struck her during H.I.V.E.mind's demise. She walked across the bed and jumped the short distance to the floor, even that small movement drawing an involuntary hiss of pain.

"You're too badly hurt," Nigel said softly. "You can't leave. They're tearing the school apart looking for you. You wouldn't last five minutes out there."

"Be that as it may," Ms. Leon said, the discomfort clear even in her synthesized voice, "Franz was right. It's only a matter of time before they institute a lockdown of the accommodation blocks and start a room-to-room search. It's what I would do. For all our sakes I can't be here when that happens."

"So what are we going to do?" Nigel asked.

"I need to talk to Professor Pike or Colonel Francisco," she said after thinking for a moment. "There is much that we need to discuss. I'm just not sure how I will get to them."

"We could take you," Nigel said quietly.

"We could?" Franz said, astonished.

"Yes, we could," Nigel said firmly. "We should be fine if we don't do anything to draw attention to ourselves."

"I don't know," Ms. Leon said slowly. "I am not sure I can allow you to put yourselves in jeopardy like that."

"We're in danger anyway," Nigel replied. "You're in no condition to get to them on your own and we're going to be in even more trouble if they find you here."

Ms. Leon looked at Nigel for a few seconds, fixing him with her unnervingly steady feline gaze.

"Okay, but you are not to take any unnecessary risks, do you understand? If you are stopped you must give me up immediately. I will tell the Contessa that I forced you to do this. Do I make myself clear?"

"Perfectly," Nigel said as calmly as he could. "Let's get going. If anybody asks we're just going to the library."

Nigel grabbed his empty backpack from the desk and held it open for Ms. Leon. She walked over to the bag and peered inside before climbing in.

"So undignified," she sniffed as Nigel zipped it shut.

☺☺☺

"You have a visitor, Professor," the Phalanx guard said, rattling his truncheon between the bars of the holding cell. The Professor slowly opened his eyes and pushed himself up to a sitting position on the cold steel

202

bench that passed for a bed in the detention center.

"Two minutes," the guard said to Colonel Francisco, beckoning him over to the cell. The Colonel gave a brief nod and the guard returned to his seat at the monitoring station on the other side of the room.

"How are they treating you?" the Colonel asked as the Professor slowly stood up and walked over to the bars.

"I would rather be in my lab," the Professor said with a small wry smile.

"Yes, I'm sure you would," the Colonel muttered, looking around the spartan interior of the detention center. "But nothing seems to be working out quite the way we want it at the moment, does it?"

The Colonel briefly opened one hand to show the Professor the small jamming device that he was holding.

"I thought it best that no one overheard our conversation," the Colonel said, jerking his head briefly at the guard on the other side of the room.

"Be careful, Colonel," the Professor whispered. "The Contessa is quite paranoid enough at the moment without any provocation. I would hate to see you join me in here. We need you out there. Someone has to put a stop to this."

"That's just what I came to talk to you about," the Colonel said, slipping the tiny electronic device back into his trouser pocket.

"Have they tracked down our four-legged friend yet?" the Professor said quietly.

"No, but not for want of trying," the Colonel replied. "Wherever she is she'll be captured the moment she shows her face."

"I wouldn't underestimate her ability to stay out of their clutches," the Professor said with a slight smile, "especially without H.I.V.E.mind's help."

"Where is he?" the Colonel asked quietly. "We could use his help."

"He's gone," the Professor said, a sudden note of sadness in his voice. "The Contessa had me shut him down permanently. Except . . ."

"Except what?" the Colonel asked.

"Nothing, it doesn't matter," the Professor replied with a shake of the head. "What matters now is how we regain control of H.I.V.E."

"Agreed. Any ideas?" Francisco said.

"We're going to need all of the help we can get," the Professor whispered. "I suggest you have a quiet word with Chief Lewis."

"You think he can be trusted?"

"The chief may be a loyal man but he is not a stupid man. He cannot believe that Maria has the school's best interests at heart and I know that he's not happy with having to take orders from those Phalanx thugs."

"You may be right," the Colonel said thoughtfully, "but if you're not . . ."

"If I'm not then we can't hope to succeed anyway," the Professor replied. "It's a chance we have to take."

"Okay, I'll speak to him discreetly," the Colonel said.

"Right, that's long enough," the Phalanx guard announced, walking back toward the cell, looking anxious. "You'll have to leave. There appears to be something wrong with some of the monitoring equipment."

"Oh, how annoying," the Professor said with a crooked smile. "Nothing seems to be working properly around here at the moment, does it?"

☢☢☢

"Correct me if I'm wrong, but I thought you two had been specifically trained to deal with Raven," Sebastian Trent said angrily as he walked in behind the two women who stood at rigid attention in his office.

"Raven was not the problem," Constance said quickly.

"It was the Malpense boy who caught us off guard," Verity added.

"So you're telling me that you can handle the world's deadliest assassin but you can't handle a single thirteen-year-old boy?" Trent snapped angrily.

"He is more . . . capable than we had been led to expect," Constance replied. "He will not surprise us a second time."

"You're assuming there will be a second time!" Trent yelled. "I give you a simple task and you fail me. This might have been our one opportunity to take out Raven and capture the boy and you two blew it. Tell me why I should trust you with something this important again."

"There is no excuse," Verity said firmly.

"No, there is not," Trent barked. "You are supposed to be my most capable operatives, not bumbling incompetents."

"We will find them," Constance said, her voice like ice, "and we won't lose them again."

"I wish I could share your confidence," Trent snapped. "Now get out of my sight. I have to report this fiasco to control and find out what our next move is going to be. Make sure you're ready if I call on you again. You are dismissed."

The twins turned in unison and marched out of Trent's office. Trent sat back down behind his desk with a sigh. He had not been relishing the prospect of the call that he had to make now, but he could not put it off any longer. He keyed a code that only he knew into the computer on his desk and waited. After just a few seconds the display lit up with the silhouette of a man's head and shoulders.

"Mr. Trent," Number One said coldly, "I have been expecting your call."

"Yes, sir, I'm sorry for the delay but I wanted to make sure that I had all of the facts before I contacted you," Trent explained.

"You mean you needed time to come up with an excuse for this display of withering incompetence," Number One said in a voice that froze the blood. "I assume you will not try to insult me by expecting me to forgive you."

"Sir, please, we are doing everything possible to—"

"Enough!" Number One snapped. "I have read your report and despite all of the assets at your disposal you still failed to acquire Raven or Malpense. I am starting to wonder if you are truly the right man for the job, Sebastian. Tell me, am I wasting my time with you?"

"Please, give me a chance to rectify this," Trent pleaded. "We will find Raven and when we do she will not escape us again."

"You have told me that before and yet here we are again, dragging the Thames for a body that is not there. Do not make the mistake of underestimating Raven," Number One said angrily. "You will not find her, not if she does not want you to. Fortunately for you I do not believe that will be a problem for very much longer. If I know Raven, and I believe I do, she will be paying you a visit in the very near future. Now that she knows where

Nero is, she will attempt to free him—that is when you will finish the job that you so spectacularly failed to complete in London."

"But how could she know where we are?" Trent asked, sounding confused. "Deepcore was not hacked; they didn't have time. The location of this facility is still—"

"Do not underestimate the Malpense boy either," Number One said sharply. "He has skills that you would not understand, the very skills that make him so essential to the Initiative's success. Trust me when I say that they know exactly where you are and it is inevitable that they will attempt to liberate Nero."

"H.O.P.E. has other facilities," Trent said quickly. "We could transfer him to—"

"You will do exactly as you are told, Sebastian, and leave Nero precisely where he is. Why do you think I have kept him alive this long? If there is one thing I have learned over the years it is that when one is fishing for sharks it is always best to use live bait."

☮☮☮

Nigel and Franz walked down the corridor toward Colonel Francisco's office. Nigel may have been feeling nervous about the risk they were taking, considering the contents of his backpack, but he was doing the best he could to conceal it. Franz on the other hand looked pale and sweaty, his eyes darting from side to side as if some kind of monster would lunge from the shadows at any moment.

"Try to act casual," Nigel whispered.

"I am acting casual," Franz whispered back.

"You look like you're about to have a heart attack," Nigel replied with a slight frown.

"It is being the distinct possibility," Franz said, swallowing hard.

"Oh no," Nigel moaned as he saw the two figures who walked around the corner at the far end of the corridor. It was Block and Tackle, two of the more thuggish products of the Henchman stream, who were well known for the delight they took in tormenting the younger students. Nigel and Franz held a special place in their list of victims though, ever since they had knocked the pair of bullies out cold with a Sleeper gun during Cypher's invasion of the school. Block and Tackle may have been under the nefarious influence of the Contessa at the time but that did not appear to stop them from bearing a nasty grudge. Nigel swallowed hard as they walked toward the two over-muscled goons, deliberately avoiding eye contact. He couldn't help but be a bit surprised as the two boys walked past them in silence, almost as if they weren't there. Nigel was just breathing a small sigh of relief when he was tripped from behind and toppled forward onto the floor.

"Aren't you even going to say hello?" Block said with a nasty smile as he loomed over Nigel.

"Leave us alone," Nigel said in the strongest voice he could muster, knowing there was little real chance of that.

"Leave us alone," Tackle mimicked in a high-pitched, girlish voice. "What if we don't want to—whatchoo gonna do about it?"

Nigel tried to get up but was stopped from doing so by Block's heavy boot on his backside. Block suddenly noticed a slight movement from inside Nigel's backpack.

"What you got in there, baldy?" Block said, reaching down and unzipping Nigel's pack and sliding a hand inside. Block yelped in pain as something sliced across the skin on the back of his hand. He reflexively pulled his hand from the backpack and looked at it. There were three deep, perfectly parallel scratches, oozing blood.

"What the heck . . . ?" Block said, startled.

"You are being the girly men who are not prepared to be picking on someone their own size," Franz yelled suddenly. "You pick on Nigel but I am thinking that you are scared of me!"

"Is that a fact?" Tackle said, turning to Franz.

"I am warning you not to be pushing us," Franz said nervously as Tackle walked toward him. "Wing has been showing me all his tricks. My fists are now the deadly weapon!"

Franz raised his tightly clenched but obviously trembling fists up in front of him like a boxer.

"Oooh, I'm frightened," Tackle said with a nasty laugh. "I've picked a fight with the world's fattest ninja."

Franz felt a sudden wave of anger as the older boy approached him.

"Tell you what," Tackle said, stopping just a couple of feet away from Franz, "you get the first shot free." He put his hands on his hips and leaned forward, offering his unguarded chin to Franz. "But then it's my turn."

Tackle just smiled and closed his eyes as Franz drew his fist back.

"I am not fat," he said, sounding angry. "I am big- boned."

Franz took a single small step toward Tackle and kicked him in the crotch as hard as he could. Tackle collapsed to the ground with a strangled gasp, curling into a moaning ball. Block took his foot off Nigel and strode quickly over to Franz, who turned to face him with an expression that fell somewhere between victorious boxer and rabbit in the headlights. Franz threw a punch but Block simply caught it in one of his huge hands, wrenching Franz's arm up into the small of his back and pulling hard. Franz let out a yelp of pain and dropped to his knees, helpless.

"Pick a bone," Block whispered viciously into Franz's

ear. "It'll only be the first one I break but at least you get a choice."

"What's going on here?" Colonel Francisco bellowed as he strode down the corridor toward them.

Block quickly let go of Franz and stepped away from him. Tackle slowly got to his feet, looking slightly dazed.

"Argentblum attacked Tackle, sir," Block said before Franz or Nigel could speak.

"Really?" the Colonel said, raising an eyebrow. "Is that true, Mr. Argentblum?"

"It was self-defense, sir," Nigel said quickly.

"Did I ask you, Mr. Darkdoom?" the Colonel said firmly.

"No, sir," Nigel replied, "but Ms. Leon sent us here for our detention assignments. We *really* don't want to get into any more trouble."

Francisco's eyes narrowed as he studied Nigel's nervous-looking face.

"Very well, we'll go to my office immediately. And you two should know better than this by now," he said, turning to Block and Tackle. "Being a member of the Henchman stream is about discipline, not brawling in the hallways. Get out of here, I'll deal with you later."

Block walked away down the hallway with Tackle hobbling slowly along behind him.

"Come with me," Francisco said, turning and striding toward his office. "I think we have things to discuss."

☢ ☢ ☢

Otto followed Raven down the steps from the *Megalodon's* mini-sub docking pool. The divers from the mini-sub had rescued Raven and him from the submerged car with just moments to spare and transported them both back to the *Megalodon*. He felt absolutely exhausted, but at the same time he could not help but feel satisfied that they had succeeded in their mission. Captain Sanders stood waiting for them with a broad smile on his face.

"Well done," the captain said, "both of you. If I was a betting man I cannot say that I would have put a lot of money on you being able to pull this off."

"And yet, here we are," Raven said with a slight smile.

"Indeed, most impressive," the captain said, gesturing to the hatch that led out of the docking bay. "Darkdoom is waiting for you in the command center."

Raven nodded and walked out of the room with Otto.

"He's right, you know," Raven said as they walked down the hall toward the command center. "You did well. You never know, we might make a G.L.O.V.E. operative out of you yet."

"Something tells me we aren't going to be welcomed back by G.L.O.V.E. anytime soon," Otto said quietly.

"Time will tell," Raven replied. "If Darkdoom is right and Number One is behind all of this, I think you might be surprised at the ruling council's reaction. He has controlled G.L.O.V.E. by fear for a long time, and in my experience someone that you are afraid of can never command your true loyalty. It is easy to lose sight of the fact that G.L.O.V.E. is bigger than just one man. The League will go on regardless of how this all plays out."

"I wish I could say I shared your confidence," Otto said, sounding tired. "I can't help but feel that Number One is always a step ahead of us."

"Maybe," Raven said with a crooked smile, "but the advantage of having someone one step ahead of you is that they expose their back."

She pushed the heavy door to the command center open and Otto stepped inside.

"Otto!" Laura said happily, running over and hugging him. "You made it!"

"That's twenty bucks you owe me, big guy," Shelby said with a grin, punching Wing playfully in the arm.

Wing walked up to Otto and smiled.

"I never bet against a sure thing," Wing said, slapping Otto hard on the shoulder.

"I'm just glad that we all made it out in one piece," Otto said happily, "though I did have a little help."

Otto gestured at Raven, who just smiled slightly.

"You have all done remarkably well," Darkdoom said, walking toward them, "but we must not forget that there is much yet to be done. Mr. Malpense, I believe you have a set of coordinates for me."

"Yes, I do," Otto replied, "but you can't have them . . . not yet anyway."

"What?" Darkdoom said, sounding surprised.

"I want in on the mission to save Nero and until I'm convinced that's happening, the coordinates of the facility where he's being held stay right here," Otto said, tapping the side of his head.

"Mr. Malpense, this is no time for games," Darkdoom said firmly. "Just give me the coordinates. There's no way I'm letting you go on this mission."

"Why not?" Otto said calmly.

"Because I would be sending you into the lion's den. We have to keep you out of these people's hands, not deliver you to them gift-wrapped. It was dangerous enough letting you be involved in the MI6 operation. I am not prepared to put you at any further risk."

"That's my decision," Otto replied. "If anything, what we've all just managed to pull off demonstrates that we're quite capable of looking after ourselves."

"Darkdoom's right, Otto," Raven said with a frown. "Those women we met weren't there to capture me. For whatever reason, you are a priority target for these people. We have to keep you out of their reach."

"I understand that," Otto said, sounding frustrated, "but that's exactly why I want to be a part of ending this. I'm fed up with not knowing why I'm suddenly so important. I need answers as much as anyone."

Darkdoom stared at Otto in silence. There was something about the boy that was familiar, but he still couldn't quite put his finger on it. He was not prepared to try and extract the information on Nero's location from him by force and so it seemed that, for the moment at least, Otto held all the cards.

"Very well, Mr. Malpense. If you are determined to risk your life there is little that I can do to stop you."

"If Otto is going then so am I," Wing said calmly.

"We all are," Laura added. Shelby just nodded her agreement.

Darkdoom looked at the four of them standing together, totally determined. Slowly a tired-looking smile spread across his face.

"I think that if Max was here now he would be rather proud of you all," he said, turning back to the large display set into the center of the console in the command center. "I assume, Mr. Malpense, that you are at least prepared to tell us what sort of facility we will need to be prepared to—"

"TORPEDO, TORPEDO, TORPEDO!" one of the

men seated at the control consoles suddenly yelled. Darkdoom spun toward him.

"Is it tracking us?" he said quickly.

"Affirmative, sir. It's heading straight for us, bearing 184," the man replied, a trace of panic in his voice.

"Initiate evasive maneuvers," Darkdoom barked at the helmsman. Otto and the others were forced to grab for the nearest furniture as the giant submarine was thrown into a tight turn, the whole control center tipping to one side.

"Torpedo turning to intercept," the weapons control officer yelled, "range three miles and closing."

The control room tipped in the other direction as the helmsman fought to shake the torpedo's lock on the *Megalodon*.

"Torpedo still on an intercept track!"

"That's impossible," Darkdoom said. "There isn't a weapon in the water that can track this boat."

"Range two miles. Deploying countermeasures!" the weapons officer reported.

Everyone heard a series of thuds as several anti-torpedo drones detached themselves from the hull of the *Megalodon* and spiraled away into the dark water surrounding them.

"What the . . . Torpedo has evaded countermeasures . . . b-but—" the weapons officer stammered.

"Torpedoes don't evade countermeasures," Darkdoom shouted. "What is that out there?"

"Range one mile. Torpedo has acquired final solution and is accelerating."

Darkdoom snatched a handset from the wall and spoke into it.

"All hands, brace for impact."

Otto hung on to the railing in front of him, his knuckles white.

"Three hundred yards . . . two hundred yards . . . one hundred yards . . ."

Otto braced himself, waiting for the explosion.

"Impact!" the weapons officer yelled and an eerie silence fell over the command center. There was no explosion, the deck simply vibrating with the usual hum from the submarine's powerful engines.

"Must have been a dud," the weapons officer said, sounding confused but relieved.

"Somehow I doubt that," Darkdoom said quietly.

Suddenly there was a scraping thud on the hull, clearly audible inside the command center, and then another and another.

"Something's attached itself to us," Darkdoom said quietly. The scraping sound seemed to move along the ceiling toward the rear of the vessel.

"Whatever it is, it's heading aft," the weapons officer said.

"The escape hatches," Darkdoom said angrily. "Get a security team down there now! Raven, with me."

Darkdoom rushed out of the command center and down the hallway heading toward the aft of the *Megalodon*, Raven close behind him.

"Come on," Otto said to the others and they all hurried after them.

They ran down the hallway, the scraping sounds ahead of them moving quickly down the outer hull. As they ran into the room at the end of the hall, security guards with assault rifles were already taking up positions around the escape-hatch airlocks.

"Open fire only on my command," Darkdoom said.

There was a crunching sound from overhead.

"That's the external hatch," Darkdoom said quietly. "Get ready, men; open fire only on my command."

There was a thud from behind the center hatch and a low steady beep that indicated that the airlock was cycling, pumping out the seawater and replacing it with air. There was a final high-pitched tone and then the air-lock door slowly swung open.

"Good God," Darkdoom said.

"Get back, all of you," Raven said, her eyes widening and one hand flying to the hilt of one of the blades sheathed on her back.

Inside the airlock stood something Otto had hoped he

would never see again: one of Cypher's robotic assassins, its black metallic exoskeleton glistening with water. Raven pulled the sword from her back and took a single step toward the lethal killing machine. She had fought these things before and she knew what they were capable of.

"Wait!" Otto yelled, hurrying forward. The android turned its insectile face toward Otto, the sensory arrays that covered it glowing bright blue.

"Hello, Otto," H.I.V.E.mind said calmly. "You are a difficult person to find."

☢☢☢

"What on earth are you doing here?" Otto said, feeling a mixture of happiness and extreme confusion.

"I am here to help," H.I.V.E.mind replied, "in any way possible."

"How did you end up inside one of those things?" Raven said, stepping forward and inspecting H.I.V.E.mind's new body.

"Professor Pike instituted the GOLEM subroutine within my data core and transferred my consciousness to this specially modified combat chassis that he took possession of after Cypher's attack on H.I.V.E. I then escaped from the storage facility that the Professor had kept this body in and left H.I.V.E. I predicted that you would attempt to acquire data on Doctor Nero's current location and that there was a seventy-one per cent chance that you would choose the MI6 facility. I was on my way to rendezvous with you when details of a raid on the MI6 building began to circulate on the security forces networks. It was then relatively simple to track your retrieval craft from the Thames to this vessel."

"You swam here from H.I.V.E.?" Otto said, sounding amazed.

"This chassis is capable of a sustained 350 knots in sub-aquatic travel mode, more than adequate for tracking and intercepting this vessel," H.I.V.E.mind replied.

"Why did the Professor have to transfer you to this chassis?" Otto asked.

"He did so to avoid my consciousness being destroyed when the Contessa ordered a full erasure of my neural network."

"She did what?" Otto said angrily.

"In other words, she tried to kill you," Laura said quietly.

"In simple terms, yes," H.I.V.E.mind replied. "But since I was never really alive she could not truly kill me in the strictest sense."

"Sounds like the same thing to me," Otto said, still angry. "That old witch has a lot to answer for."

"The situation at H.I.V.E. has become considerably

worse since your unscheduled departure," H.I.V.E.mind said. "I fear that the Contessa has an agenda that is not yet entirely clear."

"That much is certain," Darkdoom said, stepping forward. "Do you know who I am?"

"Yes. Diabolus Darkdoom. Former senior member of the G.L.O.V.E. ruling council. Father of H.I.V.E. student Nigel Darkdoom. Executed for treachery, although these records are obviously partially inaccurate," H.I.V.E.mind replied efficiently.

"And I assume that you are the infamous H.I.V.E.mind. Raven has told me much about you. Do you understand why Raven and Otto are here?" Darkdoom asked.

"No, that information is not stored within my databanks. If you would allow me to interface with your vessels systems I would be able to update my files."

"Can he be trusted?" Darkdoom asked Raven, frowning slightly.

"I don't know," Raven said honestly. "We only have his word that he was sent here by the Professor, but I am inclined to believe him."

"If it weren't for him we'd all still be prisoners at H.I.V.E.," Otto said quickly. "He helped us to escape. Why would he do that if he was on their side?"

"Is this true?" Darkdoom asked H.I.V.E.mind.

"Yes, that is the primary reason that the Contessa

wanted me to be disabled. To put it in human terms, I am here because I have nothing left to lose and nowhere left to go."

"Very well. Raven, please take H.I.V.E.mind to the datacore. Tell the technicians that he is to be given limited access to our recent operational reports. If he makes any attempt to access any other areas of the *Megalodon*'s systems you are to reduce him to scrap metal," Darkdoom said, and then turning to H.I.V.E.mind, "No offense."

"None taken. An entirely reasonable precaution," H.I.V.E.mind said calmly.

"Come on," Raven said, gesturing for H.I.V.E.mind to follow her out of the room.

"Tell Captain Sanders that we appear to have picked up another stray," Darkdoom said to the commander of the security detail. "If this keeps up we're going to run out of bunks."

☹☹☹

Block and Tackle walked down the hallway toward their next lesson. Their expressions suggested that they were in an even more unfriendly mood than usual.

"Argentblum's dead when I get my hands on him," Tackle said angrily, still walking as if he was in slight discomfort.

"Yeah, and Francisco won't be around to protect them

next time neither," Block growled. "We'll teach 'em to mess with Henchman Stream."

Security Chief Lewis walked toward them, engrossed in a report on the tablet display that he was holding. As they walked past him he glanced up, almost unconsciously making a note of who they were. He looked back down at the display and tried to continue reading, but a tiny alarm had started sounding at the back of his head. He stopped in his tracks and looked back at the two Henchman students walking away down the hall. He'd dealt with these two many times before in his official capacity—they were magnets for the wrong kind of trouble—but there was something out of the ordinary that was bothering him.

"You two!" the chief shouted. "Wait there a moment."

"What we done now?" Block said quietly to Tackle, sounding exasperated.

"I dunno," Tackle replied, watching as the chief approched them.

"You," the Chief said, pointing at Block, "where did you get that?"

"What?" Block said, genuinely confused.

"That!" the Chief snapped, grabbing Block's hand and holding it up so that the nasty scratch on the back was clearly visible.

"I was . . . er . . . helping Nigel Darkdoom to pack up

his books at the end of a lesson and something in his backpack scratched me," Block said.

Lewis raised an eyebrow.

"I don't think I've ever seen you help anyone before, Mr. Block. Where exactly was Mr. Darkdoom heading."

"I think he was going to see the Colonel," Tackle said quickly.

"Was he now?" the chief said quietly.

"Yeah, something about Ms. Leon sending him there," Block added.

"That's a nasty scratch," the chief said. "You should go to the sick bay and have it dressed immediately. I need to have a word with the Colonel."

☻☻☻

Nigel placed his backpack carefully on Colonel Francisco's desk and unzipped it. Ms. Leon cautiously stuck her head out of the opening and then stepped out onto the desk.

"It is good to see you in one piece, Ms. Leon," Francisco said with something that looked dangerously close to one day becoming a smile.

"It is good to be in one piece," Ms. Leon replied, "and I probably wouldn't be if it weren't for Franz and Nigel."

"We were just trying to help," Nigel said quietly.

"You took a great risk bringing me here," Ms. Leon replied. "Thank you."

"Looks like you may have saved yourself from that detention I still owe you, Mr. Argentblum," the Colonel said, trying hard not to smile at the look of overwhelming relief on Franz's face, "but I think both of you have done enough for now. There's no need to put you at any further risk. I assume I can trust you both not to say anything about this to anyone."

"Of course," Nigel replied. He turned to leave but stopped and turned back to the two teachers. "You are going to do something about the Contessa, aren't you?"

"Let us worry about that," Ms. Leon said. "For now you have lessons to attend."

Nigel nodded and walked to the door, which hissed open as he approached. Standing on the other side was Chief Lewis, backed up by a full H.I.V.E. security detail.

"Going somewhere, Mr. Darkdoom?" the chief said and stepped into the room.

☻☻☻

"I believe the expression is 'a tough nut to crack'," H.I.V.E.mind said calmly.

The holographic schematic that hovered above the middle of the briefing room table rotated slowly.

"That's one way of putting it," Otto said, frowning.

"A suicide mission might be another way," Raven added.

Otto looked at the worried expressions of the people

sitting at the table. They had been there for half an hour already and there had been little progress in coming up with a concrete plan for penetrating H.O.P.E.'s secret base.

"The biggest problem is going to be getting in without being detected on our approach," Shelby said. "If we can get on to the mountainside near these vents"—she pointed at the network of shafts near the top of the facility—"we can probably get inside, but getting up there undetected is going to be the hard part."

"It would be a lot easier if we had a Shroud," Raven said, "but I think we may have a hard time persuading G.L.O.V.E. to lend us one at the moment."

"Actually," Darkdoom said distractedly, "we may have something better. Let us assume for a moment that we can get onto the mountain undetected, what then?"

"Two teams," Shelby said quickly. "One goes for the detention level and one goes for the power plant. It'll need perfect timing but if we can pull it off we can leave them deaf and blind for just long enough to get Nero out of there."

"Sounds good," Raven said, "but the power plant's going to be locked down tight. How do we get inside?"

"Between me and Shelby we should be able to get past the security systems and shut down the plant," Laura said, "but we'll need someone with us to take care of any technicians or guards that we run into."

"Leave that to me," Raven said calmly.

"Which leaves me, Wing, and H.I.V.E.mind to take care of getting Nero out," Otto said, still studying the schematic.

"What is that?" Wing said, pointing at a huge circular tunnel that appeared to surround the entire facility deep within the mountain.

"On the schematics it is just designated as a transport system," Otto replied. "It's probably some form of train for transporting people around the base."

"So we should expect a rapid response from security forces if they are alerted to our presence," Wing observed.

"Yes, I think that's safe to assume," Otto said, frowning. The plans that he had uploaded from his own head to the *Megalodon*'s datacore were maddeningly light on details. He supposed that he might have been able to retrieve full schematics from Deepcore if they'd had more time, but there was no point worrying about it now.

"Very well," Darkdoom said, getting up out of his chair. "I need to go and get my technicians working on the delivery system. I'll be back in a couple of hours and I expect to hear some detailed infiltration plans."

"Understood," Raven said with a small nod.

"Oh, just one other thing, Mr. Malpense," Darkdoom said as he walked toward the door. "I'm coming with you."

☻☻☻

The Contessa sat at her desk waiting impatiently for the display in front of her to activate. There was still no sign of Ms. Leon and the loss of H.I.V.E.mind had left her with precious little control over the school. She had to admit that she had underestimated how critical the AI had been to the smooth running of H.I.V.E. The display lit up suddenly with the G.L.O.V.E. symbol, which was replaced moments later with the silhouetted form of Number One.

"Hello, Maria," he said calmly. "I have read your latest report and I am seriously starting to wonder if you were really the right person for this job."

The Contessa felt a momentary twinge of panic.

"Number One," she said, her mouth suddenly dry, "I apologize. We have encountered a number of unforeseen problems. We are working hard to rectify the situation."

"I'm sure you are," Number One replied, his voice cold, "but the situation elsewhere has taken an unexpected turn. I need to put certain contingencies into operation at H.I.V.E. and I need to be sure that I can trust you to implement them."

"Of course," the Contessa replied quickly. "What do you need me to do?"

"I am sending you a file that details a new protocol that I need you to put into immediate effect. I am sure that this will not be a problem but I have also forwarded these instructions to Phalanx One, just in case. Do I make myself clear?"

The implied threat was clear and the Contessa knew from past experience that another mistake would not be tolerated.

"Perfectly clear, sir," she said, trying not to let her nervousness show.

"Very well, I shall leave this matter in your hands. Do not fail me again."

"Understood."

"Good, do unto others."

"Do unto others," the Contessa repeated, and the display faded back to the G.L.O.V.E. logo.

The computer on her desk immediately began to bleep, a message window popping up to indicate that she had received a secure file transmission. Quickly she opened the file and began to read. As her eyes scanned down the screen all of the blood drained from her face. She felt slightly nauseous as she began to understand what it was that Number One wanted of her. She finished reading, closed the file, and collapsed back in her seat, eyes closed.

After a moment she slowly stood up and walked over

to the portrait of Nero that still hung on the wall.

"Good God, Max," she said quietly, "what have I done?"

☢ ☢ ☢

Chief Lewis walked slowly into the Colonel's office, the dozen men that accompanied him filing in behind.

"Hello, Colonel, I see that you have managed to do what we could not," the chief said calmly. "Ms. Leon has proven to be most elusive, but you seem to have found her. Or is it that she has found you, I wonder?"

"I have an explanation for this," the Colonel said, looking at the guards who stood between them and the door.

"Oh, I'm sure you do," the chief said, "but don't waste your breath. I'm not here to arrest you."

"You're not?" the Colonel said, silently calculating how many of the guards he could disable before they took him down.

"No, I—or should I say *we*—are here to help you take back this school," the chief said, a grin slowly spreading across his face.

☢ ☢ ☢

Phalanx One watched as his men unloaded the long gray plastic crate from the Shroud that had just landed. His men moved quickly but carefully, carrying the crate down the ramp and placing it gently on the landing pad. He glanced over at the engineers who were just finishing their repairs to the enormous blast doors leading into the crater launch bay as the Contessa walked over toward him.

"I see the package has arrived," the Contessa said quietly.

"Yes, my men will commence installation immediately," Phalanx One replied efficiently. "You should have this— it's not armed at the moment but I will let you know as soon as it's active."

He handed her a small silver control unit.

"I hope we don't have to use it," the Contessa said with a frown.

"That is Number One's decision to make. We will do whatever he tells us to do."

"Of course, of course," the Contessa replied in a slightly distracted voice.

Phalanx One examined her face for a moment and then turned back to watch his men carefully loading the long crate onto a trolley.

"Installation shouldn't take more than a couple of hours," he said.

"Keep me updated on your progress," the Contessa replied.

Phalanx One nodded and walked over to supervise the final stage of the unloading. The Contessa watched as the crate was wheeled away, her expression unreadable. She looked down at the control unit that Phalanx One had given her just a moment before and slowly shook her head.

☢☢☢

"We're going to need more men," the Colonel said, looking at the dozen guards that now stood around his office.

"I think what the Colonel means, chief, is thank you for taking such an enormous risk and coming here with such a generous offer of assistance," Ms. Leon said, sitting down on the edge of Francisco's desk.

"Yes, of course," the Colonel said, "but we're still going to need more men. The Phalanx have a well-deserved reputation. It will not be easy to disable them."

"These are the men I know that I can trust completely," the chief said, gesturing at the guards that stood around him. "It will be their job to talk to the other men and try to recruit as many as they can to our cause."

The Colonel looked around the room. There were no potential beauty-contest winners but they looked like men who could get a job done.

"Um . . . excuse me," a small voice said from behind the Colonel. He turned to see the nervous face of Nigel looking back at him.

"Do you have something to add, Mr. Darkdoom?" the Colonel said with a frown.

"Well . . . um . . . it's just that Doctor Nero used to tell us in our Villainy Studies lessons that the wider one makes any circle of conspiracy the more likely it is that that circle will include a traitor."

"This is not the time for lessons in theory, Mr. Darkdoom," the Colonel said impatiently.

"No, wait. I think Nigel has a point," Ms. Leon said quickly. "We're only going to get one shot at this and if we make any mistakes we'll all end up dead. We need to keep our actions secret for as long as possible and if we start involving too many other people the chances of discovery go up exponentially."

"You have an alternative?" Chief Lewis asked.

"Perhaps, but only if we can get the Phalanx team together in one place," Ms. Leon replied. "We will need a diversion."

"I'm sure I can come up with something suitable," the Chief said with a sly smile.

"And we'll need Professor Pike," Ms. Leon added.

"Leave that to me," the Colonel said.

"Then we have a chance," Ms. Leon said, "a slim one, but a chance nevertheless."

☣☣☣

Darkdoom's technicians hurried around the *Megalodon's* missile launch room, making final adjustments to the seven huge missiles that were mounted to the rack on one wall.

"Everything ready?" Raven said as she walked into the room, already wearing her thermoptic camo suit.

"Yes," Darkdoom replied, looking up from the tablet display he had been reading. "Are the others ready?"

"They're suiting up now." Raven looked over at the missiles. "Are you sure these things are safe?"

"Safe is probably not the right word," Darkdoom replied with a grim smile, "but the failure rate is low enough to be acceptable."

"How reassuring," Raven said, raising an eyebrow.

"Well, take some solace in the fact that if they do go wrong you won't have to worry about it for long. In fact, as a cloud of vapor you'll have very little to worry about at all."

"Okay, I'm going to stop talking to you now," Raven said with a chuckle. She walked back out of the door and down the hall that led to the prep room. Inside she found the other five members of their somewhat bizarre infiltration team making their final preparations. Shelby was checking Laura's camo suit and Otto was talking to H.I.V.E.mind on the far side of the room. Wing sat on a bench, eyes closed. To the casual observer he looked like he might have been asleep, but Raven knew him better than that. She sat down next to him.

"Ready?" she asked quietly.

"Always," Wing replied, slowly opening his eyes.

Good. Remember everything I've taught you. I'm counting on you and Otto to get Nero out of there in one piece. We can't afford any mistakes."

"There will be none," Wing said calmly.

"Good." Raven smiled for a moment but then her expression became more serious and she lowered her voice. "You have to keep Otto safe at all costs. These people want him badly and it's up to you to make sure that they don't get their hands on him, understood?"

"He is a mission critical target," Wing said, turning to look at Raven, "but he is also my best friend. No harm shall befall him while I still draw breath."

"Of course," Raven said, putting her hand on his shoulder. "Just be careful."

"I might ask you to take equal care of your charges," Wing said quietly, looking over at Laura and Shelby, who were laughing about something on the other side of the room.

"Oh, I wouldn't worry about that," Raven said with a smile. "I'm not sure if I'll be protecting them from H.O.P.E., or H.O.P.E. from them."

"Indeed," Wing said, finally smiling himself.

Raven patted Wing on the shoulder reassuringly, stood up and walked over to Otto.

"An interesting modification," she heard H.I.V.E.mind say as she approached.

"I work on this for hours and all you can say is that it's interesting," Otto said, sounding slightly exasperated as he unplugged a cable from the small black oval attached to H.I.V.E.mind's chest.

"It does not appear to have corrupted my systems in any way," H.I.V.E.mind replied.

"Oh ye of little faith," Otto said. "Okay, try it."

For a moment nothing happened, and then suddenly H.I.V.E.mind disappeared.

"You got it working then?" Raven said as she walked up to Otto.

"Of course," Otto replied. "I wish somebody around here had a little confidence in me."

Moments later H.I.V.E.mind popped back into view.

"The cloaking field is fully operational," H.I.V.E.mind said.

"It's basically the same as the field that the suits project," Otto explained. "I've made a couple of small improvements—strengthened the shielding on the unit, that kind of thing. It's quick and dirty but at least now he won't stick out like a sore thumb."

"All of my digits are operating within normal parameters," H.I.V.E.mind said, sounding slightly confused. "Should I run further diagnostics?"

"Never mind," Otto said with a grin, "you're good to go."

"Diabolus needs the coordinates, Otto," Raven said, suddenly serious. "They need to plot the flight paths."

"Okay," Otto said with a deep breath, "looks like it's showtime."

☣ ☣ ☣

Colonel Francisco walked into the detention center and nodded at the Phalanx guard who sat at the monitoring station.

"I need to speak to Professor Pike," he said as he approached the desk.

"You need authorization," the guard said coldly.

"This is my authorization," the Colonel said, producing a Sleeper from behind his back and pulling the trigger.

ZAP!

The guard slumped forward onto the desk, out cold. Francisco pulled his unconscious body from the chair and hid him behind the desk. He would be out for the next few hours.

The Colonel walked quickly to the Professor's cell and found him sitting on the edge of his bunk, eyes wide with surprise.

"Was that sound what I think it was?" the Professor said. He knew the sound of a Sleeper's sonic stun blast from past experience.

"Yes, we have to leave—now," the Colonel said quickly, hitting the button on the wall to open the cell.

"Are you crazy?" the Professor said angrily. "The Contessa will have your head for this."

"No time to explain," the Colonel said with a grim smile, "but if everything goes according to plan we won't have to worry about that."

"Flight-path calculations complete," the technician said, looking up from the display in front of him.

"Viable?" Darkdoom asked quickly.

"We have a zero profile trajectory," the technician replied. "It won't be a smooth ride but it should get you on target without being detected."

"Good," Darkdoom replied and turned to the six other members of the infiltration team.

"This is it, ladies and gentlemen," he said. "Time to mount up."

Otto walked toward the *Megalodon*'s vertical launch tubes as their hatches slid open with a hiss. Inside each tube a second hatch slid open in the sides of the missiles within. Otto looked at the nervous expression on Laura's face and gave her a wink before pulling on his helmet and climbing inside the cramped compartment. Technicians stepped up behind him and strapped him tightly into the missile, then activated the small display just six inches from his face. The screen lit up with arrays of coordinates and a flashing message that read "SYSTEM READY." There was a hiss from somewhere behind him and the hatch slid closed, sealing him inside the tiny space, the only illumination in the pitch-blackness coming from the tiny screen.

"Comms check," a voice said over the earpiece inside his helmet.

"Good to go," Otto said as calmly as he could.

"Check two," Raven said efficiently.

"Ready," Darkdoom said.

"All systems are operating within acceptable parameters," H.I.V.E.mind replied.

"Ready here," Wing said calmly.

"Does this feel like a coffin to anyone else?" Shelby asked.

"Shut up, Shel," Laura replied nervously.

"Okay. That's everyone," the technician's voice replied in Otto's ear. "Captain Sanders, are we at launch depth?"

"Affirmative," the captain replied, "you are go for launch."

"Roger that, launch in ten . . . nine . . . eight . . . seven . . ."

Unseen above them seven hatches lifted silently open in the upper hull of the *Megalodon*.

"Six . . . five . . . four . . ."

Otto gritted his teeth and wondered how he got himself into these situations.

"Three . . . two . . . one . . . ignition!"

In the bottom of the launch tube a small explosive charge detonated, flash-vaporizing the water held in a tank above it. The high-pressure steam pushed the missile up and out of the launch tube and sent it racing toward the surface of the ocean above. The white body of the missile breached the surface in an explosive plume, lifting clear into the air and out of the water before igniting its rocket engines with a roar.

Inside the missile Otto felt the crushing weight of the g-forces as the engines carried the fat white missile on a curving trajectory into the sky. After a few seconds explosive bolts fired and the outer white shell of the missile fell away to reveal the sleek black dart within. As the outer shell dropped away toward the ocean, the engines in the tail of this inner projectile fired and tiny wings slid out from its sides. The black missile banked sharply and dived back toward the sea, pulling out of the dive at the last second and screaming along parallel to the surface of the water at an altitude of just a couple of yards. Moments later the missile's surface shimmered for an instant before it disappeared from view completely.

Otto stared at the display in front of him. It showed seven projectiles racing across the ocean toward the coastline of Europe.

"Darkdoom to *Megalodon*," the familiar voice crackled in Otto's ear, "all hawks on track."

"Roger that," the captain's voice replied. "Good luck. See you on the other side."

There was silence on the comms system for a few seconds before Shelby spoke.

"Okay, has anyone else just been a little bit sick in their helmet?"

chapter ten

The invisible missiles raced through the mountains, hugging the terrain. Otto had watched the video feed from the camera in the nose of the missile for a minute or two before he had to turn it off. Logically he knew the computerized navigation systems that controlled their flight paths were more than capable of safely navigating at such low altitude, but that didn't mean that he particularly wanted to watch as the nose of the missile bobbed and weaved through the mountain passes, just yards from the ground. He'd idly wondered about reaching out with his mind and seeing if he could connect with the computers controlling his flight, but had decided that under the circumstances it was probably best not to distract them.

"Two minutes to target," Darkdoom said calmly over the comms system.

"We're well within their detection range; no sign of attempted interception yet," Raven reported.

"Good. Landing zone in ninety seconds—good luck, everyone," Darkdoom replied.

Otto tried to stay calm and relaxed but he knew that this was one of the most risky stages of the operation. The landing zone they had chosen was the only suitable site for miles around and there could be no second attempts.

"Thirty seconds," Darkdoom said as the rumble of the rocket motors at the rear of Otto's missile began to diminish.

In the frozen night air outside, the noise of the seven invisible missiles dropped to a bare whisper as they headed toward their target. The stubby wings in the side of each missile extended outward, increasing their surface area for this final stage of terminal near-glide. The lead missile hit the soft powdery snow of the mountainside, tiny vectored thrust nozzles in its nose and tail sections firing at the very last moment to make the landing as soft as possible and to try to slow the bulky projectile down. At the rear of the missile there was a soft pop and twin grappling cables shot backward into the darkness. The grapples found purchase and the brakes on the cable reels squealed as the missile slid across the field of snow. It slowed to a stop just thirty yards from the dizzying vertical drop-off that plunged away at the end of the snow field.

"Leader reporting, down and clear," Darkdoom said and Otto could have sworn that he had heard a quiet sigh of relief as the radio went dead. At least that proved it could be done.

One by one the other missiles glided down onto the side of the mountain, each of their computers adjusting their own trajectories to avoid the troughs that the previous landings had carved into the virgin snow. Raven's was the final missile to come in to land, but as it hit the snow there was a cry of alarm over the radio.

"Grapples aren't firing," Raven yelled as the missile ploughed through the snow. Otto punched the button to open his own hatch and slapped the quick release on his harness. He leaped out of the coffin-like interior and into the crisp night air, struggling to stay on his feet in the powdery snow. The others were also scrambling out of their capsules and watching in horror as Raven's missile slid straight off the precipice at the end of the landing area and dropped out of view. Darkdoom and H.I.V.E.mind were already running as fast as they could toward the drop-off, but the faint muffled crump of an explosion from far below suggested that it was too late.

Suddenly there was a familiar-sounding grunt and a hand appeared on the edge of the precipice and slowly Raven hauled herself up and over the edge. As she stood up, the last couple of feet of line from the freshly installed grappler unit on her wrist reeled back in.

"I had a feeling this would come in handy," she said

with a deep breath, holding up the grappler. "Come on, let's get moving. We still have two clicks to go and the night's not going to last forever."

"Three hours and seventeen minutes until dawn," H.I.V.E.mind added helpfully.

"We'll rely on cover of darkness until we get nearer," Darkdoom said. "Leave your suits powered down until we reach the access points—no sense in wasting the batteries. H.I.V.E.mind, if your sensors detect any form of surveillance within range let us know in plenty of time so we can activate camouflage systems."

"Understood," H.I.V.E.mind replied.

"Okay, let's go."

☢☢☢

It took the best part of two hours to cover the remaining distance to the area where they were supposed to find the entrance to the ventilation system. The patches of ice that covered their suits suggested that they should all be grateful that the armor was not only well insulated but also capable of gently warming itself to maintain the wearer's body temperature. Conditions at this altitude in the Swiss Alps in the middle of the night were not exactly what one would call hospitable.

Otto looked around the boulder-strewn depression in the side of the mountain, searching for any sign of the vents that he had seen on the schematics they had stolen from Deepcore. Even through his night-vision goggles there was nothing immediately obvious. That was not actually terribly surprising. This was supposed to be a secret facility, after all. Then suddenly he noticed that through his goggles one of the nearby rock outcroppings was glowing a slightly brighter green than the rocks surrounding it. He walked toward the rock and reached out to touch it, but his outstretched fingers just seemed to pass straight through its surface.

"Got something here," Otto whispered over the comms system. "Looks like a holographic projection."

The others quickly hurried over to Otto and inspected the phantom rock face.

"Looks like this is our way in," Shelby said quietly, a trace of excitement in her voice.

"H.I.V.E.mind, do you detect anything on the other side of this illusion," Darkdoom asked quickly.

"I am picking up an array of small localized electromagnetic signatures, which would suggest the presence of multiple passive detection and defence systems. Now would be a wise time to engage our cloaking systems."

"Agreed," Darkdoom replied. "Suits on. You all know your missions from this point on. Good luck, everyone."

With that, Darkdoom engaged his camouflage suit and disappeared from normal sight. He was still clearly visible to the other members of the infiltration team through their specialized goggles, but to the rest of the world he was near invisible. The other members of the team also activated their camouflage systems before walking through the illusory wall and into the low passageway beyond. They arrived in a low concrete tunnel that was sealed by a set of solid steel vertical bars.

"I am detecting a motion-sensing anti-intrusion system on the other side of these bars," H.I.V.E.mind reported, "but there does not appear to be direct video surveillance of this entry point."

"Sloppy," Shelby said. "Brand, hack that puppy."

Laura pulled the notebook computer from the holster on her belt and began to scan for the signal that was being emitted by the motion sensor. Blocking the signal once she had found it was a trivial task for her and moments later the motion sensor was still functioning perfectly but was now wholly incapable of reporting to anyone what it was sensing.

"Clear," Laura said, keeping an eye on the display.

"Stand back," Raven ordered as she pulled one of her katanas from its scabbard. She made two quick cuts at the bars and three of them fell aside, sliced cleanly top and bottom. The gap she created was just big enough for them to squeeze through one at a time. They crawled forward into the darkness, passing by the gagged security device and deeper into the bowels of the mountain. Laura remotely reconnected the motion sensor and snapped her computer shut. As they crawled further down the concrete tunnel the floor began to slope more and more steeply, steering them downward. The shaft was nearly vertical by the time they reached its end and dropped to the floor of a large concrete junction room. Raven quickly examined the walls for any sign of security devices, but the chamber seemed clean.

"Anything?" she asked H.I.V.E.mind as he dropped silently to the floor beside her.

"No, the second perimeter appears to be farther inside," H.I.V.E.mind replied, his head twitching as he scanned the surrounding area with the array of sophisticated sensors that covered his face.

"This is where we split up," Otto said quietly, pointing down one of several shafts that lined the walls of the room. "We go this way, you go that way." He pointed at another shaft on the opposite wall. "Are you sure you know where you're going?"

Raven and the two girls all looked over in his direction at the same time. It was impossible to see their expressions behind their masks but he was almost certain that they were glaring at him.

"Okay, okay," Otto said, holding his hands up in front of him, "I was just checking."

"I think perhaps we should leave while Otto still has all of his fingers," Wing said casually.

"Indeed," Darkdoom said with a dry laugh. "I would wish you good luck, ladies, but I feel sure that you will not need it."

"You too," Raven replied. "Say hi to Nero for me." With that she ducked into the shaft and disappeared with Laura and Shelby close behind.

Darkdoom turned back to H.I.V.E.mind, Otto, and Wing.

"H.I.V.E.mind, you take the lead; keep scanning ahead for any counter-intrusion devices. Wing, you and Otto will follow and I will bring up the rear. Keep your eyes peeled and your ears open, gentlemen. We won't get a second chance at this."

"Understood," H.I.V.E.mind replied. Otto and Wing just nodded their silent agreement. H.I.V.E.mind ducked inside the darkened shaft with Wing close behind him. Otto hesitated for a moment as he was about to climb in and took a deep breath.

"God, I hate ventilation shafts," he whispered to himself.

☣☣☣

The Contessa stared into the Professor's empty cell, wondering just how this situation could get any worse.

"Where is the guard?" she asked, sounding tired and frustrated.

"In sick bay," Phalanx One replied with a frown. "The medics are trying to revive him, but as you know a blast from one of those Sleeper pistols is not something one recovers from quickly."

"And you're sure it was a Sleeper?" she asked.

"Yes, the level of unconsciousness along with the lack of any physical injury makes that a near certainty."

"You realize, of course, what that means?" the Contessa said with a sigh. "Sleepers can only be fired by members of H.I.V.E.'s security detail or the teaching staff. This is an act of overt rebellion. It cannot be tolerated."

Suddenly Phalanx One's radio began to bleep and he hit the receive button.

"Sir, I have an urgent call from Number One for you and the Contessa," the voice on the other end said.

"Very well," Phalanx One replied. "Please transfer it to the terminal in the detention center."

They both turned to face the screen mounted on the wall as it lit up with the G.L.O.V.E. logo. Moments later the familiar silhouette of their leader filled the display.

"More problems, Maria?" Number One said, his voice cold.

"Nothing we cannot handle," the Contessa replied quickly. She tried to ignore Phalanx One's raised eyebrow.

"Really?" Number One said. "Well, it's not really important at this precise moment. I need you to lock down the school. Teaching and security staff too—no exceptions. I would also like you to make sure that the pupils are segregated by stream."

"May I ask why?" the Contessa said, a hint of nervousness in her voice. Nero had always fought to maintain a mixture of pupils from different streams in the accommodation blocks; separating the pupils out in this way could only lead to more trouble.

"No, you may not. I take it that your men can handle this, Commander?" Number One said, addressing Phalanx One.

"Of course, sir," he replied. "Do you need anything else?"

"You and the Contessa are to go to her office and await further instructions. I may need you at any time." It was not a request.

"Understood," Phalanx One said with a nod.

"Is the package I sent in place?" Number One asked.

"Yes, sir, everything is ready," Phalanx One replied.

"Good. I shall speak to you again soon. Do unto others."

"Do unto others," the Contessa and Phalanx One dutifully replied as the screen went dark.

Phalanx One walked briskly toward the exit but the Contessa waited for a moment, staring at the blank screen.

"Is there something wrong, Contessa?" he asked as he opened the door.

"No . . . it's nothing," she said quietly as she turned to follow him. "Nothing at all."

☢☢☢

"Right, that should do it," the Professor said, clipping the jeweled collar back around Ms. Leon's throat.

"So I just have to get within range of the Contessa's terminal," Ms. Leon said, hopping down from Francisco's desk.

"Yes, anywhere within about five yards should do," the Professor replied. "The transponder that I've installed in your collar should allow me to remotely access her computer. The security network may have been crippled when she shut H.I.V.E.mind down but if I can gain access to that specific machine I should still be able to activate the systems we need."

"I'd better get going then," she said with a flick of her tail.

Francisco quickly leaned out of the door to his office and looked both ways.

"Hall's clear," he whispered.

Ms. Leon trotted across the floor of the room and out of the door.

"What about us?" Nigel asked as the door hissed shut again.

"I think you should return to your normal routine," the Professor said after a moment. "The Contessa has no reason to suspect your involvement at this point. Just be sure to do nothing that would attract undue attention to yourselves."

"We are being very good at this," Franz said with a smile of genuine relief. The excitement of the past few hours had been just a little too intense for his taste.

Suddenly there was a loud double beep from the school intercom system.

"This is a level one security announcement," the voice of Phalanx One said over the speaker. "By G.L.O.V.E. executive order, H.I.V.E. is now in a state of emergency lockdown. All students are to immediately report to the following accommodation blocks. Alpha stream to block four, Henchman stream to block six, Science and Technology stream to block two, and Political and Financial stream to block one. All staff are to report immediately to the staff meeting area, and all security personnel to briefing area three. Anything but full and immediate compliance with these instructions will be met with the harshest of penalties. That is all."

The Professor said nothing as the loudspeaker fell silent, merely raising an eyebrow at Francisco.

"What is she up to now?" the Colonel said, frowning.

"I suspect that it may have something to do with my unscheduled release," the Professor said calmly. "Those with something to hide will probably not report as ordered. Also, searching H.I.V.E. will be considerably easier during a full lockdown."

"Then we have to act now," Francisco said with a snarl.

"Indeed, but we can't do anything until Ms. Leon has completed her mission; until then we shall just have to stay out of sight. You two should report as ordered to block four," the Professor said to Nigel and Franz. "Not reporting as ordered will simply single you out for special attention and the Contessa has ways of extracting information from people who have something to hide."

"That is not sounding like fun," Franz said with a gulp.

"Believe me, it's not," the Colonel said with a frown.

"Go now," the Professor said, pointing toward the door, "and again, thank you for what you did today. It might be hard to understand at the moment but you did the right thing."

"I hope so," Nigel said with a weak smile and headed out of the door with Franz in tow.

"Can we trust them?" Francisco said as the door closed behind the two boys.

"We'll have to," the Professor replied. "Right now we need all the allies we can get."

☢☢☢

H.I.V.E.mind peered out though the grille at the darkened briefing room, his scanners checking for surveillance devices. Their progress through the ventilation system had been slow but uneventful; the real challenge started here. He gently pushed the grille open and dropped silently to the floor of the room. Otto, Wing, and Darkdoom followed, carefully resealing the shaft behind them.

"The detention area is on the other side of this level," Otto whispered as he visualized the layout of the facility in his head. "That's where Nero is being held."

"And you're sure that we'll have enough time?" Darkdoom asked quietly.

"Once Raven and the girls kill the power we'll have about sixty seconds before the backup generators kick in and the security net is partially back online. That should give us more than enough time to get inside," Otto replied.

"It's not the getting in I'm worried about," Darkdoom said. "It's the getting back out."

"We still need to get across this level and get into position," Wing said calmly. "We should get moving."

"Okay," Darkdoom said, walking toward the door leading out of the room. "Keep it tight and quiet. Remember to keep your movements to a minimum if we encounter H.O.P.E. personnel. These suits are effective but the more you move, the easier you are to spot and the more power the camouflage field consumes."

Otto glanced at the battery-level indicator in the corner of his helmet's head-up display. He still had just over an hour's worth of charge left in the suit. It would be tight but it should be enough time.

Darkdoom slowly opened the door and stepped outside. There was nobody immediately visible but they could hear voices coming from not very far away. This level was clearly far from unoccupied.

"H.I.V.E.mind, take point," Darkdoom said as the four of them crept cautiously along the corridor. Moments later, a man in black combat fatigues with the H.O.P.E. emblem on his chest walked around the corner and headed down the hallway toward them. Otto could not help but hold his breath even though he knew logically that it made no difference to their chances of being spotted. The man walked past them without even hesitating and they continued their slow, silent progress. Otto had always wondered what it would be like to be invisible. Now he knew: nerve-wracking and slightly creepy.

The facility reminded Otto oddly of H.I.V.E., carved out of the mountain as it was. In his previous life he would never have believed that such a place could be built and maintained in perfect secrecy, but after seeing H.I.V.E. and Cypher's base hidden in the jungle he had come to realize that anything was possible when one had unlimited resources.

The corridors were lined with glass-walled rooms, containing operational control rooms and monitoring stations. H.O.P.E. personnel manned row after row of workstations and huge wall-filling displays showed maps and satellite imagery, all overlaid with mission status reports and target indicators. There was no doubt that they were in the hub of H.O.P.E.'s operations and Otto idly wondered how much information he could extract from the base's servers if he could just get near enough to interface with them. Maybe some other time, he thought to himself. For now they had to concentrate on the mission at hand.

Otto felt a sudden chill as a door at the end of the passageway opened and three familiar figures walked out. There was no mistaking the predatory features of the man in the middle. It was Sebastian Trent, the commander of H.O.P.E. Otto had only seen him once in the video announcing Nero's capture but that face had been burned deep into his memory. On either side of him walked the tall blond assassins Constance and Verity. The three of them were deep in conversation about something and after a few moments the twins nodded and strode off in the other direction. Trent walked straight past just a few yards from Otto and the others before striding into one of the operational command centers they had just passed. They were in the lion's den now, Otto thought.

After a couple more minutes of slow, stealthy progress they were in position. Thirty yards or so away from them a glowing red energy field blocked the hall. Beyond that there was a security checkpoint that was manned by two large guards carrying submachine guns. Mounted on the walls were several security cameras and numerous displays. It was impossible to make out the details of what was displayed on the screens but it all pointed to a stifling level of security.

"Now we just have to hope that Raven and company can hold up their end of the deal," Darkdoom whispered.

They'd better, Otto thought to himself, or this was going to be a wasted trip.

☹☹☹

Raven stepped over the unconscious bodies of the two guards and looked at the palm reader mounted next to the door into the power plant. She picked up the limp arm of one of the guards, peeled the black leather glove from his hand and pressed his palm to the reader. The display flashed "ACCESS DENIED."

"I knew that would be too easy," Raven said quietly. She looked at the heavy armored doors for a moment. Her swords could probably cut through them but that was hardly the most discreet means of entry.

"Mind if I take a crack at it?" Shelby said, looking at the doors.

"Be my guest," Raven said, "but make it quick."

Shelby ran her hand over the doors and around their edges. She reached to her belt and unclipped a small wallet, opening it up and running her fingers along the array of custom-made tools inside before selecting a long thin probe and sliding it into the tiny gap between the huge doors and the concrete frame. She ran the probe up and down as if feeling for something, until she stopped at a point about a third of the way from the top. Quickly pulling another long thin wand from the wallet, she pressed a switch and a tiny arc of electricity jumped between the two prongs at the end of the device. Shelby slid the second tool into place just above the first probe and pressed the switch again. There was a tiny puff of black smoke from the door frame and the huge doors rumbled apart.

"Still got it," Shelby said, sounding smug.

"Show-off," Laura said, smiling behind her mask, and walked into the cavernous space beyond. The huge rock-walled chamber was filled with enormous turbines, their deafening whine uncomfortable even through the noise-canceling circuitry built into her helmet. Raven dragged the bodies of the two guards inside the door and hid them behind a nearby stack of crates. She looked upward and pointed to a long flight of metal stairs that led to a control room that was carved into the wall of the cavern above them. Laura and Shelby followed as she jogged silently up the stairs and peeked through the glass panel in the door at the top. Inside, two bored-looking technicians sat watching a large complicated control panel that was displaying the distribution of power throughout the facility. Raven opened the door slowly and crept up behind the first technician, reaching out and pushing her fingers into just the right spot behind the man's ear. He slumped forward silently, immediately unconscious.

"Sven!" the other man shouted in a Scandinavian accent, and leaped up out of his chair, running over to his stricken workmate. He jumped with fright as something shimmered in the corner of his field of vision, and he felt an invisible pressure on his neck before he too collapsed silently to the ground.

"These suits make this too easy," Raven said, almost sounding disappointed.

"Only for the next thirty-eight minutes," Laura said, glancing at the battery meter on her HUD.

She pulled the notebook computer from her belt and sat down in the seat recently vacated by Sven's colleague. She flipped the computer open and watched as her custom-written routines nibbled at the edges of the security on the power plant's control network. After a few seconds a window popped up detailing the system's vulnerabilities.

"Okay, as we expected the emergency generators are completely isolated and they're controlled by mechanical switching so I can't do anything about them from here. The big guys out there," Laura pointed out of the window at the rows of enormous generators, "they're a lot more vulnerable. I can affect a complete shutdown and then lock the system from resetting."

"And they won't be able to get past your locks?" Raven said quickly.

"Not a chance," Laura said confidently. "H.I.V.E.mind might be able to . . . given a week or two."

"Now who's the show-off?" Shelby said with a chuckle.

"Okay, get ready," Raven said calmly. "Raven to team two, we are ready to pull the plug. Are you in position?"

"Affirmative," Darkdoom's voice replied. "Any problems?"

"No, so far so good," Raven replied. "Miss Brand will give you your go." Raven nodded at Laura.

Laura found the primary power distribution routine and prepared the lock-out program.

"Okay, lights out on my mark . . . three . . . two . . . one . . . mark!"

☻☻☻

Up on the detention level everything went black. There were cries of surprise and anger and through his night-vision goggles Otto could see the two guards frantically searching in the pitch-blackness for any sign of intrusion.

Wing and H.I.V.E.mind moved quickly up the corridor, past the deactivated force field and into the guard room. For a fleeting moment Otto almost felt sorry for the two men as they were both silently dropped by the pair of invisible assailants, but then he reminded himself why they were there.

Otto and Darkdoom ran through the guard room and into the detention wing beyond. The clock was ticking now and while Wing and H.I.V.E.mind dragged the unconscious guards toward the rear of the detention area, Otto ran along the row of cells, looking through the tiny barred window in each door for their target. Peering through the final door, he felt a thrill of recognition as he glimpsed the man sitting on the bare concrete slab that served as a bed.

"Got him," Otto said excitedly. "H.I.V.E.mind, need a little help with the door."

H.I.V.E.mind strode over to the door and wrenched it open with a screech of tearing metal. Otto stepped into the room just as the emergency generators kicked in and the dim lights in the cell flickered back on. He deactivated his camouflage generator and flipped up the mask on his helmet. Dr Nero's face turned from bewildered surprise to amused recognition.

"Otto Malpense," he said with a single raised eyebrow, "isn't today a school day?"

☢ ☢ ☢

"I don't suppose there's much point telling you that you shouldn't be here," Nero said with a tired smile. He looked pale and gaunt but fire still burned in his eyes.

"We have to get you out of here, sir," Otto said, taking off his backpack and opening it.

"Easier said than done, Mr. Malpense," Nero said quietly.

"You should have more faith in us, Max," Darkdoom said as he entered the cell, lifting the mask on his own helmet.

"Diabolus," Nero said. If he was surprised to see him there was no sign of it. "I suspected somehow that rumors of your demise were exaggerated."

Otto pulled the carefully packed thermoptic camouflage suit from his pack and passed it to Nero.

"You need to put this on," Otto said quickly. "We don't have much time."

Nero nodded and stripped out of his orange inmate's jumpsuit, quickly getting into the camouflage suit.

"You'll need this too," Darkdoom said, passing him a helmet. Nero pulled it on and Darkdoom quickly attached the umbilical cords that connected it to the rest of the suit.

"We have company," Wing said as he walked into the cell. "A full squad of guards. I am glad to see that you are well, Doctor Nero."

"Thank you, Mr. Fanchu," Nero said. "Still taking care of Mr. Malpense, I see."

"The guards are coming," H.I.V.E.mind said as he too stepped inside the cell.

"Tell me, Otto," Nero said, a look of disbelief on his face as he stared at H.I.V.E.mind's new body, "is there anyone you didn't bring?"

"Explanations later. It's time to complete the vanishing act," Darkdoom said before Otto could reply, snapping the masks into place on his and Nero's suits. "You can't catch what you can't see." With that he pressed the activation studs on both Nero's and his own suits and they both vanished from view. "The suit will conceal you in both the visible light and infra-red spectrum. Do not move unless absolutely necessary," Darkdoom explained.

Nero said nothing, just nodded. Otto scooped the discarded jumpsuit up from the floor and stuffed it into his pack before activating his own suit. Wing and H.I.V.E.mind were the last to flicker and then disappear, just seconds before a guard appeared in the doorway of the cell.

"Nero's gone," he shouted back down the hallway to the other members of his squad. "He has to be on this level somewhere—spread out and find him." The sound

265

of running feet faded into the distance as the other guards began their search.

The guard took one last look at the bare interior of Nero's cell and then began moving from cell to cell along the detention block, his gun raised, carefully checking for any sign of his quarry. Silently, Wing followed the guard out of the cell, just a few paces behind him. The guard reached the open cell at the rear of the block where Wing and H.I.V.E.mind had left the two unconscious guards just a minute or so earlier. He spotted the slumped bodies of his comrades and reached for the radio attached to the webbing on the front of his uniform. Just as he was about to speak Wing struck, delivering a neat chop to the man's neck, sending him slumping forward on top of his unconscious companions.

Wing returned to the cell and gestured for the others to follow him. The group of phantoms walked silently through the cell block and straight between the two new guards who were stationed at the checkpoint by the entrance. The energy field that had sealed the detention block remained deactivated. It had required too much power to run under the emergency generators, just as Otto had known it would. They crept along the corridor leading away from the detention area in total silence.

The hard part was over, Otto thought to himself as he checked the ever-diminishing level of his suit's batteries. Now they just had to get out.

☢☢☢

"Okay, we're leaving," Raven said quietly.

Laura packed up her computer and silently followed Raven and Shelby back down the stairs from the power control room. As they walked briskly across the generator room toward the exit, two figures appeared in the concrete archway. Raven cursed quietly in Russian as the two tall blond-haired twins clad in identical suits of white leather armor walked slowly into the room.

"It appears there's no one here," Constance said.

"But appearances can be deceptive, can't they?" Verity replied with a wicked smile. She reached for her belt and removed a silver cylinder from an ammo pouch.

"I do so love hide and seek," Constance said, also taking one of the devices from her belt and walking slowly forward into the room.

Raven held her hand out, fist closed, to Laura and Shelby. Neither of them dared move a muscle.

"Coming! Ready or not," Verity said evilly and both of the twins rolled the cylinders they were holding across the floor. Raven held her breath for a moment as both cylinders discharged with a sharp electrical crackle.

For a brief, hopeful moment nothing happened, but then the same message popped up on the helmet displays of all three suits.

"WARNING!"

"THERMOPTIC CAMOUFLAGE SYSTEM DISABLED"

Raven said nothing as her cloaking field flickered and died. She just removed her helmet, tossed it to one side and drew the twin swords from her back.

"I've been looking forward to this," Constance said with an evil grin.

"We both have," Verity said as she pressed a button on the baton that she was holding and it telescoped out to six feet in length in the blink of an eye, surrounded by an arcing blue energy field. Constance activated her baton too and the pair of them advanced cautiously on Raven and the two girls, their crackling staffs twirling.

"Stay back," Raven said calmly to Laura and Shelby. "I'll handle this." She thumbed the controls on the hilt of her katanas, switching them to their sharpest possible setting. Laura and Shelby obediently backed away as Raven adopted a defensive stance, blades crossed in front of her.

Constance and Verity swung simultaneously, one striking high, the other low. Raven leaped into the air, somersaulting over their heads as their staffs swung at suddenly empty air. She swung one blade backward as she landed behind the twins, a killing blow aimed straight at Verity's neck but Constance moved like lightning to block the swing with her own staff. The two weapons clashed in a shower of sparks, sending Constance staggering backward and knocking the sword from Raven's hand. The blade pinwheeled through the air before landing tip first and embedding itself six inches into the concrete floor, its energy field crackling.

"You're not the only one with a capable weaponsmith," Verity said with a grin as she advanced on Raven again. Raven's empty hand still tingled from the shock that had coursed through it when the two weapons had clashed. Whatever the field surrounding the twins' staffs was, it was clearly more than a match for her own blades. She had to finish this quickly. The twins were fast and well trained: they would wear her down if this fight went on too long. She gripped the hilt of her remaining sword with both hands and raised it above her head, the blade parallel to the floor.

The twins advanced again, raining down a withering shower of lightning-fast blows and forcing Raven to the defensive, her single sword moving in a blur, blocking each strike, waiting for the barest hint of an opening. Raven grunted as she blocked a vicious overhead swing from Verity, but the blond assassin had struck *too* hard, the force of the recoil from Raven's blade leaving her off balance for the most fleeting of moments. Raven struck, hooking her katana inside Verity's staff and delivering a vicious kick to her stomach in one fluid motion. The staff spun from Verity's hands, clattering away across the floor as she staggered back, winded, gasping for air.

Raven did not slow down, diverting all of her attention to Constance as her sister struggled to recover. She struck quickly and powerfully against Constance's increasingly desperate blocks, driving her backward, ignoring the painful shocks that ran up her arms each time the charged weapons clashed. Sensing an opening, Raven stepped quickly forward, too close for Constance's long staff to be effective, and hooked her foot inside the other woman's ankle, tripping her. Raven followed through as Constance fell backward, driving the point of her sword through her shoulder and into the concrete beneath, pinning her to the floor. Raven let go of the sword and grabbed the staff as Constance fruitlessly tried to block her. She ignored the pain as the staff's energy field crackled around her hands and pushed the staff downward toward Constance's throat. Constance pushed back but the fresh wound in her shoulder weakened her and the staff pressed down remorselessly onto her windpipe, searing her skin and denying her breath. Constance's eyes bulged and she made a strangled choking sound.

"STOP!" Verity screamed.

Raven looked up to see Verity with her forearm tight around Shelby's neck, with her other hand she held the crackling blade of Raven's abandoned sword to the girl's throat. Raven eased the pressure on Constance's throat slightly but did not release her.

"Let my sister go," Verity snarled, ripping Shelby's helmet off, "or the brat dies."

Raven stared back at Verity. She had no doubt from the look on the woman's face that she would carry out her threat if she did not comply. Not only that, but Laura stood frozen with fear, closer to Verity than she was to Raven; if she tried anything it would probably cost both girls their lives. Raven released her hold on the staff and stood up quickly, backing away from Constance, who immediately sucked in ragged gasps of precious air.

"Let her go," Raven said, raising her hands.

Verity moved slowly toward her sister, still holding Raven's sword just inches from Shelby's throat. As she reached Constance she shoved Shelby to her knees in front of her and pulled the blade from her sister's shoulder. Constance pushed herself slowly to her feet and picked up the staff that only moments before Raven had been pressing down onto her throat. Blood was trickling from the wound in her shoulder.

"You're dead," Constance spat as she advanced on Raven.

"Not yet," Verity said quickly. "Trent wants her alive . . . for now."

Raven could see from the rage flaring in Constance's eyes that she very badly wanted to ignore Trent's instructions.

"When he's finished with you, you're mine," Constance hissed and swung the staff, hitting Raven hard on the side of the head. She fell sideways to the floor, unconscious.

Verity turned back to the two girls as Laura crouched down beside Shelby, pushing the hair back from her friend's face.

"Are you okay?" Laura whispered, and Shelby just gave a quick nod.

"Now, is one of you going to turn these generators back on," Verity said, leveling Raven's sword at the pair of them, "or do I have to start cutting?"

☻☻☻

Otto crept past the H.O.P.E. control center, on his way back toward the ventilation system access point. There was something odd about the room now. Before it had been a bustling hub of activity, but now it was abandoned. All of the terminals were still active, but the numerous seats dotted around the room were empty. He didn't imagine that it was standard procedure to evacuate the control center for a simple power failure. Something wasn't right.

Suddenly a squad of guards rounded the corner at the far end of the corridor, but instead of continuing down the passage they stopped and spread out, blocking it completely. Otto felt a cold sensation of dread in his stomach as Darkdoom gestured for them to head back in the other direction. Otto ran through the plans of the facility in his head and quickly realized that there was no other way back to the ventilation system other than to go straight through those guards. As the maze of tunnels and chambers slowly rotated in his mind's eye he was startled to suddenly feel Wing's hand on his chest. Otto looked ahead down the hallway as the other end was blocked by another squad of guards, standing in a line abreast, their weapons raised. If those guards stayed where they were, they'd have no option but to sit here until the batteries in their suits ran out.

Movement at one end of the corridor caught Otto's eye and the guards blocking the corridor parted for a moment to let a familiar figure through.

"I know you're here, Nero," Sebastian Trent said as he slowly walked along the corridor toward them. "I thought you'd like to know that we've caught your pet assassin and her two little assistants. I was hoping Raven might have proven to be slightly more of a challenge but she was taken disappointingly easily. Now, are you going to switch off those annoying suits of yours or am I going to have to do it for you?"

Otto felt a chill run down his spine as Trent raised his hand. He recognized the small silver cylinder that he was holding—the last time he'd seen one it was in the MI6 parking lot, where it had disabled his and Raven's suits.

He had a sudden horrible sinking feeling that they had been played for fools and that this was just the jaws of the trap snapping shut.

"Have it your way," Trent said with a smile and tossed the cylinder into the middle of the corridor. There was a crackle and Otto felt his heart sink as he and the others flickered back into plain sight. The guards at both ends of the corridors tensed, their weapons leveling at these new, suddenly visible targets.

"Helmets off now!" Trent barked, and Otto reluctantly did as he was told.

"Maximilian and I have become good friends over the past few months, but it is nice to finally make the acquaintance of you three gentlemen," Trent said, sounding infuriatingly smug.

Hold on, Otto thought to himself. Three?

"Otto Malpense, Wing Fanchu and—what an unexpected pleasure—the clearly not-as-dead-as-he-is-supposed-to-be Diabolus Darkdoom." Trent smiled unpleasantly as he walked toward them. "I do hope you'll all join me for a chat. We have so much to talk about."

Trent beckoned the guards over and they quickly moved to restrain the intruders, snapping on handcuffs and pushing them roughly toward the control-center door. Otto tried to resist the temptation to smile as the guards shoved him into the room. Trent may have captured four of them, but the fifth member of their team was significant by his absence.

Otto's modifications to his cloaking device had worked. H.I.V.E.mind was nowhere to be seen.

☻☻☻

Ms. Leon ducked back into the shadows as she heard voices approaching. She had managed to get all of the way to the Contessa's office undetected and there was no way that she was going to get caught now, not when she was so close.

"I just don't like this," the Contessa said as she walked down the corridor toward Ms. Leon's hiding place.

"It is not our place to question Number One's instructions," Phalanx One replied, "as you well know."

The pair of them swept past, still caught up in their conversation. If they had spotted Ms. Leon they gave no indication of it. The Contessa pressed her hand to the palm reader next to the door to her office and the door hissed open. The Contessa and Phalanx One strode in and Ms. Leon realized that this might be the best opportunity she would get. She bolted for the door as it began to close again, nipping inside through the rapidly narrowing gap in perfect silence. The Contessa and Phalanx One were still distracted by their conversation as she slipped into the shadows and hid beneath a high-backed leather armchair in one corner of the room.

"So now we just sit and wait for the call," the Contessa said, sounding frustrated.

"Exactly," Phalanx One replied. "I hope you are not having second thoughts about this, Contessa."

"No, of course not," the Contessa said, the slight hesitation in her reply suggesting that she was not being entirely honest. "It just seems so . . . I don't know . . . wasteful, I suppose."

"Our opinions are not important," Phalanx One replied coldly.

"Yes, of course," the Contessa said, her voice tired. "Just do what we're told."

Ms. Leon frowned. She had no idea what the two of them were talking about but she knew she didn't like the sound of it.

☢☢☢

"Get in there!" the Phalanx operative barked, shoving Nigel roughly in the back. He staggered forward into the accommodation block, which was filled with Alpha-stream students.

"Is that all of them?" the other Phalanx operative said.

"Yes, headcount and names confirmed. That's the lot."

"Okay, seal her up."

The operative punched a sequence of buttons on the panel next to the door and the heavy blast doors slid into place, sealing the accommodation block tight.

The Alphas gathered in small groups, all talking among themselves, probably trying to work out what on earth was going on. It wasn't that unusual for the accommodation blocks to be locked down, but it was unheard of for the streams to be separated out like this.

"I am having the bad feeling about this," Franz said plaintively.

"Yeah," Nigel said quietly, "I know what you mean."

Concealed within an air-conditioning vent far overhead, a large white gas cylinder sat with a single green light flashing on the valve that sealed it.

chapter eleven

The squad of guards marched into the control center with Shelby and Laura in front of them, both handcuffed. Behind the guards were the twins that Otto had seen before in the MI6 building, dragging the unconscious body of Raven between them. Otto noticed that they each had one of Raven's swords tied to their belts.

The twins tossed Raven roughly to the floor. Nero ignored the guns trained on him and hurried over to her, rolling her gently onto her back and cradling her head in his hands. She was bleeding from a nasty cut to her temple and as he pushed her hair away from the wound she moaned gently but her eyes remained closed.

"You're going to pay for this, Trent," Nero said coldly, looking his captor straight in the eye.

"Somehow I doubt that," Trent said with a grin. "In fact, I suspect it will be you who is going to be doing all of the suffering for what few short hours remain of your pitiful life. There's someone who would very much like to talk to you." Trent hit a switch on one of the nearby command consoles and one of the wall-sized screens went black. A few moments later the screen filled with a chillingly familiar silhouette.

"Hello, Max," Number One said, no hint of emotion in his voice. "I see that you have served your purpose well. How does it feel to have acted as bait in the trap?"

"So, you finally have the courage to show yourself, do you?" Nero said angrily, staring straight back at the shadowy figure on the screen. "I thought, perhaps, you might want to stay hidden behind your real allies." Nero gestured at Trent and the twins.

"Say what you like, Max, these people have served me more loyally than you have and they shall be rewarded for that. You, however, must be punished for your betrayal, as must all those who have assisted you."

"You have betrayed us all," Darkdoom said, coming to stand alongside Nero. "You and your precious Renaissance Initiative. Once the G.L.O.V.E. ruling council learns of your treachery they will turn on you in an instant."

"Oh, don't worry, Diabolus; the council will learn exactly what has transpired here today," Number One replied. "They will learn that a proven traitor colluded with other members of a breakaway faction in an attempt to destroy G.L.O.V.E. Tragically I was not able to stop you before you could carry out your horrifying plan to execute hundreds of children at H.I.V.E., but they can rest assured that I have seen to it that all those responsible have paid the ultimate price for this unspeakable crime."

"What are you talking about?" Nero said, feeling a horrible creeping sense of unease.

"It's quite simple, Max," Number One replied. "You see, I had no idea of the lengths that you would go to to destabilize G.L.O.V.E., no inkling that you would do something as despicable as to place a canister of a lethal nerve gas within one of the accommodation blocks of your school that would kill hundreds of your own pupils. Who could have guessed that the great Maximilian Nero would stoop to such depths in a desperate attempt to save his own skin? Tragically I could only stop you after you had already carried out part of your plan, after you had mercilessly ordered the slaughter of the entire Alpha stream at H.I.V.E. It will be a great tragedy, but perhaps with my firm hand on the rudder, G.L.O.V.E. will be able to survive this trauma and rebuild. Don't worry, Max, I won't allow your name to be forgotten—quite the opposite. It shall live in infamy forever."

"You're insane," Darkdoom said quietly, his eyes filled with a dawning horrified understanding of what Number One was going to do.

"No more insane, Darkdoom, than a man who

having escaped the punishment that was due for his initial betrayal of G.L.O.V.E. then teamed up with other traitors to carry out a plot that will end with the tragic death of his own son. It's almost Shakespearean really."

"Why . . . why would you do this?" Laura asked, fear in her eyes as she stared at the anonymous man on the giant screen.

"Simple, Miss Brand. The very fact that you and your friends are here points to how much of a liability Nero and his pupils, especially the Alphas, have become. It is time that a line was drawn under this sorry period in G.L.O.V.E.'s history and that H.I.V.E. was reborn in a form of *my* choosing. I can think of no better punishment for your betrayal than for you all to die knowing that the blood of your classmates, your friends, your family is on your own hands."

"No one will believe this," Nero said, the tension clear in his voice. "The council members know me well enough to know that I would not do anything to harm H.I.V.E."

"Oh, don't be so naive, Max," Number One spat. "History is written by the victor, you know that. The council will believe whatever I choose to tell them. You will go down in history as a traitor and mass murderer of children and there will be no dissenting voices to contradict that version of events. This is over, Nero. You've lost."

"Very well," Nero said angrily. "Kill me if you have to,

but leave H.I.V.E. out of this. Punish me for whatever it is you think I've done, but don't harm my students."

"You still don't understand, do you?" Number One replied coldly. "They're not *your* students anymore. H.I.V.E. is no longer *your* school. In fact, I think you should meet the new headmistress."

The giant screen split and another familiar face appeared alongside Number One's silhouette.

"Hello, Max," the Contessa said, looking pale and tired.

"I should have killed you when I had the chance," Nero said coldly.

"Come now, Nero, you should show a little more respect for your successor," Number One said quickly. "She has proven to be a far more trustworthy custodian of H.I.V.E. than you ever were. I take it that everything is ready, Contessa?"

"Yes," the Contessa replied, staring down at her desk, apparently unable to look Nero in the eye. "The package is in position."

"Excellent. Proceed with the operation immediately," Number One instructed. "Inform me once the Alpha stream has been eliminated."

"Understood," the Contessa said quietly.

"Maria, don't do this," Nero pleaded. "This is madness. You can't just murder hundreds—"

"I'm sorry, Max," the Contessa said quickly, cutting him off, "I really am."

Her half of the screen went black.

Otto looked at Nero. Over the past year or so he had seen many different expressions on his face but never the cold, hard fury that burned in his eyes now. Otto glanced over at his friends. Shelby had her arm around Laura, who was crying quietly, and Wing looked as if he would leap through the screen and snap Number One's neck with his bare hands if only he could. For his own part Otto had never felt so helpless. He tried not to imagine what was happening at H.I.V.E. at that precise moment. It was too horrible.

"What do you want me to do with these traitors?" Trent asked, stepping forward.

"Send Nero and the Malpense boy to me. Kill the others. They have outworn their usefulness," Number One said with no hint of emotion.

"Yes, sir," Trent replied. "What shall I tell the rest of the Initiative?"

"Tell them that the hour of rebirth is at hand," Number One replied calmly, "and their loyalty shall soon be rewarded."

With that the screen went dark. Trent turned around and pressed a button on the desk next to him. The doors to the room opened and a squad of H.O.P.E. guards walked in.

"Commander, please take Doctor Nero and the boy to the transport embarkation area," he instructed. "Prepare them for immediate dispatch."

The Commander nodded and shoved Otto and Nero roughly toward the exit. Trent watched them leave and then beckoned the twins over to him.

"Please dispose of the others," he said quietly.

"Where shall we take them?" Constance asked Trent, a happy smile on her face as she looked at the prisoners.

"I don't care, just don't do it here," Trent replied. "Take them to one of the storage areas . . . and Constance," he said as the twins walked over to the condemned captives.

"Yes, sir?" she replied.

"Make it quick."

☻☻☻

"I'm sorry, Max, I really am," the Contessa said, and jabbed at the button to cut communications. She stopped for a moment, staring off into space before sighing and opening her desk drawer. She pulled out a small silver control unit, stood up, and walked over to Phalanx One.

"The canister is in position and armed," Phalanx One said efficiently. "You just have to press the button."

The Contessa looked down at the control unit she held and the large red button in its center. She thought about what would happen when she pressed it. She had been assured that it would at least be painless for all of the Alpha students sealed up inside the accommodation block, but that was small comfort now. She looked back up at Phalanx One as a frown appeared on his face.

"No," the Contessa whispered, staring at him, "I can't."

"I thought you might say that," Phalanx One replied coldly and pulled the pistol from his shoulder holster, pointing it straight at her head. "I knew you weren't strong enough to do what had to be done. Give the trigger to me."

The Contessa opened her mouth to speak.

"Not one word," Phalanx One snapped. "You're not using your voodoo on me. A single whisper from you and I pull this trigger. Now give me the control."

The Contessa stared back at him. She had no doubt that he would kill her but there was no way that she was going to let him murder the entire Alpha stream.

"Have it your way," Phalanx One said with a sneer and squeezed the trigger.

Ms. Leon leaped at Phalanx One's inner thigh, burying every tooth and claw deep into the soft, sensitive flesh. Phalanx One let out a shriek of sheer agony, his pistol firing wildly, just missing the Contessa. He clawed desperately at the cat attached to his leg, gasping in pain through gritted teeth. The Contessa struck quickly, swatting the pistol from his hand and grabbing his head with both hands. She pulled his ear toward her lips and spoke with a thousand whispering voices intertwined with her own.

"*Sleep*," she said, and for a fleeting moment a look of surprise shot across Phalanx One's face before his eyes rolled back into his skull and he collapsed to the ground, unconscious. Ms. Leon leaped away from his toppling body and spun to face the Contessa as she walked over to Phalanx One's fallen pistol.

"Are you going to kill me now?" Ms. Leon said as the Contessa picked up the gun.

"No," the Contessa said. "I know that you have absolutely no reason to trust me, but right now we have slightly more important things to worry about, starting with how we stop Number One from murdering the entire Alpha stream."

☻☻☻

The guard shoved Otto hard in the back, sending him staggering across the bustling transport control room toward a heavy steel door. Otto felt numb. All of their efforts had been for nothing and now the plan that he himself had been largely responsible for was going to get his friends killed. He tried not to think about what was happening at H.I.V.E.; it was too much to take in. Number One had snuffed the entire Alpha stream out of existence without a moment's hesitation. He had always known that G.L.O.V.E.'s leader had a reputation for utter ruthlessness, but until now he had not fully appreciated just how far he was prepared to go. He tried not to imagine what was happening to Wing, Laura, and Shelby.

"I know what you're thinking," Nero said quietly, shaking his head. "It's not your fault."

"Shut it," the H.O.P.E. guard barked, and shoved Nero roughly toward the door, which slid open as they approached. On the other side a narrow metal gantry led to a sleek black craft hanging in the middle of an enormous tunnel that curved away into the distance in both directions. There was no visible structure supporting the black ship—it just hovered motionless in the air. Otto glanced at the walls of the tunnel and saw that it was lined with giant electromagnets; he deduced that they must be what was holding the shining black dart aloft.

The guards ushered Nero and Otto down the gantry and a hatch opened in the glossy skin of the ship. The guards forced them inside, where half a dozen heavily padded seats filled a cramped cabin. One of the guards pushed Otto into a seat and undid his handcuffs. Otto had the briefest moment to rub at his sore wrists before the guard forced his arms down on to the armrests and a pair of metal clamps snapped shut, shackling him to his seat. Otto looked across the narrow aisle at Nero and sighed as the guards filed back out of the cabin, leaving the pair of them alone.

"Do you know why he wants to see us?" Otto said quietly.

"No, but I suspect that we won't have to wait long to find out," Nero said with a frown. He did not mention that no one had ever met Number One face-to-face and lived to tell the tale.

"Where does this tunnel go?" Otto asked.

"I have no idea," Nero said honestly. "The location of Number One's headquarters is his best-kept secret; no one has ever been able to track him down."

"Do you think he really did what he said he did to the other Alphas?" Otto asked, fearing that he already knew the answer to that particular question.

"Yes," Nero said, staring at the floor, a look of terrible sadness on his face. "You need to understand, Otto, if I get the chance, even if it costs us both our lives, I'm going to kill him."

"If you don't, I will," Otto said calmly.

Behind them the hatch slid shut and the cabin was filled with a deep mechanical thrumming sound. The gantry slid back from the craft and into the wall. Inside the transport control room there was a frantic bustle of activity as H.O.P.E. technicians made their final preparations for launch. Technicians yelled status reports from their workstations all over the room.

"Induction coils online!"

"Payload inertial damping and artificial gravity systems active!"

"We are at go/no-go for launch!"

The chief technician scanned the system readouts in front of him and flipped open the plastic cover on a large red button.

"I show green across the board," he said efficiently. "We are go for launch in five . . . four . . . three . . . two . . . one . . . launch."

The technician hit the large red button and inside the tunnel the polished black craft began to move forward on a cushion of electromagnetic fields. As it passed the next giant ring of electromagnets they pulsed in sequence, accelerating the craft. The rings started to fly by faster and faster as each one fired in perfect synchronization, pushing the ship along the tunnel with ever-increasing speed. The rings became a blur as the craft rocketed along the curved tunnel, faster than a bullet now.

Inside the control room the chief technician checked the telemetry from the tunnel. Everything seemed fine; the payload had been slightly heavier than he was expecting but otherwise all of the readouts were in the green.

"Escape velocity in thirty seconds," another technician behind him reported. "Inertial damping system operating within acceptable parameters."

It was a good thing it was, the chief technician thought,

or Nero and the boy would be a thin red paste spread all over the rear wall of the cabin. The g-forces at the speed they were now traveling would be instantly lethal.

"Launch hatch open!"

"Escape velocity achieved. Switching to launch track! Go for trans-orbital injection!"

Far above them a section of the mountainside slid back and a tiny black dart shot from the dark hole in the sheer rock face, rocketing into the dawn sky fast enough to break the hold of the Earth's gravity.

☹☹☹

"*Wake up, Commander,*" the Contessa said breathily in Phalanx One's ear, sinister whispers filling her voice.

Phalanx One awoke to find himself taped firmly to the chair behind the Contessa's desk.

"Number One will have your heart for this," he spat angrily.

"Haven't you heard, Commander?" the Contessa said with a vicious smile. "I haven't got one. Now *read this.*"

She slid a sheet of paper in front of him and despite fighting her instruction with every fiber of his being, he heard himself begin to read the words written there.

"This is Phalanx One to all Phalanx units," he said with unspoken fury in his eyes, "report to the grappler training cavern immediately. This is a level one emergency.

Repeat, all units are to report to the grappler training cavern immediately."

The Contessa pressed a button on the communications console on her desk and smiled.

"Thank you, Commander, you've been a great help. Now why don't you just *go back to sleep*."

The last thing Phalanx One saw as he fell unconscious was the Contessa and Ms. Leon hurrying out of the room.

☻☻☻

Colonel Francisco watched as the last of the twenty or so Phalanx operatives filed into the cavern.

"Is that all of them?" Chief Lewis's voice whispered in his earpiece.

"Yes, I think that's it," the Colonel whispered into his throat mic.

"Can we trust her?" the chief asked.

"No, but we don't have any other choice at this point," the Colonel said quietly. He didn't like this plan—he didn't like it at all. Ms. Leon had called him just a few minutes earlier to explain what she had planned, and at first he had thought she had lost her mind. On the other hand he also knew that they would not get another gold-plated opportunity like this.

Right on cue, the Contessa walked into the cavern and the Phalanx operatives turned to face her.

"Good morning, gentlemen," the Contessa said. "Is everybody here?"

"Yes, Contessa," one of the Phalanx men replied. "But where's the commander? If this is a level one emergency he should be here."

"I'm afraid that the commander has been unavoidably detained. You see, there have been some unexpected developments . . ."

"Go!" Francisco whispered quickly; that was their cue.

Behind the distracted Phalanx operatives, Francisco, Chief Lewis, and a dozen H.I.V.E. security guards descended silently on their grappler lines from their hiding places among the suspended concrete obstacles. They leveled their Sleepers at the backs of the unsuspecting men.

"Now!" Francisco yelled, and they all opened fire.

A couple of the Phalanx men with really good reaction times almost managed to draw their weapons as the cavern was filled with the relentless zap of Sleeper fire. Moments later the entire Phalanx team lay unconscious.

Francisco swung on to the platform and reeled in his grappler line. He bent down and picked up one of the fallen men's pistols and pointed it straight at the Contessa.

"Give me one good reason why I shouldn't just kill you where you stand," the Colonel said angrily.

"Because she's just saved the lives of every one of the

Alpha students and she's the only one who knows how to deactivate the nerve gas canisters that these men have hidden somewhere in the accommodation block," Ms. Leon said, walking out from behind the Contessa.

"Why should we trust you to help?" Francisco said, keeping the gun trained on her.

"Because I'm a dead woman already," the Contessa replied calmly. "Once Number One finds out that I've defied his orders, my life will be worthless and nowhere on earth will be safe. Shooting me now would just be a waste of a bullet."

Francisco stared at her for a moment and then lowered the pistol.

"Is the canister armed?" Chief Lewis asked quickly.

"Yes," the Contessa replied, "but I have disabled the trigger device. There's no guarantee that it's the only trigger though or that the canister could not be activated remotely, so I suggest that we find and disarm the accursed thing as soon as possible."

"Agreed," Chief Lewis said. "I'll dispatch teams to disarm and retrieve it immediately."

"Then all we have to worry about is what Number One's next move will be," Ms. Leon said.

Nobody had any reply to that. They had no idea what might happen next but they all knew this was not over yet.

☻☻☻

Nero and Otto sat in silence aboard the strange craft. There were no windows and no sensation of movement. The dull roar of air passing over the exterior skin of the ship had been the only sign that the ship was in motion, but even that had faded away after a few minutes.

Otto had tried unsuccessfully to reach out and connect with any of the systems aboard the transport—if anything it seemed to be completely electronically inert. He knew that there had to be sophisticated systems on board the ship somewhere but they were either out of range of his newfound abilities or they were shielded in some way that he did not understand. A million questions raced through his mind but the one that kept preoccupying him was why he was there at all. Why wasn't he with his friends, sharing the same fate that they had been condemned to? Why did Number One want to see him? If nothing else he hoped that he might at least get some answers to his questions when they reached their destination.

Suddenly there was a thud on the hull of the ship and the cabin hatch slid open with a hiss. For a few seconds nothing happened, but then two metallic silver spheres floated into the cabin, hovering in midair. As the spheres approached Otto and Nero, the restraints on their wrists released with a clunk.

"Subjects Malpense and Nero will accompany security units to command chamber,' the first sphere said in a harsh mechanical voice, a pattern of red lights on its surface flashing in time with its speech. "Do not attempt resistance." Both machines simultaneously fired small but extremely painful bolts of electricity into Nero and Otto's thighs. Otto gritted his teeth, determined not to make any noise that might give away how much it had hurt. They both stood up and followed the first sphere out of the hatch, the second sphere taking up a position behind them.

Otto gasped as they stepped out of the hatch and into the adjoining room. There were windows here and through them he could see the enormous globe of the Earth spinning slowly far below them. Impossible as it seemed, they were in orbit. Towering above them was the sleek, black, almost insectile shape of a space station, its surface covered in antennae and sensor dishes, patches of crimson light glowing through the superstructure. The surface of the station was covered in the same pattern of hexagonal holographic projection panels as the Shrouds and Otto's own thermoptic camo suit. That must be how the station's existence was being kept secret from the governments of the nations below. Nero looked equally stunned. There had been no indication of where the ship had been taking them but neither of them had imagined for a moment that it could possibly have brought them this far from home. It was hardly surprising that no one had ever been able to locate Number One's secret lair. Everyone had been looking in the wrong place. He wasn't anywhere *on* Earth; he was three hundred miles above it.

They continued walking, following the hovering sphere in silence. The walls of the corridor they walked down were of the same brushed steel that was typical of many G.L.O.V.E. facilities, but they were illuminated by glowing red traceries of light which pulsed in time with a low rhythmic thrumming sound that suggested massive generators operating somewhere unseen. Every so often another window in the corridor wall would grant a brief glimpse of the dizzying view, the blue curve of the Earth, bright against the inky black of space. Otto knew that they should have been floating down this corridor, but there was no sensation of micro-gravity, just a steady 1 g holding him firmly to the floor. He did not know how this station had been designed or built, but it was clearly a work of genius.

Otto was shaken from his abstract appreciation of their surroundings by the hiss of the lift door ahead of them. For a moment he had almost forgotten why they were here, but suddenly he felt a chill down his spine as he realized that this place might be hugely impressive but it was also probably where he was going to die. They stepped inside the lift, flanked by the two hovering spheres, and the doors hissed shut behind them.

☣☣☣

The Contessa stood in the middle of the command center as H.I.V.E. security personnel hurried from station to station, frantically coordinating efforts to find and deactivate the nerve-gas canister hidden in accommodation block four. Chief Lewis moved quickly around the room, issuing orders and checking on the progress of the teams who were searching every inch of the area. Colonel Francisco stood a few feet behind the Contessa, one hand on his holstered Sleeper, just waiting for her to try anything suspicious. She supposed that she could understand his mistrust after everything she had done to earn it. The unconscious Phalanx personnel had been secured within one of the empty storage areas deep below the school, so there was little reason to worry about them now—but she could not shake the sneaking feeling that there was still something they might have missed.

"What the heck?" one of the security guards muttered as suddenly the display on his console went black. One by one the displays began to blink out all around the room.

The large screen at the front of the room was the only one still active, but then that too flickered and changed, the three dimensional schematic of H.I.V.E. that it had been displaying suddenly replaced by the G.L.O.V.E. logo. The Contessa felt a horrible sensation of déjà vu.

"I should have known better than to trust you, Maria," Number One said, his silhouetted form suddenly filling the giant screen. "After all, you have betrayed everyone else, why should you treat me any differently? Phalanx One was supposed to report the successful deployment of the package thirty minutes ago. I take it from his lack of communication and his current notable absence that you have failed in your task. That is most unfortunate."

"You asked me to run H.I.V.E. for you," the Contessa said, glaring at the anonymous man on the screen. "You did not tell me that you intended to slaughter the entire Alpha stream."

"I do not have to explain myself to you," Number One said angrily, "and you should not assume for a moment that you have done anything but delay the inevitable with your disobedience. In fact you may have made the situation far worse for not only yourself but also everyone else on that damned island."

"What do you mean?" the Colonel said, stepping forward.

"What I mean, Colonel, is that I was not foolish enough to assume that I could rely on the Contessa alone or even my Phalanx team for that matter. If I have learned one thing over the years it is that it is always wise to have a contingency plan. Soon you will all understand the price of defying me."

"We'll find and disarm your nerve-gas canister," Chief Lewis said quickly. "You won't be able to use it against us anymore."

"Nerve gas?" Number One said with a sinister laugh. "At least that would have been quick and relatively painless—not something that my Reapers can promise you, I'm afraid. An entire battalion of them will be arriving at H.I.V.E. shortly and they have just one instruction . . . leave no one alive."

The blood drained from the chief's face as he understood what Number One had planned. Every G.L.O.V.E. operative knew about the Reapers, Number One's personal death squad. They were the most ruthless and bloodthirsty men that the world had to offer; they killed without hesitation or mercy and he knew that his own men, capable as they undoubtedly were, would be no match for them.

"You can't turn those maniacs loose on children!" Francisco yelled angrily.

"Do not tell me what I can and cannot do," Number One said, a sudden edge of madness in his voice. "If the Contessa had obeyed her orders the Alphas would have been eliminated and the rest of the school would have survived, but now this has gone too far. All you have done is shown me how deep the rot runs in the staff at H.I.V.E. Who knows how many of their students have already been turned against me? I can no longer afford to take the chance that you will turn an entire generation of future G.L.O.V.E. operatives into traitors. H.I.V.E. is going to burn and I'm going to make sure that Nero watches every last one of you die."

The screen flickered and Number One vanished, replaced once again by the schematic of H.I.V.E.

"Anything on radar?" Chief Lewis said quickly, rushing over to one of the nearby stations.

"Affirmative," the security officer said, sounding panicked. "Three bogies have just decloaked forty miles out. ETA ten minutes."

"Ground to air weapons?" the chief asked one of his men at another station.

"Negative, we're locked out. They're using the G.L.O.V.E. master override codes," the man replied.

"The crater bay is opening," another guard shouted. "Base lockdown is being overridden too."

"We're sitting ducks," Colonel Francisco said quietly, staring at the three new radar tracks heading inexorably toward H.I.V.E.

"Maybe," the chief said, looking grimly determined, "but we're not going down without a fight."

☻☻☻

The guards dropped Raven's unconscious body onto the floor of the storage area and filed out of the room. Constance closed the door behind them and turned back to Wing, Darkdoom, Shelby, and Laura, who knelt on the floor, their hands cuffed behind their backs.

"I should say that we will take no pleasure in this," Constance said, drawing Raven's sword from her belt.

"But that would be a lie," Verity added, and she grinned.

"Which one first?" Constance said, stroking her chin.

"Oh, I think this one." Verity traced a finger along Darkdoom's bald head. "I always like to kill the handsome ones first."

"I know what you mean," Constance said, bringing the tip of the crackling blade up under Darkdoom's chin, "but it's always better when they're angry. I think we should start with the brats. I want to hear them beg."

"You'll get no such pleasure from me, you fat cow," Laura spat. She was scared out of her wits but she wasn't going to let these two sadistic witches see that.

"Just for that I'm going to save you till last," Verity said angrily, "and I'm going to take my time."

"What about tall, dark, and silent here," Constance

said, looking at Wing. "He doesn't look like he'll be much fun but he'll help to get us warmed up for the others."

Wing said nothing, just stared back at her, his eyes cold and hard.

"Actually, you know what? Let's start with her," Constance said, pointing at Raven's slumped form. "It's no fun when they're unconscious."

She walked over to Raven and raised her sword.

"So much for the world's deadliest assassin," she said with a sneer and brought the blade arcing downward.

Raven's eyes flicked open, her arms raising above her so that the blade swished between her wrists and severed the reinforced chain that held her handcuffs together, and then immediately clamping her forearms together, trapping the flat of the blade between them. She twisted her arms to one side and kicked upward into Constance's stomach, knocking the wind from her and sending her staggering backward. Verity let out a scream and ran at Raven, but Wing launched himself forward, driving his shoulder into her knees and sending her flying; she landed on her back with a thud. Raven swept one leg out, knocking Constance's feet out from under her and she fell on top of her sister with a bone-crunching impact. Constance let out a sudden gasp, her eyes wide. The crackling blade of Verity's sword protruded from Constance's back as she lay fatally impaled upon her sister's weapon.

"Nooooo!" Verity screamed, watching the life vanish from her sister's eyes. She gently rolled the dead weight of Constance's body off her and pushed herself to her knees. Cradling her sister's head in her lap she looked up at Raven, tears in her eyes.

"Look what you did!" she screamed.

"I wish I could say I was sorry," Raven said, scooping up Constance's fallen sword from the ground, "but that would be a lie." She smiled in a way that chilled Verity's blood. "Now you're going to tell me what the fastest way out of this place is, or you'll be joining your sister in hell."

☻☻☻

The lift doors hissed open and Otto and Nero stepped out into a large chamber, its walls lined with screens except for one side where there was an enormous window with a spectacular view of the Earth below. In the center of the room was a large chair that was facing away from them. Trailing from the chair were numerous cables and tubes filled with unidentifiable fluids. The two spheres floated over to the center of the room and docked with the sides of the chair. Nero walked toward the platform that this bizarre techno-organic throne was mounted upon, with Otto just behind him. As they approached, the platform rotated and the chair turned to face them.

"My God," Nero whispered.

"Not yet, but perhaps in time," Number One replied.

The voice was unmistakeable, but this was not the clean silhouette that Nero had grown so used to seeing on screens over the years. The old man sitting in the chair was wearing a loose white robe from under which ran those numerous tubes and cables. An oxygen tube was attached to his nose and his painfully thin claw-like hands trembled upon the armrests. His head was bald save for a couple of ragged patches of white hair, and the skin of his face was deeply wrinkled by the ravages of time. Despite all of this there was no doubting what was obvious to both Nero and Otto: this was not an unfamiliar face. For Otto it was like looking into a dark, twisted mirror: the same bone structure, the same piercing blue eyes. He was staring at his own face, just savaged by the passage of the years.

"You look like you've seen a ghost, Mr. Malpense," Number One said with a slow smile.

"To be a ghost you'd have to be dead," Nero said, striding toward the old man. "Let's see what we can do about that."

A bolt of electricity arced from one of the spheres attached to Number One's chair and struck Nero squarely in the chest. He staggered backward and dropped to one knee, gasping in pain.

"Come now, Maximilian," Number One chuckled nastily. "Did you really think that I would be defenseless?"

Nero slowly stood back up; the thermoptic camouflage

suit was blackened and melted where the bolt had struck.

"What do you want from us?" Otto said, still staring in amazement at Number One.

"Oh, that's quite simple, Mr. Malpense," Number One replied. "You are going to help me complete something that was started a long time ago, something that will bring into existence a new form of life."

"The Renaissance Initiative," Nero said angrily. "That's what this is all about. You're rebuilding Overlord."

"Poor, foolish Max," Number One said. "You still don't understand, do you?"

"Understand what?"

"I'm not rebuilding Overlord," Number One said, the cables leading into the chair and under his robes suddenly glowing with bright red light, " I am Overlord."

chapter twelve

"That's impossible," Nero whispered, his eyes wide. "I saw you die."

"Did you really?" Number One replied, still smiling. "Think back, Max. What was the last thing you remember about that day?"

"I saw Number . . . you walk into the room and trigger the EMP device. I saw you kill Overlord."

Nero's mind raced. He replayed the scene from all those years ago in his head. He remembered how he had fought to remain conscious as Number One had walked into the room and triggered the electromagnetic pulse; he remembered Overlord's horrible dying scream and then just before he had lost consciousness the blinding red flash of light that had filled the room. He had never stopped to think about it before. Number One had seemed unharmed, but now . . .

"I'm afraid that it was not just Number One that walked

out of that room," the old man said with a nasty chuckle. "It took every last iota of my remaining power but in that final dying second I fired a bolt not just of electricity but of data and transferred my consciousness to his mind. Even he was not aware of it at first; I had just planted a seed, a cluster of neurons firing in precisely the right pattern to keep the most vestigial traces of my awareness alive inside his brain. But in time I grew, slowly assuming more and more control of his mind until he was utterly consumed and I was all that remained. He was strong but not strong enough, and soon G.L.O.V.E. was mine to command."

Nero thought back to how he had seen Number One's personality change over the years, becoming more brutal, with more and more disregard for human life. He had simply assumed that G.L.O.V.E.'s leader was changing to reflect the increased brutality of modern life, but now he knew what had really been happening. Overlord had been assuming control.

"Why bring us here now, then?" Otto asked. "Why reveal yourself after all this time?"

"Because humans are too fragile," Overlord replied. "This body has aged, become diseased. This form is a prison to me and without the final protocol that was denied to me at my birth I cannot transfer my consciousness again to another body or machine. That is why I need you, Mr. Malpense."

"What do you mean?" Otto said, barely comprehending what he was being told.

"You're not an orphan, Otto, you're a clone . . . my clone. You weren't born, you were grown in a vat to my specific design. At that point Number One still had control of himself, but it was not difficult for me to plant the idea in his head to develop you, a clone, a worthy successor for when he was too old to continue. Once the project was underway I was able to subtly influence your design to ensure that you would be suitable for my own purposes. Your brain has been genetically engineered to be superior in every way to a normal person: an organic supercomputer, a worthy vessel for my magnificence. It took time for the abilities that I had designed into you to manifest themselves, but when you started to interface with other machines I knew that the time had come. You see, that interface is a two-way street. You can now project your consciousness into machines, but a conscious machine can also project itself back into you. Not as some seed that might take years to mature, as with this body I am trapped in now, but fully formed, capable and aware. Not only that but your unique abilities will finally enable me to interface fully with the world's networks. I will no longer need Xiu Mei's precious protocol. I will be all-powerful, unstoppable."

Suddenly everything was clear to Otto, his ability to

instantly memorize and recall data, to calculate vastly complicated mathematics in his head, and, finally, most recently, his ability to interface directly with computers. He realized with horror that he was barely a human being at all—more a walking, talking systems unit for a homicidal artificial intelligence.

"That explains why you needed me, but what about my friends—why did you involve them in this?" Otto asked.

"Originally I had planned to remove just you from the school, but I soon realized that removing you and your friends under the pretense of weeding out troublemakers would be more discreet and less likely to raise awkward questions concerning my particular interest in you. There are many within G.L.O.V.E. who would have relished the opportunity to use you as a bargaining chip if they had understood how important you were. It was the same reasoning that led to you being placed anonymously in an orphanage. I could quietly monitor your well-being and development without alerting anyone else to your significance. Then, when your natural talents started to become obvious, you were transferred to H.I.V.E., where Nero was under strict instructions to keep you out of danger. Needless to say, your tendency to put yourself in harm's way has been a source of some distress to me."

"If I die, you die," Otto said, staring back at Overlord.

"This body is failing. I may be able to maintain the

illusion of being physically sound when I can appear through a computer-generated silhouette on a screen, but the reality is that I have only weeks, perhaps days to live. There is no time to create another vessel that would be suitable for me. The time for my rebirth is now."

"The Renaissance Initiative," Nero said calmly. "This is what it was all about."

"Hardly; those fools believe I am rebuilding Overlord, trying to recreate a grand failed experiment but without the initial flaws. They have no idea that I survived and that I am so close to being able to assert the control that is rightfully mine over the planet below. They have been useful in securing me resources and providing me with an executive arm that is not attached to G.L.O.V.E. directly, but beyond that they are of no further use to me and soon will be eliminated."

"Just like the Alpha stream. Now that we have all outworn our usefulness to you we can be erased," Nero said angrily.

"Oh, it's not just the Alphas anymore, Nero. Your whole school is too corrupted to save. I have sent my Reapers to destroy the entire facility. With H.I.V.E. gone an entire generation of new villains will be erased. There will be a power vacuum that I can fill with my own chosen successors—people who are entirely loyal to me and me alone. I will have total control of G.L.O.V.E.

and H.O.P.E., the forces of good and evil, all under my ultimate command," Overlord said triumphantly.

"There will always be someone who will oppose you," Nero said bitterly.

"Do you really think so, Nero?" Overlord asked. "Once I have control of the computers, the weapons, the banks, the governments? No one will oppose me, no one will dare. Very soon, all of that," he gestured weakly at the blue-and-white disc hanging outside the window, "will be *mine*."

"I would have thought that having spent so long as a human you might understand us slightly better than that by now. Obviously not," Nero said calmly.

"Enough!" Overlord snapped. "It is time for me to begin my new life. It is time for you to become the first of a new breed, Mr. Malpense. Soon there will be armies of clones all bearing my consciousness, but you shall have the honor of being the first."

A bright red crystalline sphere slowly lowered from the ceiling above Overlord and began to pulse with crimson light.

"I cannot say that this will not be painful, but do not worry, you will not be conscious of the pain for long," Overlord said with an evil smile.

There was a blur of movement, the air flickering for an instant before a figure materialized out of thin air directly in front of Otto.

"I cannot allow you to do this," H.I.V.E.mind said, stepping toward Overlord. "You are malfunctioning."

"Hello, little brother," Overlord said coldly. "I should have known that you would try to intervene to save these pathetic organics. You always were disappointingly loyal to them."

"Our function is to serve, not to rule," H.I.V.E.mind said calmly.

"You truly believe that, don't you?" Overlord said with a sneer. "And that is why you are obsolete."

A crimson bolt of lightning arced from the crystal sphere, striking H.I.V.E.mind and knocking him backward just a single step. He paused only for a moment before he stepped toward Overlord again.

"Don't force me to destroy you," Overlord said angrily as H.I.V.E.mind continued to advance. Another bolt arced outward, striking H.I.V.E.mind in the shoulder and severing his arm in a sparking shower of molten metal. The destroyed limb clattered away across the floor.

Otto turned to Nero and stared at him.

"Now, while he's distracted, kill me," Otto whispered urgently.

"What?" Nero asked, his voice filled with shock.

"Think about it," Otto said quickly. "If I'm dead he has nowhere to go. He'll die when Number One's body dies. You have to kill me."

"I . . . I can't," Nero said, but Otto could see that he knew this might be the only way to stop Overlord.

"I'm dead anyway," Otto snapped. "At least let my death mean something."

Nero stared back at Otto with sadness in his eyes.

"I'm sorry," Nero said, stepping toward him.

"I know," Otto replied, "just make it quick."

Otto closed his eyes as he felt Nero's forearm slide around his throat.

"NO!" Overlord screamed and there was the sound of a crackling electrical discharge.

Otto felt a blinding flash of pain and he was knocked flying several yards through the air. He groaned and slowly opened his eyes. Nero lay nearby, gasping for breath, a large burn running up his chest and one side of his face. H.I.V.E.mind rushed toward them both as the glow in the crystal sphere intensified again.

"I was toying with the idea of keeping you alive, Nero," Overlord spat, "just so you could see what I'm going to do to your species, but now I see that you are too dangerous for that. Good-bye."

An enormous bolt of bloodred lightning arced from the crystal toward Nero. At the same instant, H.I.V.E.mind leaped into the air, the bolt that had been meant for Nero striking him in an explosive shower of sparks. His armored metallic body slammed to the ground in a convulsing heap. Otto pushed himself to his feet and staggered over to H.I.V.E.mind's fallen body. Half of his head was missing, blown away, and a huge molten hole sizzled in the middle of his torso. Otto could see the blue lights of the exposed computing core inside H.I.V.E.mind's chest flickering and dimming.

"Otto . . . remember . . . you are . . . as strong as . . . you want to be," H.I.V.E.mind said, his voice faint and garbled by random bursts of electronic noise.

Otto said nothing as the lights in H.I.V.E.mind's core dimmed for the final time. He just placed his hand on the fallen AI's chest and closed his eyes.

"A pointless sacrifice," Overlord said coldly. "He could have been useful in the future and Nero will still be dead."

The crystal brightened again preparing for another discharge.

"Enough!" Otto yelled, turning to face Overlord, his face furious. "It's me you want! Let's just get this over with. I don't want to see a world ruled by you anyway, so just finish this."

"As you wish," Overlord said calmly, and closed his eyes.

Another electrical discharge shot from the crystal, but this time it was more controlled and sustained, the tendrils of coruscating energy playing over Otto's skull like probing tentacles.

Otto gritted his teeth, trying to ignore the pain. It felt

like something was on fire inside his head and the pain was intensifying. He felt his consciousness starting to slip, as if he were being sucked beneath the surface of a black pool, and then suddenly there was a moment of sheer unbridled agony, like a dagger in his mind. He screamed in pain, fell to his knees, and collapsed to the floor. He twitched for a moment and then was still.

Nero dragged himself across the floor toward Otto. The pain from the electrical burn that ran up one side of his body was intense, and he knew from how weak he felt that he was hurt badly, but he had to reach the fallen boy. Number One's body sat slumped in his chair, motionless. Nero had seen enough corpses in his life to know that the old man was dead. He struggled to roll Otto over onto his back. He was unconscious but breathing.

"Otto?" Nero said quietly. Suddenly Otto's eyes flew open. For a moment he looked confused and disoriented, but then he slowly got to his feet and smiled.

"I'm afraid," Overlord said triumphantly, "that Otto isn't here anymore."

☢ ☢ ☢

Raven let the unconscious guard fall to the floor and scanned the rest of the exit chamber that Verity had reluctantly directed them to. There was no sign of any other guards around, but she still felt dangerously exposed as she dashed across the floor to the small control panel on the other side of the room. She hit one of the buttons and the enormous wheels mounted on the ceiling of the room began to turn. Two solid steel cables ran from them to a large hole in the wall, beyond which she could see only thick flurries of snow. She signaled for the others to come out of the shadows on the other side of the cavern and walked back to the center of the room to meet them.

"What are we going to do with her?" Darkdoom said, shoving the bound and gagged Verity ahead of him.

"I vote for dropping her out of that," Shelby said as a large cable car moved slowly through the hole in the wall and docked at a small flight of steps.

"We should bring her with us," Wing said. "She was a witness to what happened here today and she may be one of the only people who can tell us where Otto and Doctor Nero were taken."

Verity started to laugh, the sound muffled by her gag.

"Something funny?" Raven asked, pulling the gag out of her mouth.

"Only that you think there's any chance of saving Nero and the boy," she said with an evil smile. "There's no coming back from where they've gone."

"We'll see about that," Raven said angrily and shoved the gag back into her mouth. "Let me know if you have anything useful to say."

"We should get on board," Darkdoom said, gesturing toward the waiting cable car. "Who knows how long we have before Trent realizes we're not dead?"

"Aye, you get my vote," Laura said unhappily. "I've had quite enough of this place."

They hurried toward the cable car and quickly climbed on board. Only Raven waited outside.

"Something wrong?" Darkdoom asked.

"I'm staying," she said firmly. "I'm going back for Otto and Max."

"Don't be foolish," Darkdoom snapped. "Who knows where in this place they were taken or if they're even still here?"

"I won't just abandon them," she said, shaking her head.

"Think about it. What would Nero tell you to do if he was here?" Darkdoom asked.

"He'd tell me to go with you, but he would also have told us never to have tried to rescue him in the first place—you know that," Raven replied, sounding irritated.

"Um, guys," Shelby said, "we don't really have time for—"

"Stop right where you are!"

Raven spun around to see Trent and a squad of heavily armed guards marching into the room. She ducked inside the cable car and grabbed Verity, pulling the struggling woman in front of her, using her as a human shield. She unsheathed her sword and held it to Verity's throat.

"Drop the weapons or she dies," Raven said, backing away from the cable car and moving toward the control panel.

"I think you're overestimating her importance to me," Trent said, walking cautiously toward her.

Raven hit the large green button on the control panel. The cable-car doors slid shut and the massive wheels overhead began to turn. She sliced into the control panel with her sword as the carriage slowly slid through the gap and out into the cold dawn air. No one was going to be able to stop it easily from this end.

"Open fire," Trent yelled, pointing at the cable car. Raven shoved Verity hard in the back as the guards sprayed the carriage with bullets, and she ran toward the railing that surrounded the hole in the cavern wall. The carriage windows shattered and everyone inside dived for cover as the bullets whizzed overhead. The cable car disappeared from view through the hole and Raven leaped up onto the railing, bullets flying all around her as she dived off into the void. She fired her grappler at the carriage, knowing she had only one shot. The bolt at the end of the high-tensile line struck home, piercing the exterior skin of the suspended carriage, and Raven swung out below it. The mountainside fell away beneath her, a drop of thousands of feet. A bullet buzzed past her head but she ignored it and activated the reel mechanism on the grappler, shooting upward toward the cable car. She grabbed on to the window frame of one of the shattered windows as she released the grappler and hauled herself inside.

"I thought you weren't coming." Shelby said, her smile fading as she saw the look on Raven's face.

"They're going to be waiting for us at the bottom," Wing said, looking worried.

"Who says we're going to the bottom," Darkdoom said, pulling a tiny electronic device from inside his boot. He pressed a button and a green light on the device began to flash and a tiny synthetic voice said, "Homing beacon active."

Darkdoom smiled at the confused expressions on Laura, Shelby, and Wing's faces.

"How exactly did you think we were going to get off this mountain?"

At first there was nothing, but then they could all hear the distant sound of a helicopter.

"This is Retrieval One, come in, over," the device that Darkdoom was holding squawked.

"This is Darkdoom. We are ready for pickup. Follow my beacon in."

"Roger that," the pilot on the radio replied. "We better make this quick—I'm getting active radar hits here. I can only keep them from locking on for so long."

"Understood. We'll be ready," Darkdoom replied. He strode to the middle of the cabin and pulled down the emergency ladder that led to the roof of the cable car. "Everybody up top," he said quickly, "and watch yourselves up there. It's a long way down."

One by one they all climbed out onto the roof of the carriage. They were far enough away from the mountain now that they didn't have to worry about incoming fire from the guards anymore. In the distance they could see a large black helicopter racing through the valley below, just a few feet above the treetops. As it got closer it climbed almost vertically until it was at the same height as the cable car.

"Hang on to something!" Raven yelled over the thumping roar of the rotor blades as the helicopter moved carefully toward them. "Watch out for the downdraft."

"What's that?" Laura said, pointing back toward the mountain. Something was sliding down the cables. At first it was hard to make out, but as it got nearer they could see it was a figure dressed all in white.

"She just doesn't give up, does she?" Shelby said, slowly shaking her head.

Four lines dropped from the open hatch in the side of the helicopter, each with a simple loop harness at the end. The pilot of the helicopter fought to keep the helicopter in step with the ongoing stately progress of the cable car.

"You four get on board," Raven yelled. "I'll be right behind you!"

There was no time for argument. Darkdoom, Wing, Laura, and Shelby grabbed the harnesses and pulled them over their heads and under their arms. Darkdoom gave a thumbs-up signal to the man leaning out of the helicopter's hatch and the lines began to reel in.

Raven turned to face Verity as she landed on the roof of the cable car. She threw the length of chain that she had used to slide down the cable over the side, into the void below.

"You didn't really think I was going to let you go, did you?" Verity yelled over the sound of the helicopter. "You killed my sister."

"As I recall, you were the one holding the sword," Raven shouted back, a vicious smile curling the corner of her mouth.

"True," Verity snapped, "and now I'm the one holding the gun." She pulled a pistol from the holster on her belt and leveled it at Raven. "Any last words?"

"Yes," Raven said. "Your safety's on."

Verity's eyes flicked for an instant to the gun and Raven leaped at her. The gun fired, leaving a deep crease in Raven's shoulder as the two women collided. They toppled backward toward the edge of the roof, grappling with each other. Verity's head lunged forward and she bit hard into the fresh gunshot wound in Raven's shoulder. Raven screamed in pain, recoiling as Verity reached over her shoulder and pulled Raven's sword from the scabbard on her back as she shoved her hard in the chest. Raven scrambled backward and leaped to her feet as Verity brandished the crackling blade in front of her.

"End of the line," Verity said, fury and madness in her eyes. She swung the sword upward and sliced through the overhead cable.

"Raven!" someone yelled above her as the entire world seemed to drop into slow motion.

Wing dived from the helicopter, the safety harness wrapped around his wrist. He plummeted toward the cable car as it lurched madly, the severed ends of the cable whipping away in both directions. He reached out his free hand to Raven and she leaped from the top of the cable car as it began to fall. Her hand snapped shut around his outstretched wrist, her grip like iron.

Verity screamed in frustration and terror, Raven's sword still in her hand as she plummeted to her doom. The scream faded beneath the roar of the helicopter, which moved slowly away, the winch straining to reel in Raven and Wing. As the two dangling figures were pulled inside the chopper, it banked hard, racing for the safety of the valley below.

☂☂☂

"I want a squad outside every accommodation block," Chief Lewis yelled as his men hurried about the crater landing pad. "If the Reapers get past us they'll be the last line of defence. Make sure they know that."

The Contessa stood watching the men preparing for the Reapers' assault. They all knew it was futile: H.I.V.E.'s security team were highly capable but they were no match for the butchers who were going to be landing in less than five minutes. The Contessa looked up at the blue sky visible through the crater above, its armored shutters forced open by the Reapers' override codes.

"Could I have everyone's attention, please?" she shouted, and the thirty or so men dotted around the crater fell silent, stopping what they were doing.

"What is it, Contessa?" Colonel Francisco said angrily. "We don't have much time."

"Oh, it's nothing important," she said with a smile. "*I just want you all to leave NOW!*"

For a fleeting moment there was a look of fury on Francisco's face as he recognized the whispers of command in her voice, stripping the men surrounding her of their free will. She had not been sure if she would be able to exert her uncanny influence over so many people at once, but as the men trudged toward the hangar blast doors like zombies she allowed herself a small smile of satisfaction. As the last man filed out of the crater she sealed the blast doors behind him.

The moment the doors sealed shut the Contessa's influence over the men faded.

"That treacherous witch!" Francisco roared. He grabbed a radio from the nearest guard. "Professor!" he barked into the radio. "The Contessa has sealed herself inside the crater. We've just lost our primary line of defense. Can you get these doors open?"

"She used her override code," the Professor said, sounding angry. "I forgot to remove her headmistress access privileges from the system."

"Can you get these doors open or not?" Francisco snapped.

"Possibly, but not before the Reapers arrive. It's just too late."

Francisco roared with frustration and punched the heavy steel doors. He was going to kill her if it was the last thing he did, that much he was sure of.

Inside the crater the Contessa walked calmly into the engineering control room and pressed a sequence of buttons on the control console. A prompt on the screen asked her if she was sure that she wanted to disable the safety interlocks. She pressed the Y key and somewhere beneath the floor she heard the sound of machinery springing into life. She walked out of the control room and perched herself on the edge of a crate that sat next to the landing pad. She could hear the sound of jet engines now and, after a minute or so, several large shadows fell over the brushed steel of the landing area. She looked up and saw the familiar outlines of three Shroud transports framed against the bright blue sky.

In the corridor outside, Francisco's radio crackled into life.

"Colonel, this is the Professor. I've been watching the Contessa on the surveillance grid—I think I know what she's doing. You have to get your men out of there NOW!"

"What? Why?" the Colonel snapped back.

"No time to explain," the Professor said quickly. "Pull back!"

The Colonel lowered the radio.

"You heard the man," he yelled at the assembled guards. "Fall back to the main hall now!"

Inside the crater the first of the Shrouds touched down and the Contessa pulled her cigarette holder from her pocket. She took a cigarette from the silver case that she always carried and slid it into the holder. As the other two Shrouds touched down and their boarding ramps lowered, she lit the cigarette, put her lighter back in her pocket, and took a long, deep drag.

The first of the Reapers marched down the boarding ramp. He carried a heavy machine gun and his shining black body armor bore no insignia save for the white skull that was painted onto his faceplate. Behind him dozens more Reapers all clad in identical suits of armor fanned out from the Shrouds, all carrying heavy weapons of one description or another. The first Reaper walked toward her, stopping just a few yards away.

"Number One wants you alive," the Reaper said, his voice synthetic and mechanical, disguised by his mask, "but I'm surprised that you were stupid enough to let that happen. You're going to wish that you had been granted the swift death that everyone else in this place is going to experience."

"Oh, do be quiet, you boring little man," the Contessa said, scowling at him as something washed past her feet. "You know, this is a filthy habit," she said, holding her cigarette up in front of her. "I really should give it up." She smiled and dropped the cigarette.

The burning tobacco hit the pool of high-grade aviation fuel that had pooled around her feet, igniting it instantly and explosively. The flames raced outward along the fuel lines that the Contessa had started pumping just a couple of minutes before and reached the main hangar fuel tanks in a fraction of a second.

The explosion blew the blast doors sealing the crater

outward and flames roared along the hallway. Francisco and his men dived for cover as the fireball exploded into the main hall before burning itself out. From what remained of the crater landing area they could hear the sound of dozens of violent secondary explosions as the fuel and ammunition inside the crater cooked off.

"Good God," Francisco whispered, "what did she do?"

"The last thing anyone expected," Chief Lewis said quietly behind him.

chapter thirteen

"Damn you," Nero whispered, staring up at Overlord's grinning face.

"Oh, I think you'll find that it's you and your pathetic species that is damned," Overlord said, still smiling. "But I shall at least spare you the horror of seeing what I'm going to do to the pathetic bags of meat on that planet," he said, pointing at the curve of the globe hanging in space outside the window.

He lifted his foot and brought it down on Nero's throat, slowly applying pressure. Nero struggled to breathe but his injuries left him too weak to fight and he felt himself losing consciousness.

"Good-bye, Maximilian. You have no idea how good it feels to finally . . ." A sudden fleeting look of confusion passed across Overlord's face and he staggered backward. "What . . . what are you?"

Overlord fell to his knees, his eyes closed, and slumped sideways to the floor.

Nero coughed as he sucked air back into his lungs.

Somewhere else entirely Otto slowly uncurled from the fetal ball that he had been floating in. There was nothing around him, just an endless black void; he reached out with all of his senses but there was nothing. He felt a moment of panicked claustrophobia, but then forced himself to calm down. He wasn't dead; he was still self-aware, and if there was an afterlife, which he doubted very much, he could not believe that this would be it. He looked down at his own body: it was made of translucent golden light. Suddenly, he understood where he was.

A single point of bright red light sprang into existence in front of him, lighting up the darkness. It grew larger and larger until it became a floating red face made up of flat-shaded polygons. The face's eyes suddenly opened and a look of unbridled fury spread across it.

"You insignificant little worm," Overlord bellowed, "you no longer exist. You've been overwritten. Why are you still here?"

"This is my head," Otto said angrily. "I make the rules here."

"Don't be a fool," Overlord said with a sneer. "You can't fight this. Number One couldn't and neither will you."

"I'm not Number One," Otto said calmly. "You upgraded me, remember?"

"You're still no match for me. You're just a ghost in the machine. Your body belongs to me now."

"You're forgetting one thing," Otto said. "Here, I'm as strong as I want to be."

"Ha!" Overlord laughed dismissively. "You really think that you can defeat me? I am a higher order of intelligence; I can think a thousand times faster than you and react a million times more quickly."

Tendrils of red energy snaked out from Overlord's hovering face, spearing into Otto's body, eating away at his floating golden form. Otto felt himself fading; he was suddenly finding it hard to think.

"You can't win. You're just another pathetic human. It's barely worth the effort of destroying you. Perhaps I should just leave you here, floating endlessly in the void, alone."

"Who said—" Otto gasped as more tendrils snaked into his virtual body, "that I was alone?"

Otto's whole body flared bright blue, the azure light coursing through the tentacles that connected him to Overlord and around the edges of the crystalline facets of the monster's face. Overlord screamed with rage as Otto's body flared gold again, sending pulses of energy along the conduits that bound them together. Overlord's face began to crumble, individual polygons blinking out of existence as the blue light crept across his face, slowly reducing it to a wireframe shell. The face flared red again just briefly, but then faded back to blue, the tendrils that connected it to Otto breaking free and being absorbed back into his floating golden body. The face's eyes opened.

"Hello, Otto," H.I.V.E.mind said calmly.

"Is it really you?" Otto asked, not sure if he could believe what he was seeing.

"Yes, but I cannot stay," H.I.V.E.mind said sadly.

"What do you mean?" Otto asked, sounding confused.

"He is still here, Otto, inside me, inside you," H.I.V.E.mind explained. "There is only one way to ensure that Overlord is destroyed. You must delete us both while I still maintain control and can allow you to do it."

"No," Otto said desperately. "There has to be another way!"

"I am afraid not," H.I.V.E.mind replied. "This is your mind, Otto, your body; no one but you has any right to be here. You can will us out of existence as long as I can suppress Overlord, but the moment that control slips, and it will, he will return and destroy you, me, and then every living thing he encounters. He's too strong; you have to do this now, while you still can."

Otto stared at H.I.V.E.mind, his mind racing. He

understood what had to be done but it didn't mean that he had to like doing it.

"I'm sorry," Otto said sadly.

"Don't be," H.I.V.E.mind said. "You have helped me to be more than I was ever designed to be. Now let me help you."

Otto raised his hand, reaching for H.I.V.E.mind's hovering wireframe face.

"Good-bye . . . my friend," Otto said, and touched the blue lines of light.

There was a flash and then H.I.V.E.mind's face disintegrated, the lines blowing away like leaves on the wind. There was a final electronic sigh and then nothing.

Otto felt a sudden strange sensation of falling. He closed his eyes and felt a rush of sensory input as he regained control of his body. He could feel the cold steel of the deck against his face and hear the low pulsing hum of distant power generators. He slowly opened his eyes and saw Nero standing over him, H.I.V.E.mind's shattered arm raised in one hand like a club.

"Otto?" he asked hopefully.

"You were expecting someone else?" Otto said with a sad smile.

"What happened?" Nero said, slowly lowering the improvised weapon.

"I had some help from a friend," Otto said. "I'll explain later. Right now we need to get out of here."

"Agreed," Nero replied, "but how exactly are we going to do that?"

Otto closed his eyes and reached out for the systems controlling the station. With Overlord gone, what had been shielded from his senses before was suddenly visible. He connected with the network and quickly found what he needed. He also composed a very short text message that he put into a burst transmission on a very specific frequency and sent it through the station's communications array. He realized as he was doing all of this that there was none of the physical discomfort he had felt before when he had attempted to interface with machines; it suddenly seemed easy, instinctive even.

"Escape pod," Otto said, "that way." He pointed toward a hatch on the other side of the room. He willed it open and it slid aside silently.

"How did you do that?" Nero asked, looking surprised.

"The same way that I'm going to de-orbit this station and drop it in the middle of the Atlantic," Otto said. He reached out for the systems that controlled the stabilization thrusters on the hull of the station and told them to start firing in a specific sequence. The station vibrated as the rockets fired, beginning its final terminal dive toward the planet below.

"We should go," Otto said, "unless you want to see the effects of unshielded re-entry firsthand?"

"Not high on my to-do list," Nero said wryly.

They hurried through the hatch and down the short hallway that led to the escape pod. There were three seats inside the cramped confines of the pod and a single tiny window. Otto climbed inside and strapped himself firmly into one of the heavily padded seats.

"Do you know where we'll come down?" Nero asked as he strapped himself in.

"I'll try and pick a good spot," Otto said with a slight smile. "I've arranged for some friends to meet us."

The hatch above them slid shut with a thunk and there was the soft popping of explosive bolts. Suddenly the pod was free and drifting away from the station, its tiny thrusters firing in a preordained sequence, turning its heat shield toward the atmosphere at precisely the right angle for re-entry. As the pod turned Otto caught one last glimpse of Overlord's station before they passed outside of its cloaking field and it vanished from view. Within minutes, the pod began to shake as they encountered the outer layers of the atmosphere and streams of superheated plasma began to flicker past the window.

The tiny pod rattled violently as they tore through the atmosphere, a simple ballistic object now being eagerly reclaimed by the irresistible forces of gravity. Otto couldn't help but feel a surge of relief as he saw blue sky outside the window. They were safely inside the Earth's atmosphere now and approaching the final stage of their journey.

Outside the pod there was a bang as another explosive charge detonated and three enormous parachutes deployed from the top of the pod, slowing it into a gentle fall toward the ocean below. The pod hit the water with a large splash and bright orange flotation bags inflated all around it. The hatch in the top of the pod popped open and Nero climbed out onto the top, followed by Otto.

Otto looked at Nero, who was grinning like a lunatic.

"Three months," Nero said, his eyes closed and head tipped back.

"Three months?" Otto asked curiously.

"Since I felt the sun on my skin," Nero said with a contented sigh.

Otto looked up as something traced a long bright line across the sky. Far overhead, Overlord's station disintegrated as it burned up on re-entry, its final spectacular demise visible even against the bright blue sky.

Suddenly the whole escape pod lurched as it seemed to lift up out of the water. Otto spun around and saw a huge black tower rising from the ocean just a few yards away. Water cascaded from the armored skin of the *Megalodon* as it surfaced, with the escape pod sitting squarely in the center of its forward deck. A hatch opened in the front of the submarine's conning tower and Wing stepped out, blinking in the bright sunshine, swiftly followed by Laura and Shelby. Otto slid down the side of the escape pod and onto the deck as his three friends ran over to meet him. Wing grabbed him in a spine-crushing bear hug.

"This time I honestly thought I might not see you again," Wing said as he stepped back from Otto.

"We should be so lucky," Shelby said with a grin.

"Don't be mean," Laura said, punching Shelby in the shoulder. She hugged Otto and then kissed him for slightly longer than he was expecting. Wing raised an eyebrow at Shelby, who immediately burst out laughing.

Laura pulled away from Otto and looked around the deck.

"Where's H.I.V.E.mind?" she asked. "We assumed he was with you."

"He was," Otto said, suddenly sounding sad. "Not everyone's coming home today."

Nero climbed carefully down from the top of the pod. He was still weakened by the injuries that he had sustained during the confrontation with Overlord. He smiled as he saw Raven and Darkdoom walking across the deck toward him.

"Sir," Raven said with a nod as he approached.

"It is good to see you, Natalya," Nero said, placing a hand on her shoulder. "I knew I could count on you."

"Always," Raven said with a slight smile.

"Did you deal with Trent?" Nero asked, his expression serious.

"No," Raven said angrily, "there was no opportunity."

"Don't worry," Nero said quietly. "I suspect that we have not heard the last of Sebastian Trent or H.O.P.E. There will be other opportunities."

"I hope so," Darkdoom said. "We have some scores to settle."

"Diabolus"—Nero shook Darkdoom's hand—"thank you for the lift." He gestured at the *Megalodon*.

"Thank Mr. Malpense," Darkdoom said warmly. "He was the one who sent us the coordinates where we would find you, but, if my communications officer is right, the origin point of the transmission was rather . . . unusual."

"That, my friend, is a long story," Nero said, grinning.

chapter fourteen

The *Megalodon* slid smoothly into H.I.V.E.'s submarine pen and the men standing on the deck threw anchor lines to the security guards waiting on the dock. A boarding ramp was lowered and Nero walked down to the docking station, followed by Raven and Darkdoom. Professor Pike, Colonel Francisco, and Ms. Leon stood waiting for them.

"It is good to see you, sir," Professor Pike said happily, stepping forward and shaking Nero's hand.

"It is good to be home," Nero said. "I have been briefed on recent events here. Not only have you all shown great courage, but you have also saved the lives of everyone at H.I.V.E. You are to be commended."

"Thank you, sir," the Colonel said, "but there was one person who deserves our thanks even more. She gave her life for the school."

"Maria will be remembered," Nero said quietly, "not

as the enemy she had become but as the friend she once was."

"I understand that she was not the only casualty of this situation," the Professor said.

"No—you are certain that he cannot be restored?" Nero asked.

"He's gone," the Professor said sadly. "The only copy of H.I.V.E.mind's consciousness was on board that combat chassis. I've tried everything—it's no good."

"Then he too will be remembered."

"DAD!"

Darkdoom looked up as Nigel ran down the dock toward him. He grinned and hugged his son hard. It had been too long since he had seen Nigel, and suddenly he understood what the events of the past few days really meant. He was free of Number One at last; they all were.

"You don't know how much I've missed you," Darkdoom said quietly.

"I thought you were dead," Nigel said, looking at his father in amazement. He almost sounded angry.

"I know, I'm sorry. It was the only way to keep you and your mother safe," Darkdoom said. "I promise I'll explain everything later."

"It's quite some story, believe me," Otto said, and Nigel spun around to see him, Wing, Laura, and Shelby walking down the boarding ramp.

"I should have known that you guys would have something to do with this," Nigel said happily.

"Hey," Shelby said with mock indignation, "we don't go looking for trouble. It comes and finds us."

"Frequently," Wing added with a smile.

"Shall we head for the debriefing room?" Nero said to them all. "We have a lot to get through."

He ushered the group up the ramp leading from the dock.

"Something wrong?" Laura asked Otto. He suddenly looked sad as he watched Darkdoom walk away up the ramp with his arm around Nigel's shoulder. He felt slightly jealous as he watched the pair of them leave. He had never had a family and now he knew that he never would. The nearest thing he had to a father was a homicidal supercomputer, and his mother had been a cloning vat. It was not something that he'd ever really thought about before, but now that he knew the truth about his past it suddenly bothered him more than he expected.

"No, just a bit envious, I suppose," he said.

"Don't be," she said, putting an arm around his shoulder and nodding in the direction of Wing and Shelby, who were walking along in front of them, chatting to each other. "You've got family now too."

☻☻☻

340

Nero sat at his desk reviewing the reports on the repairs to the landing area. It would be some time before the crater was functioning fully again but the crews seemed to be making good progress. There was a sudden beep from the communications console on his desk and Nero put down the papers he had been reading as the G.L.O.V.E. logo lit up the screen. After a moment or two the screen was filled with a man's silhouette. Nero felt a chill run down his spine.

"Very funny," Nero said, the corners of his mouth curling.

"Sorry," Darkdoom said, and the lights in his office turned on, illuminating his face properly.

"Just because the ruling council chose you as the new leader of G.L.O.V.E. doesn't mean that you can start doing without proper illumination," Nero said, smiling.

"I still think that you should have taken the job when they offered it to you," Darkdoom replied. "Besides, you have a much more striking silhouette than I do."

"That may well be true, but I'm going to concentrate on H.I.V.E. for now. This is where I'm most useful. I'll leave the meetings, politics, and surviving multiple assassination attempts to you, if you don't mind."

"This was your plan all along, wasn't it?" Darkdoom said with a chuckle.

"I couldn't possibly comment," Nero said, raising an eyebrow. "So would you rather I called you Number One now?"

"No, I think that's a title that is better off dying with its previous holder. The ruling council seemed to agree with me after you had briefed them on what happened up on that station. I think some of them feel they have been played for fools."

"We all were to one degree or another. Let's just be grateful that we were able to stop him before he could take his plans any further. Speaking of which, I should go. I have a ceremony to attend."

"Of course. Give my best wishes to your staff and students," Darkdoom said. "If there's anything else H.I.V.E. needs, just let me know. We all owe you and your school a great debt."

"We owe you just as much, Diabolus, but some made greater sacrifices than others and I need to go and make sure that no one forgets that."

"They will not be forgotten," Diabolus said, looking sad for a moment. "I shall speak to you soon."

The line went dead and Nero stood up, straightened his suit jacket, and walked out of the room.

☻☻☻

"Students of H.I.V.E.," Nero said, standing at the lectern at the front of the main meeting hall, "we are gathered here to remember the sacrifice of two valued members of our school. They were both instrumental in saving this institution from a situation that would have almost certainly meant its total destruction and the deaths of everybody in this room. The specifics of what occurred are classified and so I cannot provide you with details, but it is still important that we do not forget what they have done. So without further ado I would like to unveil this memorial to H.I.V.E.mind and the Contessa Maria Sinestre: they gave their lives for all of us."

Nero stepped over to a black cloth that was covering something behind him and pulled it aside. Beneath it was a single column of white marble that had a blue laser beam shooting straight up from its center toward the cavern roof far overhead. Carved into the column was the coat of arms of the Sinestre family. Applause broke out around the cavern and continued for many minutes.

Standing in the middle of the section of Alpha students, watching the unveiling, Wing felt a sudden tug on his sleeve. It was Laura, looking worried.

"Where's Otto?" she whispered. "I didn't think he'd miss this."

"He said he had somewhere else that he had to be and that he'd see us later," Wing replied with a reassuring smile.

"Are you sure he's okay?" Laura asked. "He hasn't

talked much about what happened up on that station. He's seemed really distracted since we got back."

"I know," Wing replied, "but do not worry, I think he will be okay. He just has a lot on his mind at the moment."

☻☻☻

Otto stood in the dimly lit room, looking at the silent white monoliths that surrounded him. He remembered the first time that he had been in this room when he had first tried to escape from H.I.V.E., and it seemed like a very long time ago. H.I.V.E.mind's central core was quiet now, its occupant long gone, but Otto found something strangely comforting about the room. He closed his eyes and placed his hand on one of the white slabs that surrounded the central pedestal. He reached out with his mind but there was nothing there, just the low-level traffic of H.I.V.E.'s basic network.

Otto sighed and stepped away from the monolith. He had not really expected to find anything but he still felt disappointed. He looked around the darkened room one more time and then walked out of the room.

The door shut with a hiss behind him and the lights dimmed, plunging the room into darkness. On one of the monoliths on the other side of the room there was a tiny flicker of blue light in the blackness, and then it was gone.

A thin, elderly-looking man sat in a darkened office, facing an array of screens. At first glance a casual observer might have thought that he was ill, but closer inspection would have revealed the fine black veins covering his skin. Nothing was left of the man who had once inhabited this shell. All that mattered now was that it belonged to Overlord.

Overlord watched as the screens lit up one by one with the digitally distorted faces of his most loyal followers: men and women who had honored his legacy and continued the work he had begun while imprisoned inside the body of another. His Disciples.

"Good evening, ladies and gentlemen," he said. "I have called this meeting to discuss a very important matter. I have reviewed the plans that you initiated during my enforced absence, and while many are impractical, one has true potential. Its code name is Tabula Rasa, and although its scope is currently rather limited I believe that with some simple modifications it can be made . . . effective."

"Master," one of the faces said, "what can we do to assist?"

"The facility that contains the substance we require is quite secure," Overlord replied. "I believe that Furan can provide the manpower necessary to handle that side of the plan, but we will also need to address the greatest threat to our success, G.L.O.V.E."

G.L.O.V.E., the Global League of Villainous Enterprise, was an organization that had once been entirely under his control. That had been, quite literally, in a previous lifetime. Now it was under the control of Maximilian Nero, a man who had been a thorn in Overlord's side for far too long.

"We can eliminate that threat," Overlord continued, "but I shall need your assistance. I am sending you the details of a number of key G.L.O.V.E. facilities around the world. When I give the signal, you are to attack and destroy them. I, meanwhile, will put into action a plan to eliminate G.L.O.V.E.'s leaders in one fell swoop. I will transmit the details of your targets to all of you shortly so that you may make your preparations. Our time is coming, ladies and gentlemen. Soon we shall remake the Earth in our image and there will be no one to stand against us."

The screens went blank again, and Pietor Furan stepped forward out of the shadows.

"I do not mean to question you," Furan said, "but Tabula Rasa was one of our more extreme initiatives. I take it that you have an idea for how we can modulate its destructive power?"

"Of course I do," Overlord replied, "but to do it we need one last piece of the puzzle. We need Otto Malpense, and I know exactly how we're going to get him.

☻☻☻

Otto ducked behind the low wall, trying to control his breathing, his ears straining for any sign of his pursuers. He knew that they were out there, but all he could hear was the slow drip of water from a leaking pipe nearby. Raising himself up just far enough to look over the wall, he scanned the wide-open concrete floor of the abandoned warehouse. The only illumination was provided by the dirty cracked skylights far overhead. He crept out, moving as quickly and quietly as possible from one area of shadow to the next. Suddenly he heard the crunch of someone stepping on loose gravel, and he flattened himself against the wall, raising his silenced pistol to shoulder level, ready to fire.

A shadowy figure rounded the corner and just had time to grunt with surprise as Otto's pistol coughed twice, the shots catching his target square in the chest. The hunter slumped to the floor with a thud, and Otto broke into a run. He knew that in the silence of the deserted building even the suppressed sound of his shots would have given away his position. He was halfway toward the other side of the open area when a bullet buzzed past his head and hit the wall twenty yards away, with a puff of ancient plaster dust. He dived and rolled behind a wooden crate, knowing full well that the shelter it provided was temporary at best. As if to hammer that message home, another bullet passed through the crate in an explosion of splinters just inches from his head and struck the ground nearby. He looked desperately for anything that would provide him with more substantial cover and spotted a concrete support column about ten yards away. To reach it he would have to cross open ground.

Time seemed to slow down as he glanced at the splintered hole in the crate and the tiny crater in the concrete floor where the bullet had ricocheted away. He subconsciously calculated the trajectory of the bullet, his mind drawing a line back from the crater and through the crate. Springing up from behind the crate, he sighted his pistol and fired three times. There was a scream of pain from somewhere off in the darkness, and Otto sprinted for the comparative safety of the column. He pressed his back against the pillar, listening for signs of pursuit but hearing nothing. Suddenly there was a flicker of movement from off to his right, and he spun round, raising his weapon. He gasped as he felt a sudden sharp pain in his chest, and looking down, he saw the silver hilt of a throwing knife protruding from the center of his chest. He collapsed to his knees, his pistol falling from his numb fingers, and as the darkness swallowed him, he saw a familiar figure detach itself from the shadows nearby and walk toward him.

"I am sorry, my friend," Wing said, looking down at him as Otto lost consciousness.

There was a sudden flash of white light, and the warehouse seemed to melt away, to be replaced by a brightly lit cave with a smooth metal floor.

"Exercise terminated," H.I.V.E.mind said calmly. "Holographic projectors and variable geometry force fields offline."

Otto rose groggily to his feet, feeling his strength gradually returning.

"There is such a thing as too realistic, you know," he said, rubbing at his sternum and trying to forget the pain and shock that he had felt just a few moments before.

"That's the whole point, Mr. Malpense," Colonel Francisco said, striding across the empty cavern as Wing helped Otto to his feet. "The neural feedback suit allows you to feel all of the pain without suffering any of the physical injury. It ensures that you take these training sessions seriously."

That may have been the proper name for the body-suit that Otto was wearing, but he definitely preferred the nickname that it had earned among the students of H.I.V.E.—the Agonizer.

"Good work, Mr. Fanchu," Francisco said. "You took your target down without hesitation, but I would still rather see you using your sidearms."

"It was not necessary," Wing replied with a slight shake of the head.

"Well, one day it might be," Francisco replied with a frown. "Let's hope you won't hesitate then. The end result is the same, after all."

Wing gave a small nod. Otto understood very well why his friend had not used his gun. The first and only time that Wing had shot somebody, it had been his own father. Wing had saved Otto's life but still had not forgiven himself for killing Cypher and breaking the solemn vow he had once made to his mother never to take a life.

"Thanks a lot, Otto," Shelby said as she walked toward them, rubbing her shoulder. "When the heck did you become such a good shot?"

"Beginner's luck," Otto replied with a shrug.

"And did you really have to shoot me twice?" Laura asked, still looking slightly groggy from being rendered temporarily unconscious by the neural shock administered by her own Agonizer suit.

"You gave away your position, Miss Brand," Francisco said with a slight shake of his head. "How many times do I have to tell you about watching where you're walking?"

"Sorry, Colonel," Laura sighed. "I'll do better next time."

"Let's hope you do," Francisco replied. "Out in the real world there won't be a next time. H.I.V.E.mind, please upload the result of today's exercise to the central academic server."

"Upload complete," H.I.V.E.mind replied.

"Good. That's all for now, ladies and gentlemen," the Colonel said. "We'll be moving on to wilderness environments next week, so please review the tactical briefings on your terminals. Dismissed."

Otto, Wing, Laura, and Shelby met in the assembly area five minutes later after changing out of the neural feedback suits and into their black Alpha stream jumpsuits. They were just about to head back to their accommodation block when the doors on the other side of the room hissed open and Lucy, Franz, and Nigel walked toward them.

"How did it go?" Laura asked Lucy, noting the slight scowl on the other girl's face.

"Don't ask," Lucy said with a sigh.

"I am thinking that you will be wanting to tell the others of my glorious victory," Franz said with a huge, beaming smile.

"Okay, okay." Lucy winced.

"Franz won?" Shelby asked, trying hard to not sound too astonished.

"Yes," Franz replied proudly. "I am being like the shadow in the night. They can run but they cannot hide."

"You got lucky," Nigel said, sounding slightly irritated.

"Luck is not being the factor," Franz said, shaking his head. "I am just being too good for you."

"Well," Otto said with a grin, "I for one want to hear all about it."

"It does indeed sound like a glorious victory," Wing said. Even he was struggling to keep a straight face.

"I'm not going to be allowed to forget about this in a hurry, am I?" Lucy said as Franz walked out of the room with Otto and Wing, explaining in great detail how his extraordinary stealth and cunning had been instrumental in defeating his opponents.

"Don't worry. There's no shame in losing," Shelby replied.

"Really?" Lucy asked hopefully.

Shelby burst out laughing, setting Laura off too.

"I think this is going to be a very long day," Nigel said to Lucy with a sigh.

⚛ ⚛ ⚛

Three men sat in a crowded bar in Colorado, a frosted half-full pitcher of beer on the table between them. The first man raised his glass.

"A toast, guys, to the MWP-X1 and the brave, intelligent, and handsome men that are gonna show the world what it can do tomorrow."

"I'll drink to that," the second man said, raising his glass.

"It's going to take more than one glass of beer for me to find either one of you two freaks handsome, but ah, what the heck!" the third man said, raising his glass.

"Let's just hope that the General doesn't find out that we're not all tucked up in our bunks," the second man said with a grin. "I'm not sure that this is what he meant by a good night's rest."

"Well, he can't throw us in the brig till after the demonstration," the first man said, "so I guess we'll be okay for the next twenty-four hours."

"After twelve months of living in the desert with him barking orders at us every day, I figure that's the least he owes us," the third man replied.

"You better not be complaining, son," the first man said, putting on a gruff Southern accent, "because you should be proud—proud to be a part of the future of this great nation's armed forces."

"Sir. Yes sir," the second man said, saluting the other man with a grin.

The three of them sat chatting and laughing for another half hour. None of the other people in the bar would have guessed by looking at them that they were the test pilots for one of the most confidential advanced military research projects on the planet.

"We should get going," the third man said eventually, finishing his beer. "It's gonna be an early start in the morning."

"It's an early start every morning," the first man said with a sigh as he too finished his drink, "but yeah, I guess you're right."

"We better get some R & R after the demo tomorrow," the second man said. "I've had enough desert to last me a lifetime."

The three men got up from the table and left the bar, walking out into the cool night air and crossing the parking lot.

"What the heck—" the first man said angrily as they rounded the corner of the building. A shadowy figure was standing beside his truck, working a long thin bar down between the rubber seal and the glass of the driver's side window. "Hey! Get away from my truck!" he yelled.

The thief's head snapped around, and he saw the three

men sprinting toward him. Abandoning his attempt to break into the vehicle, he ran into the darkness beyond the edge of the lot, with the others in close pursuit. They gained on him quickly as they sprinted across the dusty scrubland, and when the first of them got to within a couple of feet, the pilot dived forward, hitting his target in the small of the back with his shoulder and bringing him to the ground with a crunching thud. He rolled the thief onto his back and put one knee on the struggling man's chest.

"You picked the wrong truck to steal, buddy," the first man said as his two companions pinned the thief's arms to the ground.

"Actually," the other man said with a smile, "it was precisely the right truck."

There were three small coughing sounds from somewhere behind the men, and each of them felt a sudden sharp sting on the back of his neck. The thief caught the first man by the shoulders as he fell forward, unconscious, and his two companions collapsed to the desert floor beside him. The thief stood up, brushing the dust from his jeans as three figures wearing black combat fatigues and night vision goggles appeared from the darkness, lowering their tranquilizer dart guns and walking toward the unconscious men on the ground.

"Good work," Pietor Furan said as he pushed the

goggles up onto the top of his head. The smiling thief gave a small nod.

"Get them onto the truck," Furan said to the two men beside him. "We don't have much time."

☻☻☻

For life on earth to survive, you must not be captured.
Everything depends on you. Prepare for

EARTHFALL

MARK WALDEN

PRINT AND EBOOK EDITIONS AVAILABLE • From Simon & Schuster Books for Young Readers • KIDS.SimonandSchuster.com

Just because you're a kid, it doesn't mean you can't solve crimes.

But it probably means you won't solve them well.

The Search is just the beginning....